ALSO BY JON ATHAN

The Girl in the Attic (2021)

Am I Beautiful? (2021)

Do Not Disturb (2020)

The Groomer (2020)

Into the Wolves' Den (2019)

Lovesick (2019)

The Good, the Bad, and the Sadistic (2018)

Grandfather's House (2018)

The Abuse of Ashley Collins (2017)

A Family of Violence (2016)

CW01499351

The legend of La Llorona has been part of my life since my childhood. It is one of the first horror stories I was ever told. It is responsible for sparking my love for the genre. For that, I dedicate this book to my family and my culture.

WARNING

This book contains scenes of intense violence and some disturbing themes. Some parts of this book may be considered violent, cruel, disturbing, or unusual. This book is not intended for those easily offended or appalled. Please enjoy at your own discretion.

TABLE OF CONTENTS

PART I

1

GUSTAVO 'EL EMPALADOR' RIVERA

THE HUSTLE BY VAN MCCOY ECHOED THROUGH THE compound's empty hallways and rooms. Harsh, guttural screams disrupted the feel-good disco music every few seconds. All of the noise died out in the desert before reaching the tall brick partition surrounding the compound. There were no other buildings in the area—only shrubs, cacti, and dirt.

In one of the compound's hallways, a trail of fresh blood led from a doorway to a wide archway. In the hallway a console table had been knocked over. The shards from a broken blue-and-white vase were scattered across the floor, dyed red by the blood. In the doorway at the start of the bloody trail lay a big, bare, amputated foot. It was being used to prop the door open.

The foot had been chopped clean off at the ankle.

Slits of white—bone, tendon, cartilage—were visible amidst the blood at the stump.

The wide archway opened up to a spacious kitchen. Like the hallway, the linoleum floor appeared to have been mopped with blood. There was a severed hand on the long rectangular table in the kitchen. At the base of the hand, a bloody cleaver was lodged in the table. A clean machete lay next to it.

The music played from an old radio on a shelf above the stove. A crucifix hung on the wall above the kitchen archway, Jesus Christ frowning at the carnage below him. It looked like a massacre had occurred in the compound. All of the blood, all of the extremities, and all of the screams, however, came from one man: *Francisco Fuentes*.

Around the corner in the kitchen, tucked under a flight of stairs, there was a bathroom. Francisco lay on the bathroom floor, wearing only a frayed tank top and plaid boxers. With one of its straps torn, the shirt was stamped with muddy footprints from a brutal stomping. There were welts and bruises and red marks across his arms, back, and chest.

His head was beaten to a bloody, swollen pulp. Wedges of inflated flesh hid his eyes. The large lumps on his head were clearly visible thanks to his buzz cut hair. His left hand and his right foot were severed, blood spouting from the stumps at the ends of his limbs. He was flopping around on the floor, slipping and sliding on his own blood.

"*No tenía que ser así, güey,*" Gustavo Rivera said in Spanish.

'It didn't have to be like this, dumbass.'

'*Güey*' was used as an insult, but it was also frequently used in informal conversations to refer to someone without using their name.

Gustavo was a 38-year-old Mexican man. His curly black hair—streaked with gray—was slicked back under his trucker cap. He had a thick mustache with peppered stubble across his jaw. He wore a dark wind-breaker, jeans, and brown leather boots. There was a long scar on the left side of his neck. It was given to him by a rival cartel member during an attempted beheading.

He was standing in the bathroom next to Francisco. Gustavo's colleague and cousin, Ricardo Rivera, stood behind him, pushing down on an animal control pole to pin Francisco to the floor. The customized pole's barbed-wire noose was wrapped tightly around Francisco's neck. The barbed wire ate away at the captive's throat as he struggled.

Gustavo crouched next to him and said, "*Oye. Escúchame, joven. Háblame de ese gringo, 'El Ken.' O, mejor aún, háblame de tu patrón. ¿Dónde está Rafa?*"

'Hey. Listen to me, youngster. Tell me about that foreigner, 'El Ken.' Or, better yet, tell me about your boss. Where's Rafa?'

"*No se... nada,*" Francisco whimpered.

'I don't know... anything.'

He yelped and flinched as a barb on the noose pierced his neck next to his Adam's apple. His flinching motion inadvertently caused the barb to saw into his neck. He felt it grinding against his thyroid cartilage before brushing up against his jugular. The pain sent him into another frenzy, which only caused the noose to tear deeper into his neck.

Gustavo pulled a table knife out of his pocket. He crouched, then held the knife out in front of his captive and wagged it.

He said, "*Está bien, amigo, está bien. Vamos a hacerlo por las malas.*"

'Fine, friend, fine. We'll do this the hard way.'

In a raspy voice, Francisco said, "*Gus... Mátame... Mata–*"

'Gus... Kill me... Kill–'

Gustavo knelt on his upper back. Francisco gagged as the barbs dug into his throat, then he screamed. Blood spouted from his neck, landing in the walk-in shower in front of him.

Gustavo pulled the man's right arm back as if he were going to try to handcuff him. With a firm grip on his forearm, he started sawing into Francisco's inner wrist with the serrated edge of the table knife. Francisco's clenched fist came undone as the blade went through his flexor tendons and veins. It gave him a case of involuntary spirit fingers, his digits shaking uncontrollably. Then the blade stopped *in* his wrist, stuck amidst his carpal bones, bursae, and ligaments.

Blood squirted out from the arteries at the sides of his wrists. It splashed on the cupboard to their left and the wall to their right.

"*¿Necesitas una mano?*" Ricardo asked as he tightened his grip on the animal pole.

'Need a hand?'

Wiggling the knife around, Gustavo said, "No... no..." He grunted as he pushed the knife, breaking some bones and tearing a ligament with an unnerving crunching sound. While pulling on the silverware, he repeated, "No, no."

Francisco gasped for air, although it sounded like he was hiccupping. His vision blurred and darkened. He still caught sight of the blood swirling down the drain, though. For a moment he didn't recognize it as his own. It looked like the blood from his slain comrades, from his murdered family members, from his victims. All blood looked the same. The tremendous pain shooting through his right arm also made him forget about his mutilated neck. Yet, he found himself incapable of falling unconscious. He had been injected with amphetamines and other drugs prior to the torture to ensure he remained awake and felt everything.

The music changed to *Funkytown* by Lipps Inc.

The blade came to a stop again a little over halfway through his wrist. Gustavo stood on one foot on top of Francisco's back. With his other foot, he stomped on the knife's handle. A geyser of blood leapt out of Francisco's wrist. He stomped on the handle two more times, missed the third kick and planted his boot on Francisco's palm instead, then kicked the handle a fourth time. Francisco's hand was severed, leaving a jagged stump at the end of his arm. The captive screamed for a measly three seconds, then began to gasp for air again.

Gustavo picked up the hand and, chuckling, he said, "*No necesito una mano, primo. Tengo uno aquí mismo.*"

'I don't need a hand, cousin. I have one right here.'

Ricardo laughed with him. The gore didn't faze them. Violence was part of their everyday lives, as if written in their job descriptions or embedded in their DNA. Murder was an occupational hazard. *Sicarios*—hitmen—like Gustavo amputated more limbs than life-long surgeons and murdered more people than the average serial killer. Francisco was just a slab of meat to them.

Gustavo slapped the back of Francisco's head with the amputated hand, then shouted, "*¡Mira lo que me estás haciendo hacerte, güey! ¡Háblame de El Ken o Rafa y te terminaré con una bala en la cabeza! ¿Dónde están? ¡Dime!*"

'Look at what you're making me do to you, idiot! Tell me about El Ken or Rafa and I'll finish you with a bullet to the head! Where are they? Tell me!'

He smacked the back of Francisco's head with his own amputated hand repeatedly while saying his last word—*¡Dime! ¡Dime!*—over and over. He wanted Francisco to talk, but the victim could only mumble and whine and gasp in response.

"*Pinche pendejo. ¿Crees que esto ha terminado? Todavía tienes un pie más, puta,*" Gustavo said.

'Fucking idiot. You think this is over? You still have one more foot, bitch.'

He grabbed the table knife. As he reached for his captive's ankle, he noticed the blade was bent. He tossed it aside, letting it *clang* on the floor.

He looked at the doorway and yelled, "*¡David! ¡David, trae el machete!*"

'David! David, bring the machete!'

David Carrillo, a pudgy guy with a mullet, stood in the kitchen. He was making a sandwich at a counter. Despite all of the gore and screaming around him, his appetite remained healthy.

He sighed as he tossed another slice of ham on his sandwich, then he muttered, "*Chingada madre...*"

The term translated to 'motherfucker' or 'damn it.'

He grabbed the machete from the table in the kitchen. While walking over to the bathroom, the song on the radio changed to *Maniac* by Michael Sembello.

"*¿Aún no has terminado con él?*" he asked as he handed the machete to Gustavo.

'You're not finished with him yet?'

Gustavo responded, "*Cállate la boca, güey.*"

'Shut the hell up, asshole.'

David said, "*Solo–*"

In Spanish, he was about to say 'I'm just saying' when Gustavo raised the machete and looked daggers at him. David puckered his lips, raised his hands in surrender, and stepped back.

"*Cállate,*" Gustavo said sternly.

He swung the machete at Francisco's left heel. His Achilles tendon was immediately severed. Francisco felt it bobbling around in his leg like a bungee cord. He gritted his teeth and held his breath as he convulsed violently. The barbed-wire noose, tightening as he fought, was now partially obscured under folds of his bloody, torn skin. With Gustavo's second mighty swing, the victim's foot was lopped off.

Francisco's head fell limp. He continued grinding his teeth, thick strings of foamy saliva hanging from his mouth. The amputation happened so fast and the pain was so immense that he didn't even realize he had lost all of his extremities. He knew one thing and one thing only: *Agony*. He felt the hot pain flowing through every inch of his body, as if his blood had been replaced with acid.

Yet, he remained conscious.

Gustavo grabbed the back of Francisco's head and lifted it up to stop him from inadvertently suffocating and cutting himself with the noose. Ricardo stood on his tiptoes and moved the animal pole to his left to give Gustavo some space. Meanwhile, David went back to the kitchen, topped his sandwich off with another slice of bread, then returned to the bathroom doorway. He took a bite of his sandwich just as *Maniac* was coming to an end on the radio. *What is Love* by Haddaway was up next.

Leaning close to Francisco's ear, Gustavo said, "*¿No quieres hablarme de tu patrón? Está bien, amigo. Háblame de Él Ken. ¿Cuál es el verdadero nombre del gringo? ¿Cuáles son sus rutas? Dime algo y te daré una bala en vez de esto.*"

'You don't want to tell me about your boss? Fine, friend. Tell me about El Ken. What's the American's real name? What are his routes? Tell me something and I'll give you a bullet instead of this.'

Eyelids flickering, Francisco stared vacantly at the shower drain. He mouthed: '*Mátame.*' He sought death —nothing more, nothing less.

"*Chingada madre,*" Gustavo said.

He got up to a half crouch and directed his attention to his captive's lower body. He swung the machete at the back of his right knee. The blade tore through the flesh and bone with ease. It only took three powerful chops to detach his lower leg. Split ligaments and veins hung from the stumps. Blood spewed out and puddled under them, reaching the cupboard and the toilet.

Gustavo picked up the hairy lower leg. He swung it down at Francisco's upper back and barked, "*¡Pinche idiota! ¡Habla! ¡Habla, cabrón! ¡Habla!*"

'Fucking idiot! Talk! Talk, bastard! Talk!'

Francisco could only groan and whine. The sound of his ribs and spine cracking was louder, though.

Large red marks and knots developed across his upper back. And with each blow, the barbed-wire noose slid around in his neck, widening and stretching the massive gash across his throat. A piece of his thyroid cartilage was visible in the wound.

Frustrated, Gustavo threw the severed leg to the side. It hit the mirror above the sink, shattering it upon impact. He took the animal pole out of Ricardo's hands and tossed it aside. The noose was still wrapped around Francisco's neck, so the pole landed on the toilet next to them. Then he rolled Francisco onto his back.

"*Deberías haber dicho algo, hijo de puta,*" Gustavo said as he took a utility knife out of his pocket. It translated to: 'You should have said something, you son of a bitch.' He beckoned to his cousin and said, "*Ayúdame.*"

'*Help me.*'

Gustavo thumbed the utility knife's slider, causing the blade to shoot out of the handle with a rapid succession of *clicks*. He swung it at Francisco's mutilated neck, unwittingly cutting the noose. With his own box cutter, Ricardo joined him. They sliced away at his neck with the sharp blades, one after the other.

Within seconds Francisco's neck resembled the jagged, craggy surface of a mountain, crisscrossed with deep, bloody crevices. He tried to scream, his mouth open as wide as humanly possible, but his larynx was ruptured by one of the blades. Awful gurgling and squelching and groaning sounds came out of the wounds on his throat instead.

Francisco reached for his neck, as if he had forgotten he had no hands. His arms shook on his chest, blood spraying out from the stumps and splashing on his face. Blood fountained out of his severed jugulars in wide crimson arcs, too. It hit his executioners, the shower door, the toilet, and the walls. Some drops from one of the blades even hit the ceiling.

In a sudden jerk, he curled up into the fetal position. He rolled onto his side while his head swung every which way. It was a last-ditch effort to hide from the blades—a subconscious effort to survive.

Gustavo kicked him in the chest twice, then pushed him onto his back with his foot. Ricardo stepped on Francisco's face, pinning the back of his head down against the shower floor, and continued slicing away at his neck. By then, David was more than halfway done with his sandwich and the song on the radio changed again.

A Fifth of Beethoven by Walter Murphy.

Gustavo stopped two minutes later after hearing his blade screech against Francisco's spine. Ricardo kept going. Francisco's limbs trembled, but his torso finally stopped moving. The loud gurgling noise continued to come out of Francisco's neck, but he was no longer breathing. His head, which was sliding under Ricardo's boot like a wet bar of soap, was only attached to his body by his spinal cord and some flimsy flaps of flesh.

As he walked out of the bathroom, Gustavo said, "*Encuentren el gringo de Rafa. Cuando lo atrapamos, tenemos El Decapitador.*" It translated to: 'Find Rafa's American. Once we have him, we have The Decapitator.' He stopped outside of the bathroom and jabbed his index finger at David's chest. He said, "*Deja su cabeza en la puerta de su familia. Pero limpia este lugar antes de irte. Déjalo impecable. ¿Me oyes, güey?*"

'Leave his head at his family's doorstep. But clean this mess up before you leave. Leave it spotless. You hear me, asshole?'

Holding the last quarter of his sandwich close to his mouth, David nodded and said, "*Pues sí, patrón. Te oigo. Ya está hecho.*"

'Well yes, boss. I hear you. It's already done.'

Gustavo looked back and sneered at Francisco's corpse, then he uttered a *tsk* and walked away while shaking his head in annoyance. David wolfed down the rest of his food and rubbed his palms together, then he drew a hunting knife from a sheath on his waistband. He entered the bathroom and helped Ricardo behead their dead rival.

2

THE PRICE OF HOPE

VANESSA RAMIREZ WALKED ACROSS THE EMPTY PARKING lot while holding her son's hand. His name was Joaquín, and he was five years old. Her eleven-year-old daughter Lucía skipped ahead of them. They were making their way to a strip mall to visit Vanessa's workplace, a beauty salon called Chuy's Studio. Upon reaching the sidewalk in front of the stores, they heard a faint burst of gunfire, quickly followed by another.

They didn't react to it, though. A person shooting a rifle in the distance was equivalent to a child playing with maracas. It was only a cause of concern when the shooter was close enough to target them or hit them with strays.

The door chime rang as Vanessa opened the door to Chuy's Studio. Her kids ran straight to the seating area to the right. Lucía took a seat and grabbed a fashion magazine from the table in front of her.

Joaquín went to the gumball machine nearby. He tried to turn its handle, but it didn't budge.

There were two employees and three customers beyond the front desk. Two of the customers were getting their hair dyed and the other one—an elderly woman with gray hair—was getting ready for a perm.

"*Vani,*" the elderly woman said, frowning. "*Pensé que no trabajabas los sábados. Si hubiera sabido que venías, te habría esperado, mija. ¿Por qué no pudiste peinarme? Me gusta cómo lo haces.*"

'Vani. I thought you didn't work on Saturdays. If I knew you were coming, I would have waited, honey. Why couldn't you do my hair? I like the way you do it.'

'*Mija*' literally translated to 'my daughter,' but it was also used as an affectionate term to address young females in Spanish. '*Mijo*' was used in the same way to address young males.

"*Hoy no estoy trabajando, Gloria. Solo estoy aquí para hablar con Alicia,*" Vanessa said, snickering. It translated to: 'I'm not working today, Gloria. I'm just here to speak to Alicia.' She snapped her fingers at her son and said, "*Oye, deja de jugar con eso.*"

'Hey, stop playing with that.'

Moping, Gloria said, "*Quiero que lo hagas tú. No me gusta cómo lo hace esta chica. Le tiemblan mucho los dedos.*"

'I want you to do it. I don't like the way this girl does it. Her fingers shake too much.'

Her stylist, who was standing right behind her

throughout the conversation, looked at her with wide eyes, as if to say: *Oh, is that how you really feel?* She started bickering with Gloria, but they kept a friendly tone.

Standing on the opposite side of the salon, Alicia Cortes beckoned to Vanessa and said, "*Vamos, hablemos en la oficina.*"

'C'mon, let's talk in the office.'

"*Oye, pórtate bien. Ahora vuelvo,*" Vanessa said to her children before walking away. It translated to: 'Hey, behave yourselves. I'll be right back.' As she made her way to the back of the salon, she looked at the woman styling Gloria's hair and said, "*Cuídalos, por favor.*"

'Look after them, please.'

Vanessa entered the office. To the left, there were two desks. Each desk had a desktop computer and a collection of binders and notebooks on them. To her right, there was a table for two. Beyond the table, wedged in the corner of the room, there was a mini fridge with a cheap coffee machine on top.

Vanessa took one last peek out into the salon through the crack between the door and the jamb before shutting and locking it. She was always looking over her shoulder—always expecting the worst.

Standing next to the fridge, Alicia asked, "*¿Quieres café?*"

'You want some coffee?'

Vanessa turned to look at her. They were both twenty-eight years old, but Alicia always seemed

calmer and happier than Vanessa. Alicia wasn't bothered by the brutal violence plaguing her country. The
rampant femicide saddened her, but she didn't let it
scare her. Like the cartel members, she accepted
violence as a regular part of life. She was born there, so
she figured she might as well die there, too. Vanessa
had other plans, though.

"*No, gracias,*" she said.

'No, thank you.'

Alicia served herself a cup of coffee, then with a
smile, she said, "*Entonces siéntate. Vayamos al grano.*"

'Then sit. Let's get down to business.'

Vanessa appeared to hesitate, inspecting her friend
as if she didn't recognize her. Alicia's curly hair—dyed
blonde—reached down to her waist. About three
inches taller than Vanessa, she stood five-three with a
curvy, athletic figure. Vanessa kept her hair short and
black. The wavy tresses barely touched her shoulders.
They both had dark brown eyes. Although they viewed
their world differently, they saw the same glitter of
kindness sparkling in each other's eyes.

As Vanessa sat across from her at the table, Alicia
said, "*Hablé con mis contactos–*"

In Spanish, she was going to say 'I spoke to my
connections about the trip' when Vanessa shushed her
mid-sentence.

Vanessa said, "*En inglés. Siempre en inglés.*"

'In English. Always in English.'

Alicia nodded and smiled slightly as she recalled

their agreement. Vanessa only wanted to discuss those 'business' matters in English to lower the chances of any eavesdroppers understanding them. She didn't want anyone to know she was looking to hire *coyotes*—people smugglers—to get her and her family out of Mexico and into the United States.

In English, Alicia said, "Yeah, okay. Um… I spoke to my friends about the trip and… there's been some changes."

"What do you mean 'changes?' What changed? Are they taking us or not?"

Alicia bit her lower lip and stared down at the table. Although she hadn't heard the news yet, Vanessa let her shoulders sink as she exhaled in dismay. Her friend's silence spoke volumes about the situation.

Vanessa said, "Alicia, I have the money. I'm ready to go. *We're* ready to go. What's wrong? What happened?"

"The money," Alicia replied.

"One hundred seventy-five thousand pesos for my family. That's what you said and that's what I have. I'm ready. What's the problem?"

Alicia said, "I was wrong. I know what I told you, but there was a, um… How do you say?" She scrunched half her face up and twirled her pointer finger around, then said, "Oh, a *misunderstanding*."

"A misunderstanding?" Vanessa repeated, her voice softening with sorrow. "Please tell me it was a small one."

Alicia shook her head slowly. Vanessa put her hand

over her forehead and muttered indistinctly. She was afraid to ask her next question because she already knew she wasn't going to like the answer. But she had to know the truth. She couldn't move forward without knowing the true price of hope.

"How much?" she asked. Alicia remained quiet. Vanessa touched her hand, looked her friend in the eye, and repeated, "How much?"

Switching back to Spanish, Alicia said, "*Trescientos cincuenta mil pesos más.*"

'Three hundred fifty thousand pesos more.'

"*No me jodas,*" Vanessa muttered. It translated to: 'Don't fuck with me.' Returning to English, she said, "That's... That's three times what you told me, Alicia. What are you saying? Wha–What are you trying to do to me? Are you trying to cheat me? Are you working with those bastards to steal from me?"

Angered by the suggestion, Alicia scooted forward in her seat, glared at Vanessa, and yelled, "Hey! I would never do that! You're like family to me, Vani. I love you and Lucía and Joaquín. I would never do anything to hurt you. I can't believe you'd say that. I can't fucking believe it! What's wrong with you?"

She leaned back in her seat and crossed her arms. Vanessa could see she was genuinely offended by her words. She didn't have any reason to distrust her. She just didn't trust the people around her. And she knew money could make people betray themselves and the ones they loved the most.

Breaking the silence between them, Alicia said, "I didn't even want to get involved in this in the first place. *You* asked *me* to hook you up. That's what I'm trying to do. But these guys... They only see money in desperate people. They know you'll pay anything to get out of here, so they'll keep asking for more and more."

Fear was the name of the game in Mexico. It influenced politicians and kept civilians in line. It corrupted law enforcement and crippled the economy. It fueled barbaric violence and drove desperate citizens out of the country. Fear kept Mexico under the reign of the cartels and on the brink of self-destruction.

Vanessa said, "I'm sorry. I was just... surprised. Surprised and angry. I know it's not your fault."

"It's okay," Alicia replied, sounding sincere and disappointed at the same time.

"So, what am I supposed to do now? It will take years before I have enough money to pay them. By then, they'll already be looking at Joaquín. They're taking them in younger and younger these days. My neighbor's boy—Juanita's kid, Jorge—got picked up and he's only ten. Joaquín can't grow up here or he'll end up like him. Or worse, he'll end up like his dad. And Lucía is growing so fast—so, so fast. You've seen what they're doing to our girls, Alicia... I can't let them hurt Lucía. I *won't* let them."

"I know, I know. You can always look for someone else to take you. You can find a better deal. Or you can try to cross on your own. My cousin did it before. Two times, actually."

"It's too dangerous. Joaquín isn't strong enough to cross. I don't even know if Lucía can make it."

A ruminative silence befell the office. The sound of Joaquín and Lucía roughhousing in the salon barely seeped into the room.

Alicia grunted to clear her throat, then asked, "Have you thought about that other, um... 'thing' I told you about? I heard that they're still looking for girls, and my friend can get you a job. They also say that *burdel*—Enrique's Bar—is a lot safer than some of the other places. Much better than working on the street."

'*Burdel*' translated to 'brothel.'

Vanessa stuttered, "I–I... I can't do that. What if I get hurt? Or killed? Or raped? Or sick?"

"I can't say that it's not possible, but I know that this place is safer than the others. You'd have your own room upstairs and people downstairs."

"But what if something does happen? What would I tell Joaquín and Lucía?"

"Tell them the truth, Vani. Tell them you're fighting for them. Tell them you have to do some 'bad' things to make good things happen. Maybe they won't understand now, but they will later."

Vanessa considered the option deeply. Prostitution was legal in Mexico, but legalization alone couldn't create a safe environment for sex workers. In sex work, danger could come from anyone and anything. A handsome man could portray himself as a gentleman on the surface while hiding the sickest, most depraved mind in his skull, and the cleanest cock could spread the deadliest diseases.

Noticing her deep conflict, Alicia said, "You can try being a drug dealer."

"I can't do that. I can't be part of this drug war. I know too many people who have died from this... this craziness. They killed–"

"I was kidding."

"–Tomás, Alicia. They say it was an accident, but it still happened. He wasn't the perfect man, he was bad in his own way, but no one deserves to die like that. It isn't–"

"Vani, I was kidding. *Perdón*."

'*Perdón*' was used for ordinary apologies in Spanish.

They went silent again. Alicia took a sip of her coffee. In the salon, Gloria scolded the children about their arguing. She treated them like her real grandchildren.

Vanessa thought about her late husband, Tomás Ramirez. He had been killed three years earlier, a victim of collateral damage during a shootout between rival cartels in a casino. They didn't have the best relationship, more downs than ups, but she still cared about him since he was the father of her children. His violent accidental death told her that it didn't matter if they stayed away from the cartels. As long as they stayed in Mexico, the cartels would find their way to them.

"So, what are you going to do?" Alicia asked.

Vanessa looked back at the door and listened to her children's muffled voices for a few seconds. *Anything for them,* she thought.

She looked back at Alicia and said, "I don't know yet. Just give me the number to your friend at that bar. I'll think about giving them a call." She smiled wearily and said, "It's better to give them my body than to give them my kids, no?"

3

PINHEAD

"Get me the fuck outta here, man! I ain't telling you shit, motherfuckers!"

The loud, shaky male voice echoed through the desolate desert. The area was overgrown with dry shrubs and cacti.

Gustavo and Ricardo sat on a black pickup truck's cargo bed, feet hanging from the back. In front of them, there was an abandoned gasoline station with an auto repair service garage. The doors and windows were removed, replaced with sheets of dilapidated plywood. There was a rusty Coca-Cola sign on the side of the structure. Two decrepit cars were left on cinder blocks in front of the building. One of them was riddled with bullet holes. There was no pavement in sight. The dirt roads had been swallowed by the desert vegetation.

"Ivan Navarro," Gustavo said, an American passport in one hand and a Texas driver's license in the other. "*De McAllen, Texas, Estados Unidos. Veintiún años. No mames, todavía eres un niño.*"

'From McAllen, Texas, USA. Twenty-one years old. No shit, you're still a boy.'

Between the pickup truck and the gas station, Ivan Navarro was buried from the neck down in the dirt, only his head sticking out like a barrel cactus. All covered in beads of sweat, he had a smooth, boyish face with a shaved scalp. The sun and the dry weather left his cheeks rosy and his lips chapped and bloody. A curved tattoo over the tail of his left eyebrow read: *RSK*. It was the acronym for a gang he had joined in high school. After dropping out of high school, a life of crime, albeit short, led him to Mexico.

"Let me go!" Ivan yelled, his voice continuing to quaver and echo. "Fuck, man! Do you know who I work for, homie?! You know who... who..."

His voice faltered due to the pressure on his chest and the lump of anxiety in his throat. He was beginning to feel claustrophobic.

"Homie," Gustavo repeated mockingly as he hopped off the truck. He pointed at Ivan's head, looked back at Ricardo, and said, "*Este pinche pocho.*"

'This fucking pocho.'

'*Pocho*' was used as an insult towards Mexican people accused of being Americanized.

While strolling up to Ivan, who was only about five meters away, Gustavo looked up at the sky. He saw a flock of vultures flying in circles far above them. He stopped in front of their captive, towering over him. His shadow gave Ivan some temporary relief from the scorching sun. He wiggled around in the dirt, but he couldn't muster the energy to dig himself out. He was starved and dehydrated prior to his partial burial.

"*¿Hablas español, joven?*" Gustavo asked as he crouched.

'Do you speak Spanish, young man?'

In a tight voice, Ivan said, "*Un... poco.*"

'A... little.'

Speaking slowly and clearly so as not to be misunderstood, Gustavo said, "Okay then. We'll do this in English. I used to live in America, you know? Twenty years ago in East Los Angeles. Maybe it's been a little longer than that. I thought I was going to get rich over there. Get the money, the power, the women. Like Tony Montana, you know? But no. *La migra* caught me after two years. I went to prison for a while, then got kicked out of the country with nothing but my clothes and a little bit of cash in my pocket. Like you Americans say, 'back to square one,' huh?"

'*La migra*' was a slang term used to refer to the U.S. Immigration and Customs Enforcement agency.

"Let me... go," Ivan said.

Ignoring him, Gustavo said, "*Volver al infierno.* Do you know what that means, *pocho?* It means 'back to hell.' That's what this place is: *Hell.* Some people don't want to admit it, but life is much better down here when you do. It's better to live free than to live like a slave. Better to be a demon than a fallen angel. And you want to know something else, Ivan? In this hell... *Yo soy el diablo.*"

'*Yo soy el diablo*' translated to 'I am the devil.'

"I don't care, motherfucker!" Ivan barked. "Shoot me, bitch! Kill me! Fucking do it, pussy!"

He thrust his head forward and tried to spit, but no saliva came out due to his dehydration. The gesture was enough to infuriate Ricardo, though.

"*¡¿Qué chingados te pasa, cabrón?!*" he shouted as he jumped off the truck's cargo bed.

'What the fuck is wrong with you, asshole?!'

He ran up to the men, then punted the side of Ivan's head like a soccer player getting a free kick. Ivan clenched his eyes shut, ground his teeth, and moaned. His right ear was ringing while his head spun. Ricardo was about to kick him again when Gustavo stood up and stepped between them.

He pushed Ricardo back and said, "*Cálmate, güey.*"

'Calm down, man.'

Ricardo raised his hands and shrugged. As Gustavo turned away, he hocked a loogie at Ivan. The blob landed on top of their captive's head.

Ivan didn't notice it. The kick to the head left him nauseated and disoriented, whining and writhing. He wasn't as tough as he wanted to sound. He was only hoping to earn himself a quick death—a bullet to the back of the head or a hanging from an overpass—through his disrespectful behavior. He was well aware of the cartel members' cruel torture tactics. He had heard the stories from friends and seen the videos online.

Gustavo returned to a squatting position in front of Ivan. He said, "My cousin wants to kick your head until it pops like a melon, but I won't let him do that. Not yet anyway. First, I'm going to give you the chance to take the easy way out. All you have to do is answer my questions. And what's the easy way? Well, I'll let you pick. It's a great deal, no? Think about it. Most people in the world don't get to pick how they'll die. Some are unlucky enough to end up here in *el infierno* with us... like you."

"Fuck, man," Ivan whined.

"Tell me, Ivan, who's your boss?"

"You know already."

"Then tell me."

"*El Decapitador.*"

It translated to: 'The Decapitator.'

Gustavo said, "Say his real name."

"You know it already!" Ivan shouted.

"This isn't about what *I* know, kid. This is about you. Say his name."

"Rafael Vàsquez! Rafael '*El Decapitador*' Vàsquez!"

Gustavo hummed and nodded with approval. The information sparked a fire of determination in his eyes. Ricardo, who had been pacing around behind his boss, grew attentive. Hands on his hips, he stopped next to Gustavo and squinted down at Ivan.

Gustavo said, "You work with another American. They call him 'El Ken.' Like the Barbie doll, no? What's his real name?"

Ivan said, "His name... His name is... Shit, man, just shoot me! Please!"

"Tell me his real name and I'll give you a bullet. It's that easy."

"You don't know who you're fucking with. You have no fuckin' idea. Rafa's going to fuck you up, man. Whatever you're going to do to me, he'll do worse to my family if he finds out I talked."

With a smile, Gustavo said, "They'll be fine in America."

"They won't be. You know it."

Gustavo shrugged and said, "Yeah, you're right. I was only trying to make you feel better."

He chuckled. Ricardo laughed with him, although he didn't understand most of the conversation. He spoke enough to get by, but his English skills weren't as honed as his cousin's.

Gustavo said, "But there's no point in thinking about your family now. You should have thought about them before you joined this business. You knew you were putting them in danger when you signed up. Think about yourself now, Ivan, because nothing else will matter when you're dead. There is no heaven for men like us. You'll never see your family again and you'll never know what happened to them. So, tell me: Do you want to do this the easy way or the hard way?"

Ivan wasn't a very religious person. He hadn't visited a church in over a decade, and he only prayed when he needed something. But he had always believed in heaven and hell—reward and punishment. Buried neck down in a Mexican desert, he knew death was certain. He didn't want to drag his family into his business and share his suffering with them before his scheduled meeting with God. So, he stayed silent.

"The hard way then," Gustavo said. He glanced over at Ricardo and said, "*La pistola.*"

Ricardo moseyed over to the pickup truck. Ivan knew '*la pistola*' translated to 'the pistol.' Although he was scared of death, he was hoping Ricardo was going to return with a handgun. *Maybe they were bluffing,* he told himself. *Maybe these guys aren't as hard as they look.* His hopes were swiftly dashed when he saw the cord-less roofing nail gun in Ricardo's hand. Ricardo handed Gustavo the tool, then went back to the truck.

"Oh fuck!" Ivan cried. The hard dirt cracked and crumbled around him as he attempted to move his buried limbs. Looking left and right, he yelled, "Help me! Help! *¡Ayúdenme!*"

'*Ayúdenme*' translated to 'help me.'

No one was around to hear him, except for the vultures flying overhead. They flew a little lower, as if watching the show.

Gustavo held the nail gun about a centimeter away

from Ivan's forehead. With a squeeze of the trigger, a one-and-a-half-inch nail shot out. It hit Ivan with just enough pressure to skewer the bulging vein at the center of his forehead and fracture his skull. Blood spurted out of his forehead for a few seconds, landing on the ground and Gustavo's arms, then it slowed to a dribble and ran down his face.

The flooring nail gun wasn't strong enough to penetrate the bone. But the pain from the shot was so immense, so constant, that he felt like the nail was ricocheting around in his skull, ripping through his brain from every angle.

Ricardo approached them with a hammer and a small pouch full of rusty nails. He took a knee behind Ivan and went straight to work. He held one of the nails up to the back of Ivan's head and swung his hammer at it. It instantly cut through his skin and scraped his skull. He hit the nail's head again. Over Ivan's screaming, they heard a weak *cracking* sound come from his parietal bone.

"*No lo hagas con tanta fuerza,*" Gustavo said.

'Not so hard.'

Ricardo said, "*Mmm, pues, apenas lo toqué.*"

'Mmm, well, I barely touched it.'

Gustavo shot a nail at the capitalized 'K' tattooed on the left side of Ivan's forehead, then another on the opposite side. Blood from those wounds soaked his eyebrows before dripping into his eye sockets. Ricardo hammered another nail into the back of Ivan's head.

He hit it hard the first time, then tapped it the second time to make sure it wouldn't fall out. He was going to hit it a third time, but Ivan started swinging his head frantically, so he ended up tapping his scalp with the hammer instead.

"*Cálmate, puta,*" Ricardo said.

'Calm down, bitch.'

Ivan shouted, "No! Ahhh! Ow! Fuck! Stop!"

"You should have talked," Gustavo said.

He pressed his thumb down on Ivan's left ear to pin it to his head, then he fired a nail at it. The nail pierced his outer ear and his scalp, once again cracking his skull. Gustavo shot his other ear with the nail gun, too. Both of Ivan's ears were pulled back and nailed to his scalp. Meanwhile, Ricardo was making his way to the top of his head. He was using less force, so some of his nails fell out of his skull.

Although none of the nails had completely penetrated his skull, Ivan was in danger of suffering from a subarachnoid hemorrhage due to all of the fractures and all of his bleeding. Blood rushed into his left ear canal, muffling his hearing. Ivan felt the warmth of the liquid spreading behind his eye. More blood dripped from his jaw, the back of his head, and his earlobes, soaking the dirt around his neck.

He was in so much pain that he couldn't speak anymore. He could only pant and groan and cry. He didn't even have the energy to scream. His head throbbed, sickening pulses of pain coming from every direction. Although the rest of his body hadn't been touched, everything hurt. His heart was beating so hard that his entire chest ached. He felt like his sternum was going to burst open like a door. Lower in his torso his stomach was knotting up.

Once they were finished, twelve nails stuck out of Ivan's head. Three bloody nails, dislodged during the torture, lay on the ground around his neck.

Using his thumb and index finger, Gustavo pried Ivan's left eye open. He could see he was still conscious.

He pointed the nail gun at his eyeball and said, "What's El Ken's real name?" Ivan's lips flapped, but only a shaky exhale came out. Gustavo shook his captive's head gently and said, "If you don't start talking, I'm going to shoot nails through your eyes. Then I'm going to pull those nails out. If your eyes come out, too... *Pues, qué lástima.* What's his name?"

The Spanish translated to: 'Well, what a shame.'

Ivan snorted, then in a pain-induced trance, he mumbled, "Ca... Ca –Caleb... Car..."

"*Car?*" Ricardo repeated, brow furrowed. "*¿Cómo un carro?*"

'Like a car?'

Gustavo shook Ivan's head again and said, "Caleb what?"

"Carter," Ivan replied in a slow, quiet voice.

"Caleb Carter. Okay, okay. That's good. Where can I find him?"

"I... don't... know."

"Think about it, Ivan. You know we're only getting started. We can dig you out of there and take you to one of our doctors. We can keep you alive and keep going with this for a very long time. We can cover your body with nails before you die. I don't want to do that. I have other shit to do. But I *will* do it if I have to. Give me a real answer, boy."

Ivan's eyes rolled back while his head bobbed. Another nail fell from the back of his head. Blood spritzed out of the hole like a spray of perfume.

As his eyes rolled back down, eyelids twitching against Gustavo's fingers, Ivan said, "Bars... clubs... Strip... Strip clubs."

"Where?"

"Everywhere."

Gustavo said, "Tell me his favorite."

"Zacatecas," Ivan responded. "Enrique's... Bar."

"Good, *mijo,* good. And what about Rafael? Where can we find him?"

"I don't... know."

"Think about it."

"I really... don't know. I never... seen him. Please, man, kill... kill me."

Gustavo studied his face, hoping to find a telltale sign of lying—darting eyes, a facial tic, a change in his breathing. He couldn't see much through all of the blood, though. Ivan's entire head was painted red by it.

Gustavo said, "Okay, okay. You can die now." As he stood up, he beckoned to Ricardo and said, "*Vámonos.*"

'Let's go.'

"Wa–Wait," Ivan stuttered. "Whe–Where are you...
going? Wait... God, plee–please wait."

Gustavo and Ricardo placed their tools in a duffel
bag in the truck's cargo bed. Then Ricardo climbed
into the driver's seat and Gustavo got into the
passenger seat.

As the truck cruised away, using the last bit of his
energy, Ivan shouted, "Don't leave me!"

The truck jounced across the overgrown dirt road.
About an eighth of a mile away, it turned left. Ivan's
head swiveled as he followed the vehicle's path. Almost
half a mile away, they took another left. The truck
came to a stop atop a hill overlooking the gas station.

The men got out and sat on the hood of the truck.
With a pair of binoculars, Gustavo cast his gaze at
Ivan's head. He could see his mouth moving, but they
could no longer hear his cries. He moved the binoculars up and watched as the vultures slowly descended,
still flying in circles above the gas station.

"¿Conoces este... Enrique's Bar?" Gustavo asked.

'Do you know this... Enrique's Bar?'

Ricardo said, "Lo conozco."

'I know it.'

Ivan's eyes widened with fear as one of the vultures
landed next to him. The vulture glanced around, as if
checking for other people, then walked towards him.

"Stay away from me!" Ivan cried.

The vulture expanded its wings and squawked. To

Ivan, the loud, raspy hissing noise sounded like some-thing from a dinosaur out of a Jurassic Park movie.

He yelled, "No! Somebody–"

The vulture thrust its beak at Ivan's face. It pecked at the nail sticking out from the left side of his fore-head. With a second peck, the nail came out. Blood gushing out of the wound, Ivan yelped sharply. Another vulture landed behind him and another to his right, surrounding him from all sides. They squawked and pecked away at his head.

With their beaks the vultures in front of him targeted his soft tissue first. One of them ripped the tail of his eyebrow off before severing his upper eyelid. His exposed eyeball, spinning wildly in its socket, was glazed with blood. The vulture made a hissing sound, then nipped at his eye. The left side of Ivan's vision dimmed immediately as its beak pierced it. The bird started pulling on his eye, causing it to protrude from its socket. It only took the vulture a few seconds to bite a large hole into the eye, splitting it open. The front half of the eye fell forward, sitting on his cheekbone.

If it were still functioning, he would have been staring at the bloody dirt under him. But he couldn't see a thing from his left eye now.

The other vulture in front of him pecked away at his nose. It tore his nostrils open before nibbling and pulling on his nasal septum. After reducing his nose to bloody mush, the bird moved on to his lips. It plucked his upper lip off with one peck. His lower lip was more resilient, tearing slowly—*millimeter* by *millimeter*. Blood coated his exposed teeth and gums. The bird devoured his lips, then attempted to grab his tongue, chipping some of his teeth with its beak.

Meanwhile, the vulture behind him pecked at the rusty nails sticking out of his scalp, extracting them one by one. Once most of the nails were gone, it thrust its beak at the back of his head, as if it were trying to break a coconut open. And due to fractures from the previous torture, the vulture succeeded. The back of his skull broke to pieces. The bird's beak punctured his brain, but he remained conscious.

He didn't think about anything—his life, his family, God, the afterlife, *nothing*. At that moment, he existed only to suffer. He passed away after his forehead was caved in by one of the vultures' beaks. Shards of bone, covered in bloody skin, fell to the ground. The vultures feasted on his brain. The squawking and hissing and crunching and gulping echoed through the empty desert.

Gustavo watched until the vultures finished eating the top half of his head. He put the binoculars down but kept staring in Ivan's direction. He felt nothing for the young thug. He existed only to cause suffering.

He said, "*Vamos por el gringo.*"

'Let's go grab the American.'

4

ALTERNATIVE MEANS

YELLOW VOMIT SPLASHED IN THE TOILET, DROPS OF water and bile hitting the bottom of the seat. The trash bin between the toilet and bathtub was filled with crumpled tissue paper and used condoms. The light in the bathroom *hummed* ceaselessly while the floor vibrated due to the loud music playing downstairs. Some voices from the drunkards and bar-hoppers on the street reached the second floor, too.

Vanessa was on her knees in front of the toilet, gasping and grimacing in disgust. She had accepted the job offer from one of Alicia's friends. It was only her second night working as a prostitute, and she was already revolted with herself. Although some treated her with respect, most of her Johns were ill-mannered and rough. She hated the idea of being reduced to nothing more than a breathing sex toy for horny men. She didn't feel human around these people.

Alicia had advised her to think about her children when things got rough. But Vanessa didn't feel right thinking about her kids while on the clock. Her children didn't belong in the brothel, physically or in memory.

One hand on the counter to her left and the other on the edge of the bathtub to her right, she pushed herself up to her feet. She lowered the lid while looking away, then she flushed the toilet. At the sink to her left, she washed her face, then brushed her teeth. She kept her head down to avoid her reflection in the grungy, cracked mirror in front of her. She had never judged anyone for choosing that line of work, but she was her own harshest critic.

Maldita puta, a voice in the back of her head said.

It translated to 'fucking whore,' and the voice sounded a lot like her mother's.

She dropped the toothbrush and, voice trembling, she said, "*Perdóneme.*"

'Forgive me.'

Before she could dissolve into tears, a woman knocked on the room's door and called out to her, "Vani!"

Vanessa rinsed her mouth and splashed some more water on her face. Patting her face dry with a small towel, she opened the bathroom door. The bedroom looked like a typical hotel room. Nightstands stood to the left and right of the bed in front of her. To the right of the bed, there was a tattered leather sofa and a rickety coffee table. Next to the bathroom door, a dresser hugged the wall. The television on top of the dresser was off, but there was a stack of pornographic DVDs next to it. The red glow from a neon sign outside shone through the curtains.

She put on a pair of jeans and peeked out from behind the curtains, as if she didn't recognize her environment. The neon sign read: *Enrique's Bar*. Under it, another neon sign advertised the availability of Corona Extra beer at the establishment. She could see a couple of people loitering near the bar's entrance. Sober, buzzed, or shit-faced, they all seemed happy.

"Vani!" the woman repeated as she banged on the door—harder, *angrier*.

Vanessa opened the door and found a woman named Anna standing in the hallway. The woman, a few years younger than Vanessa, was wearing a tight black mini dress—so short that the lower curve of her ass was always visible.

"*¿Qué te tomo tanto tiempo?*" Anna asked.

'What took you so long?'

Vanessa said, "*Sólo estaba... Perdón, no te oí. ¿Qué pasa?*"

'I was just... Sorry, I didn't hear you. What's up?'

Anna said, "*Tiempo para trabajar. Vamos.*"

'Time to work. Let's go.'

Vanessa nodded reluctantly. She followed the other prostitute down the hall. Moaning and shouting seeped out of the other rooms. She couldn't tell if the noise was caused by pleasure or pain, though. She went down a stairwell and ended up in the bar. Along with most of the other new and unknown prostitutes, she worked as a bartender between sessions with her Johns. The popular prostitutes mingled with the patrons, attempting to seduce anyone who looked like they could afford them.

Suavemente by Elvis Crespo played in the bar.

Vanessa took orders and served drinks. She occasionally joined men at their tables and drank with them. She wasn't very aggressive when it came to selling herself, so when they got bored of her, the younger men pushed her aside and went for the more sexually willing prostitutes. The older men in the bar —those pushing sixty—didn't mind her quiet personality. They only wanted to fuck women half their age. She didn't want anything to do with them, though. Some women in the bar gave her dirty looks and jeered at her. She didn't want anything to do with them either.

After failing to solicit a customer for thirty minutes, she returned to the bar for a glass of water. The noise, the pressure, the abuse—it all made her head swim.

"*¿Trabajas aquí?*" a man said from the other side of the bar in a foreign accent.

'You work here?'

Vanessa glanced over at him. A man was leaning over the bar. He looked young, late twenties or early thirties. Connected to the trimmed stubble on his face, his wispy, wavy brown hair was stylishly tousled and combed back. His eyes were bright blue. In the dimly lit club, they appeared to be glowing like headlights. Although he was leaning forward, she could tell he was a tall guy—over a foot taller than her. He seemed out of place in Enrique's Bar.

"*Sí. ¿Qué puedo ofrecerle?*" Vanessa replied.

'Yes. What can I get you?'

With a little smirk, almost imperceptible in the dark, the man said, "*Tú.*"

It translated to: 'You.'

Vanessa was taken aback by his approach. He was confident, but he didn't come off as arrogant or slimy like most of the other men in the bar.

"*¿Hablas inglés?*" the man said. Before she could respond, he translated his question to English: "Do you speak English?"

Vanessa remained quiet, curious but cautious. He was obviously looking for sex, but she wasn't sure if he was trying to pick up women at the bar or if he knew she was a prostitute.

She said, "Yes. Can I get you something to drink?"

"No, thank you," the man responded. "I haven't seen you here before. You new?"

"Um... Yeah. I mean, yes. I started last night."

"You mean you started working... upstairs?" the man asked, pointing a finger gun at the ceiling with the last word.

Vanessa nodded. *A sex tourist,* she thought. Prior to her first shift, she had spoken to her coworkers about the men coming down from the United States to partake in Mexico's flourishing prostitution business. They usually stayed close to the border. She didn't expect to meet an American John so soon in north-central Mexico.

The man said, "Let's go up for an hour."

"It's 1,500 pesos. You have to pay first."

"I know the rules. It's not my first rodeo."

Unconcerned about the men around him, he pulled a wad of cash held together by a money clip out of his pocket. He peeled three 500-peso bills from the clip and handed them to Vanessa. The men next to him eyeballed his cash, then looked the foreigner up and down, and then went back to drinking their beers.

Vanessa took the money to a man behind the bar. She informed him about the client, received his approval, then walked around the bar and grabbed the foreigner's hand.

She said, "Let's go up to my room."

———

To Vanessa, sex with the foreigner was nothing special. It started with a strip show, then a blowjob led to sex. It got painful whenever the vaginal lubricant dried up, but he didn't get violent with her. He had her cycle through his favorite positions: Missionary, doggy style, cowgirl, reverse cowgirl, doggy style again, then the planking position. He ejaculated into a condom about forty minutes into their session. He paid another 500 pesos for a 20-minute extension, then finished up a second time with ten minutes to spare.

Lying in bed next to her John, Vanessa's curiosity got the best of her. She usually didn't chitchat with her clients, but this man was different. He treated her like a person, so she wanted to do the same for him.

She asked, "So, how do you like Mexico?"

"There's not much to dislike. It's a beautiful country with beautiful women. Can't ask for much more than that."

"I guess so. What's your, um… your favorite place?"

"Here."

"You mean this bar or this city?"

"Both," the man said.

Vanessa asked, "Really? You come around here often, don't you? But you know this area isn't very safe, right? It's not safe at all right now, actually."

The man turned his head to gaze into her eyes. He said, "I'm not scared."

Vanessa started laughing, then cut herself off by putting her hand over her mouth. She could see he wasn't joking. She had never heard anyone say something so absurd, though. Everyone she knew, except for her oblivious son, felt at least *some* fear in that area.

She said, "I'm sorry. I didn't mean to laugh."

"No offense taken," the man said with a half-smile.

Buck naked, he got out of bed and went over to the sofa where his clothes were waiting for him in a neatly folded stack. He put on his underwear and looked out the window, the red glow from the neon sign illuminating his muscular body.

Vanessa sat up in bed and said, "You look like a decent guy. I mean, you are... I don't know how to say what I mean, but you treated me right. I just want to tell you to be careful out here. You can talk to me however you want, but some of the guys out here—and some of the women, too—they might not like your... attitude."

The man pulled his jeans up, then he turned around to face her. Vanessa's eyes widened upon spotting the black pistol in his hand. She didn't notice when he was undressing during her strip tease. He wasn't pointing it at her, it looked like he was just trying to show it off, but it still frightened her.

She said, "Please don't–"

"What's your name?" the man interrupted.

Vanessa spoke English fluently and she heard him clearly, but she didn't know how to answer his question. Her body was telling her to get ready to run.

The man huffed, then asked, "What's wrong? You never seen a, uh... a '*pistola*' before?" He put the pistol on the coffee table. He said, "Tell me your name."

"Vanessa," the prostitute responded in a meek voice.

"And your last name?"

Vanessa opened her mouth. Only a croak of hesitation came out. She shook her head, as if to say: *No, I'm not telling you.* The firearm told her that she was either dealing with a member of law enforcement or a drug dealer—or a member of law enforcement working for drug dealers. Either way, she felt like she was in danger.

The man said, "Don't be like that. I can always go down and ask your boss, Manuel. Or is Fernando working tonight? I'm good friends with lil' Fernie, too."

Vanessa assumed her John had a better relationship with her bosses than she did. She was cornered, stuck between an enigmatic foreigner with a gun and a bar full of drunk thugs—many of whom were armed as well.

She said, "Vanessa Ramirez."

"Nice to meet you, Vanessa," the man said. "My name is–"

"Maybe you shouldn't–"

"–Caleb."

"–tell me."

The room went silent. Dozens of questions ran through Vanessa's mind, but she couldn't muster the courage to ask him anything. She could only hope her alarm would ring and end the session. But even then, with Caleb's connections to the establishment's management, she feared he could stay for as long as he pleased without consequence.

Caleb sat on the sofa and put his socks on, then his

boots, and then a tank top. He wasn't worried about losing control of the pistol in front of him.

Watching him dress himself, Vanessa said, "I don't want any trouble."

"Me neither," Caleb said. "We're just talking. I'm not going to hurt you. You understand that, don't you?"

"I don't... understand anything right now. I'm very confused. What do you want from me?"

"I want to talk."

"About what?"

Caleb threw on his flannel shirt. As he buttoned it, Vanessa's alarm went off. She let it ring for thirty seconds, hoping one of the other prostitutes would notice the ceaseless wailing and come bang on her door.

No one came to her rescue.

After he finished buttoning his shirt, he tucked his pistol in the back of his waistband and walked to Vanessa's side of the bed. He flicked his finger across her cell phone's screen to turn off her alarm. He put another 500-peso bill on the nightstand next to the phone. Vanessa scooted to the middle of the mattress, holding the bed covers tightly over her bare breasts as if Caleb hadn't already seen them.

Caleb said, "I like you, Vanessa. We have... chemistry. You feel it, too, don't you? I think we'd look like a nice couple together."

"I... I can't date customers. It–It's against the rules."

"I know, I know," Caleb replied. He sat down next

to her and said, "I didn't say I want to be a couple, I said we'd *look* like a nice couple—like a *real* couple. Listen, I'll get straight to the point. I work in the smuggling business for a very, *very* powerful man."

'*Smuggling.*' Vanessa's heart sank as soon as she heard that word. It confirmed one of her theories. She was in the presence of a *narco*—a person involved in Mexico's organized crime. She found herself incapable of moving, stiff like a corpse in rigor mortis. It was like the Grim Reaper himself was sitting next to her.

Caleb continued, "Appearance is everything in my line of work. Women like yourself can make this whole process a lot easier at the border. You look clean. You speak English. And like I said, we have chemistry. What do you say? You want to work with me? Want to make some real *dinero?*"

'*Dinero*' translated to 'money.'

Vanessa knew cartel members didn't like to take 'no' for an answer. People either complied or died. She couldn't say a word, though.

Noticing her reluctance, Caleb smiled and said, "You're in this for the money, aren't you? I don't think a girl like you would be here if you weren't desperate for some cash. No, not some cash. You're here because you need *a lot* of money, right? How much do you need? C'mon, tell me."

"*Trescientos cincuenta mil pesos,*" Vanessa said with a hint of reluctance.

Caleb's eyes went to the ceiling as he translated her

words in his head. He looked back at her and said, "Three hundred fifty thousand? For what?"

"To leave Mexico with my kids."

"*Coyotes?*"

Vanessa nodded.

Caleb said, "I knew I liked you for a reason. You're a good woman. But, shit, it's hard to give good people bad news."

"What do you mean?"

"I'll break it down for you. You say you need three hundred fifty thousand pesos to get you and your family out of here. I'll be honest: I enjoyed my time with you, you're my type of girl, but you're no bottom bitch."

"*¿Qué?*" Vanessa asked, brow raised in astonishment.

'What?'

"A bottom bitch, y'know? An earner. A *high* earner. You've got the looks for this job, but you're not selling yourself down there. You're too cold, too introverted. How many customers do you get a night? Three? Maybe four or five? At 1,500 pesos an hour, you're making 7,500 pesos on a good night. And that's before your pimp takes his cut, but let's keep it simple. Let's pretend like you get to keep all that money. At that rate, it'll take you over 45 nights to make the cash you need. But you're not going to be working every night, are you? No, you're a mother. And I can see in your eyes that you're a good one. If you show up every weekend, we're talking five to six months of work. But, again, that's all in this fake scenario where you get to keep all the money. The reality is: You're probably going to get robbed a couple of times, probably going to get beaten by some drunks and junkies, and you're probably going to catch something. It's going to take you a year or two to get that money. And you know what's going to happen then? The price is going to jump. That's the way it goes."

The speech left Vanessa in wordless awe. She agreed with him, though. She replayed her conversations with Alicia in her head, remembering all of her doubts and concerns.

"I know," she said, sounding defeated.

"So, why don't you think about working with me? I have a few big jobs coming up. If you help me, you'll have that money and more in two or three months."

Vanessa looked down at the comforter. She thought about her children's futures first, then she pictured her own. She knew that there were only two ways out of the cartels: Prison or death, in a cement box or a wooden casket, behind bars or under dirt. She was willing to sacrifice herself for her kids, but she couldn't help them if she was taken from them. She had to stay alive and free.

Although scared, she gazed into Caleb's eyes and said, "I can't. I'm sorry."

Caleb didn't immediately react to the refusal. His

face was still and his eyes remained bright—no confusion, no anger.

He patted her shoulder, causing her to recoil, then he said, "You're a good one. Good luck out here." He walked over to the door. As he opened it, he glanced back at her and said, "Maybe we'll see each other again. *Buenas noches, hermosa.*"

The Spanish translated to: 'Good night, beautiful.'

He closed the door behind him as he stepped out. Vanessa bolted into action. Naked, she lurched to the door and locked it, then she ran back to the bed. She opened the drawer on the nightstand and pulled out a pocketknife. She snatched her phone off the table and turned around with the blade drawn. Arms shaking, she dialed 911 but she didn't press the CALL prompt. She was expecting Caleb to return or another cartel member to break into her room and chop her up with a machete.

She stood there in the nude, staring at the door for three minutes that felt like three hours. To her utter surprise, no one showed up. She gasped and dropped the knife, then she fell onto the bed and sobbed. Although Caleb didn't hurt or threaten her, she felt like she had just survived an encounter with a vicious hitman. Again, she could only think about her family.

"*¿Qué estoy haciendo aquí?*" she cried.

'What am I doing here?'

5

THE LAST STRAW

Sɪᴛᴛɪɴɢ ɪɴ ᴛʜᴇ ᴅʀɪᴠᴇʀ's ꜱᴇᴀᴛ ᴏꜰ ʜᴇʀ ꜱᴇᴅᴀɴ ᴡɪᴛʜ ʜᴇʀ hands on the steering wheel, Vanessa stared at her reflection in the rearview mirror. A spasm of shame contracted her face. Thin layers of tears coated her bloodshot eyes. The steering wheel jerked left and right as her arms trembled. Her hand flew up. She moved the mirror, fearing she was going to break down if she kept seeing her reflection. She wasn't in the ideal place to lose her cool after all.

She looked out the windows. She was parked outside of an elementary school. The school had a rustic red brick exterior. The cobblestone street was lined with short buildings—mostly two and three stories tall. Across the street, there was a church. Next to the school, there was a clinic, an optician's shop, and a cellular store. Farther down the street, there were a few restaurants and a hostel. Pedestrians strolled down the sidewalks, enjoying the clear, balmy day.

A pudgy guy in a gray t-shirt—two sizes too small —blue shorts, and flip flops reminded her of a John from Enrique's Bar. A tingly sensation spread across her mouth, as if her taste buds had remembered the excessively bitter flavor of the customer's semen. She pulled a small bottle of mouthwash out of her purse, gargled a mouthful of it, then spit it out into an empty water bottle in her cupholder.

She was afraid her children would smell her night of sex through her breath or taste it in her kisses. They thought she was working the night shift at a restaurant on the weekends. She brought them breakfast from McDonald's every Monday morning to fool them.

Vanessa looked at the school and thought about her meeting with Caleb. It had been three weeks since they met. To her total disappointment, his predictions came true. She had trouble finding high-paying customers due to her cold attitude. She was meeting two clients a night—three on good nights. And she had already been robbed at knifepoint once on her way to her car after a shift. She had barely made a dent in her financial goals.

She murmured, "*Tenía razón...*"

'He was right...'

A bell rang inside of the school. The sound of doors opening and children chattering reached the sidewalk in front of the building.

Vanessa took her cell phone out of her bag and opened the calculator app. She was about to start checking Caleb's math when she heard squealing wheels behind her. She leaned back and squinted at her rearview mirror. Her eyes grew as she spotted the red pickup truck barreling down the street. Over its loud engine, she could hear the flapping from its flat tires. She could see its cracked windshield, too.

The phone fell out of Vanessa's hand as she reached for the steering wheel and the key in the ignition. Before she could start the car, the truck took a sharp left turn behind her sedan, brushing her rear bumper.

The truck crashed into a lamppost in front of the church across the street. The sound of clunking metal and shattering glass echoed through the area along with the gasps and screams from the nearby pedestrians. The front of the truck was crushed like a can of Coke, white smoke billowing out from under the squashed hood, while a small fire broke out under the vehicle.

Upon impact, the driver was ejected through the windshield. His shoulder hit the lamppost with a loud *thud*, sending him spinning through the air like a frisbee before landing on the sidewalk and rolling onto a lawn. His face was split open down the middle— from his hairline to the tip of his nose. Through the flaps of bloody skin, his cracked skull was visible in the deep wound. He squirmed on the ground.

Vanessa gaped at the site of the accident. She noticed some movement in the truck. For a second—a *split* second—she thought about getting out of her car and offering a helping hand. But her gut told her that this wasn't a normal accident. And she knew her gut was correct when she spotted the barrel of a rifle in the vehicle amidst all of the movement.

She glanced back at the rearview mirror upon hearing more squealing wheels. She saw three black pickup trucks with men standing in their cargo beds careen around the corner. She ducked down as the wrecked truck's passenger doors swung open. Peeking over the windowsill, she saw three men climb out of the truck's cab.

Two of them were carrying assault rifles and one had a shotgun slung across his back. They were covered in cuts and blood. One of the men walked with a limp due to a fresh gunshot on his thigh. Another man stood up in the cargo bed, swaying every which way. He had a pistol in his hand. As he jumped off the cargo bed, his legs gave out and he fell to his knees.

"*¡Espérenme!*" he shouted.

'Wait for me!'

He got up, turned, and dragged an unconscious man off the cargo bed. He crouched next to the guy and tried to awaken him, slapping his face and shaking his body, unaware of his obliterated spinal cord. He was yelling the same phrase over and over: '*¡Levántate, güey!*' It translated to: 'Get up, man!'

Vanessa kept her head down as the rest of the armed men ran around her sedan. She grabbed the key in the ignition and put her foot on the gas pedal. She had an opportunity to drive off, but then, from the periphery of her vision, she saw the armed men making their way to the school. *Mis hijos*, she thought. And with that thought of her children, her chance to escape slipped past her.

One of the black pickup trucks sped past her sedan and the crash site, then skidded to a stop a few meters ahead of her. The other two trucks stopped behind the wreck.

"No, no, no," Vanessa whined.

Automatic gunfire erupted in the street. Through the sideview mirror, she saw a hail of bullets pelt down on the man with the pistol. He instantly dropped his weapon and rolled into a ball. Each gunshot made his body convulse. At point-blank range, the unconscious man's head was shot with an assault rifle. Columns of blood rose from his head like water in the Fountains of Bellagio. Bits of brain flew out of the exit wounds, splattering on the cobblestone. The bullets left so many holes of so many sizes that his head now looked like a cheese grater.

From the foyer of the school, the men from the wrecked truck exchanged gunfire with the gang of assassins on the street—and Vanessa was caught in the middle. Weeping, she wrapped her arms around her head and fell over the center console. Bullets instantly shattered some of the car's windows, shards of tempered glass raining down on her and cutting her up. Cracks spread across the rear and front windshields. One of the sideview mirrors was shot off. More bullets riddled the doors.

The shootout felt endless. There wasn't a single second without gunfire. She wondered how many guns were being fired, how many bullets were being used, how many people were being hit. She wasn't even sure if she had been shot or not. She couldn't hear herself bawling her eyes out over the gunfire. The pain from the cuts on her hands, scalp, and neck at least told her that she was still alive.

After about four minutes the shooting slowed down. Some of the assassins from the black trucks were injured, but none of them were killed. They ran through the smoke and dust, shooting their targets' heads and chests two more times each, although the victims were already dead. Even the guy with the dozens of holes in his head was shot twice in the chest. While yelling obscenities in Spanish, the victors climbed back into their trucks and sped off.

Vanessa waited over the center console for fifteen seconds. She sat up in her seat, crumbs of glass falling from her head like dandruff. Her ears were ringing due to the loud gunfire. She saw civilians running through the smoke, attempting to help the victims. Although she couldn't hear them, she knew a song of tragedy always followed the music of violence—gunfire replaced by emergency sirens, battle cries by pained cries, insults by prayers, life by death.

Shaking all over, she looked down at herself. She was shocked to see she was still alive. She didn't find any gunshot wounds on her body either. She thanked God for the miracle. As her hearing returned, she started to make out some of the words outside of her car.

In front of the church, a priest yelled, "*¡Vengan aquí! ¡Vengan aquí!*"

'Come here! Come here!'

"*¡Ayúdanos!*" a man hollered from the school.

'Help us!'

Vanessa stuttered, "Lu–Lucía..." She opened the driver door, causing shards of tempered glass to fall from the windowsill. As she stumbled out of the vehicle, lightheaded and dizzy, she shouted, "Joaquín! Lucía!"

Glass crunching under her sneakers, she lurched around the sedan. She stopped on the sidewalk. Next to her car, which was damaged beyond repair, lay one of the men from the wrecked truck. He was shot through the eyes with pinpoint accuracy and twice in the chest. Blood leaked from gunshot wounds on his neck, left shoulder, and abdomen.

A few feet away from him, another man lay face-first on a small patch of grass. His polo shirt and jeans were covered in bloodstains. The blood soaked his bushy black hair and beads of it clung to the blades of glass like dew as well. There were seven gunshot wounds across his upper back.

Another man—a civilian—sat on the ground and leaned back against the tall steel fence next to the school's front gate, howling in pain. A bullet had gone through his forearm, snapping a bone and leaving a massive crater in his brachioradialis muscle. They could see the bundles of muscle fibers in the wound. His forearm and hand were drenched in blood.

"Joaquín!" Vanessa yelled as she made her way through the front gate. "Lu…"

Her voice faltered mid-word as she turned towards the walkway to her right. Between the administration building and a row of classrooms, she found a group of people. She recognized some of them as faculty members and fellow parents. Their sobbing and pleas for help broke her heart.

An older woman was on her knees between them. She held a little girl—no older than nine years old—in her arms. The girl was wearing a white polo shirt and a long plaid skirt. She had been shot in the head, arms outstretched with her hands hanging limply. The exit wound at the back of her head was the size of a golf ball. Blood and what appeared to be liquefied brain tissue dripped through the exit wound.

Two guys ran up to the group. They took the girl out of the woman's arms. The woman followed them to a van parked in front of the school. They were heading to the hospital. Hope had a way of warping reality. Deep in their minds, they knew nothing could bring that girl back to life—a piece of her brain was left on the school grounds after all—but they were *hoping* they could change that by taking the victim to the hospital.

Fearing the worst, Vanessa ran past the group and, at the top of her lungs, she shouted, "Joaquín!"

"*¡Señora Ramírez!*" a woman shouted from behind her. Vanessa slowed her run to a jog and glanced around. The woman hollered, "*¡Vanessa! ¡Aquí!*"

'Vanessa! Over here!'

Vanessa saw Claudia Valdez standing in the doorway to a classroom. Claudia taught Lucía when she was in the first grade, and she was supposed to teach Joaquín next year.

"*¿Has visto a mis hijos?*" Vanessa asked as she ran up to her.

'Have you seen my children?'

As Claudia was responding, Vanessa spotted her children—as well as other students—cowering in the classroom behind the teacher. She pushed past her and hugged her kids. She looked them over, ensuring they weren't injured by any stray bullets, then hugged them again. Crying, they kept asking her about the incident outside.

Vanessa could only apologize to them. Although she didn't squeeze any triggers, she blamed herself for the shooting. She felt like she was the reason her kids had to live in fear because she had failed to get them out of Mexico. A simultaneous sense of relief and urgency flowed through her. She was glad her kids were safe, but she knew it was only a matter of time before cartel violence affected her family again.

6

NO CHOICE

"*¡TARDE OTRA VEZ!*" FERNANDO YELLED FROM BEHIND THE bar, sneering with annoyance. "*¿Qué pasa contigo?*"

'Late again! What's happening with you?'

Vanessa had just approached the bar. *Cómo Te Voy a Olvidar* by Los Ángeles Azules played in the club. A couple of drunk guys, accompanied by two escorts, sang along to it at a booth. The evening crowd was barely settling in.

Vanessa said, "*Te lo dije, no tengo–*"

'I told you already, I don't have –'

Before she could finish reminding him about her destroyed car, Fernando snapped, "*¡No te hagas!*" It translated to something like: 'Don't play dumb with me!' He beckoned to her and said, "*Ponte a trabajar, cabróna.*"

'Just get to work, bitch.'

Although tired of the abuse, Vanessa couldn't argue

with him. He was a lanky guy, she was sure she could beat him in a fair fight, but he was affiliated with fearsome gangsters. The slightest gesture of disrespect could have put her in danger. And with her car out of the picture, she needed money now more than ever.

So, she gritted her teeth and marched away. She went into the employee locker room behind the stage, which was used for live performances from strippers and musicians—but mostly strippers. She put her belongings in a locker, then adjusted her makeup and clothes in front of a vanity mirror.

She was wearing a light blue long-sleeved top with a low neckline, revealing plenty of cleavage, and tight jeans. She felt confident and beautiful, but she knew she needed an edge to compete with the other prostitutes. She removed her bra and threw it into her locker. Her nipples stood out against the thin fabric of her top.

Vanessa returned to the bar. She served drinks and chatted up the customers. She forced a smirk, face aching after twenty minutes of nonstop smiling.

And it worked.

By midnight, she had met four Johns, breaking her previous record. They were vulgar and belligerent, but they paid their bills. In her workplace, she couldn't ask for much more than that. After her fourth client, she used her short break time to bathe, eat a sandwich in her room, and brush her teeth. Then she went back to work in the bar.

While serving drinks at the bar, she overheard a man say, "*Es él.*"

'That's him.'

Julio Espinoza, wearing a black cap and navy-blue jacket, was sitting next to him. He glanced over at the entrance to the bar. Vanessa followed his gaze. Caleb was receiving a warm welcome at the entrance, surrounded by the bar's staff and a couple of prostitutes. Two Mexican men stayed close to him. Stern-faced and vigilant, they looked like his personal bodyguards. Julio left the bar through the back entrance in a hurry.

Vanessa wondered if he was afraid of Caleb—and if she should have been afraid of him, too. Caleb approached the bar. He was about to order a drink when he finally recognized the bartender.

"Vanessa, right?" he asked.

"Yeah," Vanessa responded. "What can I get you?"

In perfect unison, they both said: "*Tú.*"

'You.'

They shared a laugh.

Caleb said, "So, what do you say? You available?"

Vanessa smiled thinly and nodded. Caleb was a confessed drug smuggler. His occupation scared her, but he had treated her better than all of her other Johns. Although she hated to admit it, she enjoyed his company. She hadn't had a repeat customer since she started working there either. His familiar face sparked a sense of comfort within her.

Once again, Caleb gave her three 500-peso bills. She took the money to her pimp and let him know about the job, then she led Caleb by the hand up to her room on the second floor.

Meanwhile, in the alley behind Enrique's Bar, Julio held a cell phone up to his ear and said, "*El Ken está aquí.*"

'El Ken is here.'

———————

The sex was different this time. Vanessa was more lively—more aggressive. She didn't just turn off the lights in her head and let her John have his way with her like she did with her other clients. Caleb was hot with passion, too. He kissed her like he meant it. Their connection grew stronger. They were comfortable with each other.

They were more than an escort and a customer but less than lovers. They were friends with benefits.

Caleb finished twice with five minutes to spare in his hour. Vanessa got comfortable under the bed covers while Caleb went to the bathroom where he tossed the used condom in the trash bin and took a piss.

As Caleb approached his clothes on the sofa, Vanessa said, "Wait." Caleb stopped and looked at her, hands hovering over his underwear. Vanessa asked, "Can you stay a little longer?"

Caleb stayed quiet. He put on his underwear while staring at her. He wasn't interested in more sex, but he *was* interested in Vanessa.

Vanessa said, "I'm sorry to ask you that. But you're... rich, right? Can I ask you to stay for twenty more minutes?"

Caleb kept gazing curiously at her, as if trying to read her mind. After a few seconds of silence, he took a clip of money out of his pants pocket. He put a 500-peso bill on the nightstand, then sat next to the prostitute.

"Thank you," Vanessa said softly. She called her pimp and informed him about the extension. After the call, she turned her attention to Caleb and repeated, "Thank you."

"*De nada,*" Caleb said. It translated to: 'You're welcome.' Switching back to English, he asked, "So, what's on your mind?"

"What? Oh, um... I just need a little break. That's all."

"I know what you mean. That's why I come here. To take a break. To get away from all the craziness out there. I know you might not love it here, it's probably like a prison for a girl like you, but for me... This place is like a safe room. I don't have to worry about anyone creeping up on me. It's not like they can get to me without getting through everyone else first."

"I thought you weren't scared."

"Don't confuse caution with fear. You wanna know

what my dad taught me when I was a kid? He said: 'Being cautious means staying one step ahead of everyone else. Being scared means cowering behind and letting the monsters get ya.' And he was right. You can't let your guard down in a place like this. You have to keep your eyes open and your feet moving. You fall behind and the 'monsters'—the gangsters, the *narcos*—will get you. And when they do... it's over."

Vanessa thought about the shootout in front of the school. She wondered if 'caution' could have saved the victims of collateral damage.

"I understand," she said.

"I thought so. You're a smart girl. So, how's your 'fundraising' going?"

"Fundraising?"

Caleb took a cigarette out of the pack on the night-stand. He clenched it between his teeth and lit it. The orange glow from the hot cherry played beautifully with the red light from the establishment's neon sign.

Holding the smoke in his lungs, he said, "The money you were saving."

"Oh. It's... bad."

Caleb blew the smoke overhead, then looked at Vanessa and asked, "Someone rob you?"

"No. There was a shooting at my kids' school. Well, outside of it. I was parked out there and... and these guys came up and started shooting at each other. I was stuck in the middle of it. My car was... It was destroyed.

I'll have to buy another one soon, so now I have to save more. It's worse than before I started working here."

Caleb took a drag on his cigarette and grabbed Vanessa's wrist. The unexpected softness of his fingers made her nervous.

"Do you know what an avalanche is?" he asked, blowing the smoke out at the headboard.

"I think so. Like a wave of snow?"

"Yeah, that's right. A *big* wave of snow. When people get hit by avalanches, it's common for them to get disoriented. They don't know which way is up or down. That's what I think about people like you. Cartel violence comes like an avalanche—destructive, violent, deadly. And when people like you get buried by it, you don't know if you're climbing out or digging yourself deeper."

"I never thought of it like that before, but I guess you're right."

Caleb looked like he was about to say something else, but he took another puff of his cigarette and looked away instead. Vanessa figured he couldn't trust her with sensitive information since she wasn't part of his criminal organization. It was understandable. She was, however, surprised that he hadn't brought up his previous offer again. She was expecting him to be much more aggressive and bitter about her initial refusal.

They sat there and savored the rare moment of tranquility. To the prostitute, the room started feeling less like a dungeon and more like a bedroom. Her trust in Caleb was growing.

Breaking the silence, she said, "If I did work with you... And I mean *if*, okay? Just *if*."

"Yeah?"

"*If* I did work with you... what would I have to do?"

Caleb crushed the cigarette in an ashtray on the nightstand and asked, "Well, who said the offer was still on the table?"

"Huh? Oh, um... I thought... I–I was just saying if–"

"Relax," Caleb interrupted. "I'm just teasing you. Look, if you work with me, you'd be assisting me in moving 'goods' through Mexico and across the border to the United States."

"Goods? You mean drugs? Guns? Stuff like that?"

"It's better if I don't say and you don't know."

"Okay. Then what do you mean across the border? You mean through the *coyote* tunnels?"

"No. I mean we'd be driving straight through the border like a couple of tourists."

"Seriously? That's very, um... risky, no? If you get caught... If *we* get caught, we could go to prison for a very long time."

Caleb said, "You're right. There is a *very* small possibility that we could go to prison for a *very* long time. But again, there's a very small chance of that happening. It would be even smaller if we worked together. Think about it. A white guy with a Mexican girl—his Mexican 'fiancé'—crossing the border looks a lot better than a white stoner crossing after traveling through Mexico alone. It's all about image, and we've got that. Chemistry, remember?"

"But I don't even have my papers. That's why I need the money to cross with the *coyotes*. And I'm not your fiancé."

"Do you have a passport?"

Vanessa nodded.

Caleb said, "Then you don't have to worry about 'papers' or any of that crap. It's not like you're moving over there. We can get you a Border Crossing Card for your 'visits.' All you have to do is sit there, look pretty and *act* like my fiancé, and answer a couple of questions every now and then. You speak English and you speak it well. It should be a piece of cake for you."

He saw the reluctance in her eyes. And like a crafty salesman, he could see he was close to breaking her.

Scooting closer to her and softening his tone, he said, "You're already risking everything in this place. Any day now, one of these guys could lose his shit and kill you. You don't want to end up like one of those women that get chopped up and flushed down a toilet, do you? Down here, they'll put the picture of your corpse under headlines just to sell newspapers and magazines. You don't want your kids to have to see something like that, do you? If you ask me, a little bit of time in prison is a whole lot better than an eternity in a casket. And think of the bright side. You're a woman, so the system will be a lot softer on you than it'll be on me. You might spend three years in prison while I'd get ten or fifteen for the same charge. And if we don't get caught—and we *won't* because it's never happened—you'll have enough money to leave Mexico within the next six months with your family. And I'm talking *legally*, Vanessa. None of that *coyote* bullshit. We have access to those resources."

Vanessa thought about her options only to come to the same conclusion she had found before she started working at the club: She didn't have many. For a widowed mother of two, there weren't a lot of legitimate ways to make a living in Mexico. On the other hand, organized crime thrived during times of economic struggle. Her phone rang on the nightstand, signaling the end of Caleb's extension.

"What's it going to be?" Caleb asked. He got up and continued dressing himself. He said, "I'm not saying this is your last chance, but... You know how it is down here. One minute, you're picking up your kids from school. The next, you might be bleeding out in your car from a gunshot. Or maybe one of your kids will–"

"Please don't talk about my kids," Vanessa said, her voice quavering.

"Yeah, sorry."

Vanessa turned off the alarm. She looked at her phone's wallpaper. It was a picture of herself and her children at a friend's birthday party. The picture was taken only three weeks before the birthday boy—one of Joaquín's classmates—was killed by a stray bullet while playing with action figures in his bedroom.

She looked back at Caleb and said, "I'll do it. I'll work with you if you promise to protect my family."

Caleb returned to the bed, gazed into her eyes, and said, "You have my word. I'll have your family out of here in the next six months. I'll protect you."

Vanessa believed him. She heard the gentleness in his tone and saw the kindness in his eyes. Her shoulders slackened as the anxiety left her body.

A smile tugging at the corners of her mouth and tears dripping across her cheeks, Vanessa sniffled and said, "Thank you."

Caleb said, "I'm going back to the States soon. I'm going to give you my phone number. I'll need some information from you to get you that Border Crossing Card. Your first job will be in a couple of weeks. I'll pick you up when everything's ready." He started heading to the door but stopped at the foot of the bed. He said, "I'm not saying anything is going to go wrong, but make sure you tell your kids you love 'em before we go. Just in case."

"I... I will."

"*Hasta la próxima, hermosa,*" Caleb said before exiting the room.

'Until next time, beautiful.'

Vanessa stayed in bed and thought about her future. Although she knew every country in the world had its fair share of issues, she imagined herself living happily ever after with her kids in the United States. Some reluctance clung to the back of her mind, though. She pictured herself climbing out of a pit of corpses with her family, but a part of her feared she was digging herself deeper.

Like Caleb had told her, she wasn't sure which way was up or down. She only knew she had to keep moving in order to survive.

7

THE FIRST TRIP

THE SILVER FORD EXPLORER CRAWLED FORWARD A FEW feet, then stopped behind the black Ford F-150 in front of it. The column of vehicles moved slowly towards a border station. Surrounded by orange traffic cones, an armored all-terrain military vehicle was parked to the side. Men in military uniforms stood guard between the lanes behind short walls of burlap sandbags. Mariachi music played in the small town behind the civilian vehicles.

Caleb sat in the driver's seat of the Ford Explorer while Vanessa sat in the passenger seat. *Goodbye* by Post Malone featuring Young Thug was playing through the radio. Vanessa was breathing loudly through her nose while staring vacantly at the side-view mirror. She felt like someone was going to open the door and pull her out of the SUV. She couldn't stop thinking about her children either. She felt like she was abandoning them by leaving the country.

She had managed to persuade Alicia to babysit Joaquín and Lucía. She told Alicia she was spending the weekend with a wealthy client, and she told her kids she was going on a small trip to explore a career opportunity.

Interrupting her thoughts, Caleb said, "Perk up. Smile a little. Remember what I told you: These inspections usually take a minute or two. It's no big deal."

He grabbed her hand. Once again, his smooth skin and gentle touch instilled a sense of confidence within her.

He said, "Everything's going to be fine. It's almost over."

Vanessa put a little smile on her face and said, "I know. I know."

The inspection of the Ford F-150 took about thirty seconds. The couple watched it cruise over the Progreso International Bridge as they pulled up to the kiosk.

Hector Ortiz, the border patrol agent, said, "Papers."

Caleb took their passports and Vanessa's Border Crossing Card out of the glove compartment. He handed them to the border patrol agent.

"Anything to declare?" Hector asked as he skimmed through Caleb's passport.

Vanessa was relieved the border patrol agent couldn't read her mind because she immediately thought about the contraband hidden in the SUV. Over $200,000 worth of black tar heroin and meth-amphetamine was stored in the Ford Explorer's gas tank, spare tire, and quarter panels.

"No, sir," Caleb responded.

Hector moved to Vanessa's documentation. He looked at her passport, then at her, then back at her passport. Then he scanned her Border Crossing Card.

He leaned forward and, looking directly at her, he asked, "*¿Hablas inglés?*"

'Speak English?'

"Yes," Vanessa said with a nod.

"You mean 'yes, sir,' don't you?"

"Oh, ye–yes, sir."

Feeling the tension in the air, Caleb asked, "Is there a problem?"

Ignoring him, Hector asked, "Anything to declare, ma'am?"

Vanessa said, "No, sir."

"Is there a problem?" Caleb repeated, raising his voice.

Hector said, "What's the purpose of your visit to the United States today, folks?"

"I live here and she's visiting."

"And what's the nature of your relationship?"

"We're engaged," Vanessa said.

She tried to match Caleb's tone, irked by the questioning but not quite defensive. She figured a real couple would have been offended by the suspicions cast on their relationship.

Another border patrol agent entered the kiosk. They spoke in hushed voices, then they reviewed the documentation again.

Caleb sighed and shook his head. Vanessa grabbed his hand and shrugged at him, as if to say: *What can you do?* Caleb had to fight the urge to smile. He was impressed by Vanessa's performance. They played well off each other, understanding each other's cues without trouble as if they had been working together for years.

Hector handed Caleb the documentation and said, "You're free to go."

"Yeah, thanks," Caleb replied.

Vanessa wanted to say: '*Really?*' But she bit her lower lip to stop herself from blurting it out. She put the documentation in the glove compartment. A cocktail of emotions—relief, excitement, astonishment, happiness—left her hands shaking. Fortunately, Caleb had already started driving forward so the border patrol agents didn't notice.

The whole process at the kiosk took less than three minutes. They had spent more time in the line to the border crossing station.

Through the rearview mirror, Vanessa saw a sign that read:

WARNING
ILLEGAL TO CARRY
FIREARMS/AMMUNITION
INTO MEXICO

She couldn't read the rest of it as they put some distance between themselves and the border. But one thing was clear to her: She was no longer in Mexico.

Afuera del infierno, she told herself.

It translated to: 'Out of hell.'

She rolled her window down and looked out. She didn't see much of interest—overgrown foliage and trees as far as the eye could see, a clear blue sky dappled with fluffy white clouds, cars cruising towards the border. The fresh air tasted the same, too.

Yet, with tears of joy welling in her eyes, she couldn't help but smile. She swallowed big gulps of air and released each one as a massive sigh of relief. The silence—*the peace*—overwhelmed her. There was no gunfire in the distance, no *narcos* patrolling the streets, no messages left on dead bodies.

"*Afuera del infierno,*" she whispered as she wiped the tears from her eyes.

Caleb smirked, amused by her innocence. He asked, "How are you feeling?"

Trying to hide her tears, Vanessa lowered her head and said, "Good. Really good."

"Easier than you thought, huh?"

"Yeah," Vanessa said with a nervous laugh.

"Well, it's only going to get easier after this. Let's drop off the car, check in to our motel, then act like a couple for a few nights before I take you back to Mexico."

"Yeah, let's do it."

They drove to a gas station outside of Progreso, Texas, and parked the SUV behind the auto repair service garage.

Caleb said, "Grab the papers from the glove compartment." He grabbed a duffel bag full of clothes from the back seat and said, "And don't forget anything."

———

Caleb and Vanessa had dinner at a Mexican restaurant. It was a small but popular eatery. From the entrance, tables for two hugged the wall to the left and there was a bar to the right. In the back, there were two tables for four. The restaurant was filled beyond capacity, customers packed tight like a crowd at a concert.

Vanessa sat at the end of the bar closest to the exit and, since there weren't enough seats, Caleb stood next to her. They ate chicken enchiladas with rice. Vanessa opted for green sauce on hers while Caleb asked for red sauce.

"How's the food?" Caleb asked. "Worse than Mexico?"

"It's good," Vanessa responded. "I've tasted better and worse back home."

"Honestly, I can't tell the difference sometimes. But I have friends who *swear* you can only get 'real' Mexican food in Mexico."

"I've heard that before, too. But I like this place. The food is good, and it feels... I don't know why, but it makes me feel like a kid."

"Reminds you of your mom's cooking? Or your '*abuela's*' maybe?"

'*Abuela*' translated to 'grandmother.'

Vanessa said, "It's not that, no."

She glanced around the restaurant. She observed the other customers—families, couples, singles. The children looked happy, kicking their feet and chatting amongst themselves. She overheard conversations in English, Spanish, and Spanglish. There was an atmosphere of normality in the restaurant.

She looked back at her food and said, "I just haven't felt 'normal' like this in a long time."

"I get what you mean. I love Mexico, but there's some, uh... some 'security' in knowing I can always come back here."

"Caleb... You know a lot about me, but I don't know that much about you. Why do you do... *this?*"

Caleb shoved another forkful of his enchilada in his mouth before scanning the bar for any eavesdroppers. Everyone seemed to be minding their own business.

He said, "I think it would be best if we didn't talk about the specifics of the business in public. But the answer is simple: *Money*." He started cutting another piece of his enchilada with a knife and fork. He said, "That's it. Money, money... and more money."

"Is it worth it?"

"Yeah. And I'm sure you'll be saying the same thing after you get your first payment."

Vanessa said, "I mean, are..." She looked over her shoulder, then she leaned closer to her partner. With her voice just above a whisper, she asked, "I mean, are you okay hurting people for money?"

Caleb stopped sawing into the enchilada. His eyes appeared to darken as he glared at her. He looked over her head. No one was looking back at them.

A slice of wet tortilla and a piece of chicken impaled on it, he held the fork up to Vanessa's face and said, "I said *don't* talk business in public."

He shoved the food in his mouth and shook his head. Vanessa was caught off guard by his aggressive reaction. But she understood his frustration. She was still afraid a border patrol agent was going to drag her out of the restaurant and throw her in a detention center. She went back to her meal, hoping she hadn't damaged their business.

"I'm sorry," Caleb said as he put his silverware down. "I'm just trying to be careful. If you want the truth, I've never hurt anyone in this business. I'm not saying I'm a pacifist or anything like that. I just haven't been put in that position. Yet."

Vanessa was skeptical at first, but then she remembered the smoothness of his hands. He was capable of violence—everyone was—but it wasn't part of his life. He wasn't like the other cartel members she had read about in Mexico.

She asked, "Do you have a family?"

"Not one of my own, no. I probably wouldn't have started a job like this if I did. I have some nephews and nieces, though. I'm going to make sure they never have to struggle. My money is theirs as much as it is mine."

"That's... That's very sweet."

Caleb said, "Just don't tell anyone about it. People love sweets, y'know? I'm not trying to get 'eaten' out there." He dabbed his face with a napkin and asked, "You ready to go back to our room?"

Vanessa grabbed his hand, smiled, and said, "Yeah. Let's go."

Vanessa and Caleb walked through the small, quiet town. They chatted about their trip and the area without mentioning their job. As soon as they arrived at their motel room, their bubble of sexual tension burst. They kissed as they disrobed, then they had their third sex session with one another.

Their connection was stronger than ever because

the sex was no longer part of a transaction. They were fucking because they *wanted* to fuck.

After the sex, they showered together, then returned to bed. Vanessa lay with her head on Caleb's firm chest.

Before she could drift to sleep, she said, "I'm scared."

"Of what?" Caleb responded, eyes fixed on the ceiling. "Me?"

"No. Everything but you."

"Good. I'm going to protect you. I gave you my word, remember?"

"I know. I just... I think too much."

Caleb massaged her shoulder and said, "Then think about something else. How are you liking your first night in the US?"

"Actually, it's not my first time here. I've never been to Texas before, but I used to visit family in California when I was a little girl."

"Really? Where?"

"Los Angeles. Bakersfield. Ventura."

"And how was it?"

Memories flashed in Vanessa's mind. She recalled playing in sprinklers with her cousins in Bakersfield, walking down the Hollywood Walk of Fame with her family in Los Angeles, and visiting her grandmother's house in Ventura. She didn't have a single bad memory of her childhood trips to the United States.

She said, "Back then, I didn't think about it a lot. It

was like a... a school field trip. It was just another place. Looking at it now... I know we only crossed a bridge to get here, but it feels like I'm in a different... world. There's a war going on in Mexico. You call it a 'Drug War,' but it's more like a... a *guerra civil*. Do you know what that means?"

"Sounds like a civil war."

"*Yes*. Yes, a civil war, Caleb. And I don't think anyone in the world cares. They only care enough to make movies and TV shows about it. I know the US isn't perfect, but it's calmer than Mexico. It's safer. I felt it as soon as we crossed. I know it can still be dangerous around here, but at least I won't have to worry about the cartels anymore. At least my kids will have a better chance at living happily here."

Something inside of Caleb wanted to tell her about his country's issues—the poverty, the racism, the gun violence, the political grandstanding, the dog-eat-dog culture. He didn't want to discourage her, though. He needed her for his work, so he had to keep her dream alive to keep her on board.

He caressed her hair and said, "Everything's going to work out for you and your kids in the end. I'll watch your back as long as you watch mine."

Vanessa looked up at his face. She couldn't find a trace of deceit in his eyes. She kissed him, then she snuggled up against his chest.

8

WELCOME TO THE FAMILY

"Who is he?" Vanessa asked from the passenger seat.

As he parked outside of an auto repair garage, Caleb said, "A friend."

They arrived in Nuevo Progreso, Mexico, in a different silver Ford Explorer. It had the same license plates as the trap car they had left in Texas two days earlier, but this new vehicle was clean. The garage in front of them was open. Inside, a man leaned back against the side of a black luxury sedan. He had a skin fade haircut, the top slicked back, and his face was clean shaven. He wore a black button-up shirt with the top three buttons unfastened and the sleeves rolled up, a gaudy belt buckle with a golden assault rifle on it, an equally flashy gold wristwatch, jeans, and cowboy boots.

He was dressed like some of the other cartel

members Vanessa had seen throughout her life. But he reminded her more of Caleb than the other thugs. He looked approachable.

"C'mon, I'll introduce you," Caleb said.

He grabbed the duffel bag from the back seat, then exited the SUV. Vanessa watched the men as they greeted each other. They seemed to be on good terms, but she was still suspicious of them. She took their travel documents out of the glove compartment, grabbed her bag, then joined them in the garage.

As she approached, Caleb said, "Vanessa, this is Diego Ruiz. He's, uh... Well, let's just say he's on our side."

Reaching out for a handshake, Diego said, "Nice to meet you. Heard a lot about you, you know?"

Vanessa shook his hand and said, "Hi."

"Hi? You speak more English than that, right? I thought you were some sorta genius."

"N–No, I'm not a... I mean, yeah, I do speak more English. I'm sorry if I sounded rude or cold. I'm just a little surprised. You weren't... part of the plan."

"What *are* you doing here, Diego?" Caleb asked. "I've got everything under control, *hermano*."

'*Hermano*' translated to 'brother.'

"*El jefe* wants to see you," Diego answered.

And '*el jefe*' translated to 'the boss.'

Caleb said, "Yeah, sure. Let me drop off Vanessa, then we'll head out."

Diego sucked his teeth and shook his head, then said, "Nah, man. *El jefe* wants to meet her, too."

Vanessa took a step back and looked over her shoulder. She was afraid she was being set up, about to be kidnapped, extorted, and tortured to death by a cartel. Two potential responses floated around in her mind, looking for a way to escape through her mouth: '*Did I do something wrong?*' and '*Help!*' But a debilitating fear stole her voice.

She found some comfort in the befuddled expression on Caleb's face. He was either a very good actor or just as confused as her. She trusted him, though, so she sidestepped until she was partially hidden behind him.

"Is there a problem?" Caleb asked, calm and unafraid.

Diego chuckled, then said, "No, *güey*. He only wants to talk to the both of you. He's been in a good mood, so he wants to 'socialize,' you know?"

'*Socialize.*' The word echoed through Vanessa's head. She wondered if the cartel's big boss really wanted to socialize with them or if it was a code word for something sexual or violent—or something sexual *and* violent.

She stuttered, "I–I have to go home. *Mis hijos...* My kids are waiting for me. Their babysitter is–"

"Your kids will be fine. That girl, the babysitter... Her name is Alicia Cortes, right? She's going to stay at your home for a little longer. She knows you're busy with your work. We'll have you back by dinner anyway, so don't trip. Now, go use the bathroom because it's a long drive and we're not stopping for anything."

Like a child, Vanessa was scared into a breath-holding spell. Her head trembled while her shoulders hitched up to her ears. She looked at Caleb for direction. He gave her a nod and a small smile, as if to say: *Go ahead. Everything's fine.* This time, however, he couldn't instill a sense of calmness within her through his cool demeanor.

With her head down so as not to give herself the opportunity to ask the other customers for help, Vanessa marched out of the garage and went to the restroom on the other side of the gas station. There were only two stalls and two sinks in there. It was empty. She entered the first stall and sat down on the toilet without pulling her jeans down.

She sobbed into her hands. Questions swirled around in her head—'*How did they find out about Alicia? Are Joaquín and Lucía safe? Am I going to die?*'—but she was afraid of finding the answers. She couldn't run to the police without jeopardizing her family's safety. She could only trust Caleb and hope for the best.

She finished her business in the restroom, then returned to the garage. From her puffy eyes to her red nose, her emotional breakdown was obvious to the men.

Diego asked, "You good?"

"Yes," Vanessa said softly.

"Then get in the back."

Diego opened the rear passenger side door for her. She took the longest inhale of her life before sitting down. Caleb sat in the seat in front of her.

Leaning into the back seat, Diego asked, "You claustrophobic?"

"No."

"Good. I'm taking you to see the boss. Right now, he trusts you enough to let you work for him, but you're not 'family.' So, I can't let you see where I'm taking you. You're going to wear earplugs, a blindfold, and a bag over your head during the drive. Don't touch *anything*. Don't even reach for your head. I don't care if your nose is itchy or you have to sneeze or you want to fix your hair. Don't do it. Okay? Huh? *¿Me oyes?*"

The Spanish translated to: 'You hear me?'

"Yes," Vanessa said in an unintentional whisper.

"You see? I knew you were a smart girl," Diego said. He reached over her and grabbed the duffel bag from the seat next to her. As he looked through the bag, he said, "Just relax and everything will be okay. Isn't that right, Caleb?"

Caleb and Vanessa made eye contact through the rearview mirror. While Vanessa was scared shitless by the change of plans, Caleb showed no fear. He had one hell of a poker face.

He said, "It's like I said: You watch my back, I watch yours. I've got you, Vani. Trust me."

"Trust *us*," Diego corrected.

Before Vanessa could respond, Diego pushed an

earplug into each of her ear canals and twisted them into place. She could see his lips moving, but she couldn't hear any of his words. Then he covered her eyes with a blindfold. Her breathing intensified as a burlap sack was tossed over her head. She heard Diego's stifled voice again, then she felt someone fasten her seat belt.

On impulse, her hands rose from her knees upon hearing the door slam next to her. Her sudden lack of hearing and sight triggered her survival instincts. She had a strong urge to reach for the sack over her head. But before she could raise her arms any farther, she felt someone touch her left hand. And she recognized those soft fingers.

Caleb, she thought as her hands went back down to her knees.

She felt the car moving. After the first turn, she lost track of their direction. She heard the men's muffled voices as well as some distorted music. She felt a fresh breeze on her damp neck, too. Unable to see or hear, she retreated into her mind.

At first, she thought about her fate. She believed she was going to be sexually violated or executed. She was hoping they wouldn't make an example out of her. She had seen the terrifying cartel snuff videos circulating on the internet and the grisly crime scene photos gracing the covers of magazines. For a moment, she saw the blindfold and earplugs as a silver lining.

At least I won't see it coming, she thought regarding her presumed execution.

Then her mind wandered to her family. Before her trip to the United States, she had told her children that she loved them, but she didn't say goodbye. She wondered if they were going to feel abandoned—if they were going to hate her for leaving them. Then pessimism darkened her thoughts. She was worried the cartel was going to kill her children as well.

Her tears soaked her blindfold and a drop of mucus rolled down to her lips. She swayed in her seat with her trembling hands hovering an inch over her knees. Now, her survival instincts were telling her to fight for her life and her maternal instincts were telling her to fight for her children. Yet, she couldn't over-power her fears.

No tiene sentido, she kept telling herself.

It meant: 'It's pointless.'

Trapped in her head, Vanessa lost track of time. She felt like she was floating through a dark abyss where the laws of nature did not apply and time was nonexistent.

The car came to a halt and the distorted music stopped. The vehicle shook and quiet *thuds* slipped past her earplugs. A breeze hit her sweaty neck and hands. Then her seat belt slid across her chest and waist.

Unable to hear herself, she stuttered, "Wha–What…"

She gasped upon feeling a hand on her right wrist. Then another hand grabbed her left shoulder. She began to babble, spewing a string of unrelated syllables slurred together. She was pulled out of the car. Another person grasped her waist and held her left hand from behind. Again, she recognized the soft touch.

"Caleb," she said, barely audible.

She was led forward. She felt soil under her sneakers for the first few steps, then they transitioned to a hard surface. She was forced to turn right. After some panicky breaths, she noticed the change from fresh air to indoor air, and she could no longer feel the sun beating down on the nape of her neck. She knew she had entered a building.

With the earplugs loosening in her ear canals, Vanessa could hear other footsteps and silverware clattering around her as they moved to the left. She heard a man greet another person in Spanish, then she was led to her right. They walked for about fifteen seconds, then took a left. And after another short stroll, they took a final right.

She was pushed down. For a brief moment, she felt like she was plummeting to the floor. She landed in a soft, comfortable chair, though. The sack was pulled off her head, then the earplugs and blindfold were removed.

In front of her there was a large desk. The computer monitor on top of it was facing the other way. Bookcases—filled with biographies, encyclopedias, and history books in English and Spanish—covered the wall beyond the desk. The bookcase in the middle had a globe, which looked like an antique, on top of it.

And on the wall above the short staircase hung a grayscale painting of a nude woman sitting in a void. The model looked depressed and hopeless, as if she had been held captive for years.

Caleb crouched in front of Vanessa, startling her. She looked back and saw Diego standing behind her. There was an open door behind him, but there were no windows in the room. She took note of her only exit, getting ready to run as soon as the opportunity arose.

"Vani," Caleb said, snatching her attention. As she looked back at him, he said, "The boss will be here any second now. Just be yourself, okay? Stay on his good side."

"Caleb, I–I don't want to be here right now."

"Relax. Nothing's going to happen to you."

"Please listen to me. I *don't* want to be here. I want to go home. I want to see my..."

Her voice trailed away and her pupils dilated with fear as she heard the approaching footsteps. It was too late.

"¡*Diego! ¡Caleb! ¿Cómo fue?*" a man said as he entered the room, his voice harsh but unusually welcoming.

'Diego! Caleb! How did it go?'

Diego responded, "*Muy bien, patrón. ¿Y tú?*"

'Fine, boss. And you?'

"*Estoy vivo y libre,*" the cartel leader said. "*No puedo quejarme.*"

'I'm free and alive. I can't complain.'

From the corner of her eye, Vanessa saw the man shake Diego's hand and pull him in for a hug. Then he greeted Caleb in Spanish, and Caleb responded in Spanglish. The men shook hands, then the leader made his way to the other side of the desk. He leaned back against the short bookcase and spun the globe.

Vanessa was expecting to meet a stout, monstrous guy with a rugged, scarred face in a cowboy costume. Instead, she found a handsome man in his mid-thirties standing before her.

His wavy hair was combed back—not too long, not too short—and his jaw was shaded with groomed stubble. He wore a dark gray dress shirt with black trousers and matching dress shoes. He accessorized with a yellow gold wristwatch and a crucifix chain under his shirt. He wasn't trying to draw too much attention to himself.

"*¿Y tú eres Vanessa, no?*" the leader asked.

'And you are Vanessa, no?'

Vanessa opened her mouth. Her teeth chattered, so she clenched her jaw and swallowed loudly. She drew a deep breath and nodded at him. The globe stopped spinning.

"*¿No puedes hablar?*" the leader asked, smiling. It translated to: 'You can't speak?' He laughed, then said, "Or do you prefer English?"

"*Habla español,*" Diego said from behind her.

'She speaks Spanish.'

"No, no," the leader said. "Let's do this in English. I don't get to practice very much anymore anyway. And besides, we don't want our friend here to feel left out. You know Caleb's Spanish still isn't very good."

While the other men laughed, Caleb smiled slightly and said, "*Perdón.*"

'Sorry.'

The leader sat in the chair across from his guests and said, "Well, let me start by saying that it is a pleasure to meet you, Vanessa. My name is Rafael Vàsquez."

'*Rafael Vàsquez.*' Vanessa's face turned to stone upon hearing the name. She had heard about him on the news. He went by the nickname '*El Decapitador,*' which translated to 'The Decapitator.' Early in his reign, he was known for terrorizing communities by ordering the beheadings of rival cartel members, their families, and random civilians. He ruled through savage violence and refused to affiliate himself with the other cartels in the region. Although it left him with a target on his head and chest, he thrived during times of war.

Vanessa had always feared crossing paths with a man like Rafael. She never wanted to meet her employers or the rest of the criminal underworld's upper echelon. She only wanted to work with Caleb until she had enough money to quit and move.

Stay on his good side, she heard Caleb's words in the back of her head, as if they were communicating telepathically.

Grunting with each pause, she said, "It's... nice to... meet you, too."

"Ahh, so you *can* speak," Rafael replied. "And such a beautiful voice. You remind me of... Well, never mind. We can talk about that some other day. Today... Today, we talk business."

'*Some other day.*' Now, those words sprinkled a pinch of relief into the concoction of fear and anxiety flowing through Vanessa. She rationalized that if he was planning on speaking to her on a different day, then she wasn't going to be executed and her family wasn't in immediate danger.

She gave a twitchy smile and said, "Sure."

"Tell me, Vanessa, how was your first job?" Rafael asked.

"It was... fine. I mean, um... It went well, I guess."

"You guess? You're alive and free, aren't you? In this line of work, life and freedom are everything. It's like the saying goes, we live to fight another day. So, let me ask you something else, *mija*: Will you be 'fighting' for me again? Do you like this job? Or do you want to go back to that whorehouse?"

Vanessa said, "I think..."

She hesitated upon feeling Caleb's hand on her

shoulder. She wanted to tell her boss about her moral struggle with the smuggling business. She didn't want to talk herself into trouble, though.

She said, "I want to continue working for you." She laughed nervously, then continued, "It was scary at first, but it was easier than I thought. Caleb is a good boss. We make a good team, I think."

Rafael wagged his index finger at her and said, "That's what I like to hear. But just remember who's the real boss around here."

He snickered and pointed at himself. The other men in the office nodded in agreement. There was no confusion amongst them. They knew better than to question Rafael's leadership.

"*Sí... patrón,*" Vanessa said, trying to copy Diego's vernacular.

'Yes... boss.'

Rafael said, "I know a lot about you, Vanessa. About your past, your family, your dreams and your nightmares. And I'm not saying that to scare you. No, no, I don't want to do that, *mija*. I'm saying it because I want you to know that I understand you. I can see the good in your heart and the fear in your eyes. You don't want to be here, but this is the only way to get to your destination, right?"

Vanessa feared answering truthfully would offend him. At the same time, she was afraid he was asking her a trick question. She didn't want to lie to him if he already knew the answer.

She nodded slowly.

Rafael said, "Right. I want to... address your concerns because I think you'll have a better time working for me if you understood the *nature* of the business. I'm sure you understand that we are a... criminal organization. That shouldn't bother you, Vanessa." He leaned forward in his seat and started tapping the desk with his index finger as he said, "This government *allows* us to operate. There are thousands of politicians, soldiers, and cops working for the cartels. If they're not in my pocket, they're in someone else's fighting for loose change."

"*Así es,*" Diego commented from the other side of the room.

'That's right.'

Rafael stopped tapping his desk and continued his speech: "When I was a child, my father beat me for stealing a piece of candy from a store. It hurt to walk for days. And you know what? A few years later, the bastard got arrested for robbery. Tried to rob a bank. It's crazy, isn't it? But I tell you this because this same thing—this same *hypocrisy*—is happening now. Corrupt politicians tell us to follow the law while they break it. They tell the people not to take drugs while they make a profit off the drug trade. Tell people not to join cartels while they're already employed by us. It's bullshit, and bullshit should not bother you. We're just following 'Dad's' example, no?"

Vanessa nodded, although she wasn't sure if she

completely agreed with him. She knew corruption was running rampant in the government, but she had her own morals. She knew the difference between right and wrong, and she didn't need the government to set an example for her.

Rafael said, "And I'll tell you something else, Vanessa. If the government took care of our people, we wouldn't be where we are today. We do more for our communities than they do for their own families. We've provided food and housing during times of need. While unemployment soars to record highs, we give people meaningful careers and help them achieve financial independence. We're here because the people want us. No, they *need* us. That is the truth."

Vanessa was impressed by Rafael's charisma and fluency. His speech made her think about smooth-talking politicians, cult leaders, and religious fanatics. He had a way with words.

She said, "I think you could run for president, and you'd probably win."

The room went quiet. An air of tension filled the office like poisonous gas. Rafael tilted his head to the side and glared at his guest. He looked her over, as if baffled by her quip.

Noticing his anger, Vanessa said, "I–I'm so–"

Rafael interrupted her with his laughter. Diego laughed with him while Caleb stayed silent and smirked.

"How'd you know I was thinking about running for office?" Rafael asked jokingly.

Forcing a smile, Vanessa said, "You're just very... likeable."

"Well, thank you for saying so, *mija*," Rafael said as he leaned back in his seat. "I think we understand each other. Follow our instructions and we'll have a long, healthy relationship. You get the same deal the rest of my people get: Stay loyal to me and I'll stay loyal to you. We're a family and we treat each other like one, but never forget who's boss. I don't make it hard to follow my rules, but if you break them... I will break you. Remember that."

"I will."

"Good girl."

Rafael opened a drawer and pulled a thick envelope out. It was filled with cash—so much that it looked like it was about to tear. He thumbed through the money, then without counting it, he took a short stack out. He placed it on the desk, then slid it towards Vanessa.

"Think of that as your signing bonus," he said. "Use it to buy yourself a gun. Something small but powerful. Get some practice with it before your next job."

"I'm sorry, sir, but a gun? I've never used one before. And I don't think I can take one to the States anyway."

"You'll still be traveling with Caleb across the border, but between those jobs, I need you to help with some local deliveries. I'm not asking you to hurt anyone. I'm only asking you to be prepared to defend yourself. These smaller jobs will keep you employed and paid. I can't have you on the payroll doing nothing, can I?"

Vanessa shook her head, uncomfortable with the idea of using a gun. Caleb prodded her shoulder gently, as if to say: *Take it.* It was too late for her to turn back.

"Thank you," she squeaked out as she took the money off the table.

9

THE CHILDREN

Vanessa parked her silver Nissan Versa in the carport next to a row of townhouses. She had purchased the vehicle at a used car dealership to replace her wrecked sedan. Having worked for Rafael for four months now, she had the money to purchase something newer and move somewhere more luxurious, but she didn't want to draw attention to herself, so her car looked like her neighbors'. Escaping from Mexico with her kids was still her primary concern.

Her tote bag slung over her shoulder, she walked around the corner to the front of the townhouses. She strolled past two homes before stopping dead in her tracks. In front of her headlights pierced the darkness of the night, the bright beams peeking over the cars parked on the street. The oncoming vehicle crawled down the road, as if the driver were lost—or searching for someone.

Heart racing, Vanessa went into a half-crouch behind a pickup truck. She reached into her bag and grabbed the small handgun next to her wallet. Her thumb instantly went to the weapon's safety lever and her index finger to the trigger.

But the car rolled past her.

Vanessa moved her finger away from the trigger while staying behind the truck and keeping her eyes glued to the passing vehicle. It sped up near the end of the street, slowed to another crawl at a stop sign, then took a right.

She stared at the intersection for another fifteen seconds. When the vehicle didn't return, she sighed in relief. Paranoia came with the job.

She hurried past two more homes, then crept into the fifth townhouse to her right. She made sure to fasten every lock on the front door.

While securing a chain lock, a woman asked, "*Vani, ¿dónde has estado?*"

'Vani, where have you been?'

Again, Vanessa's hand went straight to her tote bag. But before she could plunge into the bag, she recognized the voice. She looked back and found Alicia standing with her arms crossed next to a staircase leading to the second floor. Since Vanessa started working for the cartels, Alicia had been babysitting Joaquín and Lucía. Vanessa paid her more than she earned at Chuy's Studio for her time.

"*English,*" Vanessa said sternly. She turned to check

on the front door's locks again. She said, "We've been through this before. Only in English when we talk about this."

"Right," Alicia said. "You don't want *los pequeños* to know what you've been up to."

'*Los pequeños*' translated to 'the little ones.'

Vanessa turned to face her friend and said, "It's not like that. I'll tell them everything when they're older and they're out of here. I know they have questions, but they're not old enough for... for the truth yet."

"You can't hide it from them forever. You can't hide *yourself* from them."

"What are you talking about? I'm not hiding from them."

Alicia said, "Vani, you're barely here. You don't even know that Lucía is already learning English in school. And she likes it. She's good at it. She learned a lot of it from you because she wants to be like you." She approached Vanessa and grabbed her friend's hands, the yellow foyer light beaming down on them. She said, "It's been months since you started this. You said you were only going to work for them for a little while. You never said you were going to become one of them."

"I'm not one of them. Don't think that about me."

"People are talking. Joaquín can't understand it, but Lucía–"

"*¡No soy uno de ellos!*" Vanessa snapped in Spanish.

'I'm not one of them!'

Startled, Alicia released Vanessa's hands and

stepped back. For the first time in her life, she was scared of her lifelong friend. Vanessa saw the tears building up in Alicia's eyes. She felt bad about taking her stress out on her. Her gaze wandered to the stairs upon hearing the floorboards creaking above her. If she managed to frighten a grown woman with her roar, she figured she was also scaring her children.

Lowering her voice, she said, "I'm sorry. I'm really sorry."

"It's okay," Alicia said, choking back her tears and forcing a smile. "Forget I said anything. How did it go?"

Vanessa could tell Alicia was just trying to find a respectful way to end the conversation. She said, "It was okay."

"Good. I was worried about you. That's all."

"I know. Thank you for everything."

Vanessa took her wallet out of her bag. She paid Alicia three thousand pesos for her babysitting services, then she opened the front door and stepped aside.

As Alicia walked out, Vanessa asked, "Will you be back next week? Can you watch them for me again?"

Alicia stopped on the sidewalk and looked back at Vanessa. She glanced up at the second-story windows, then to her left and right, and then back at her friend. She wanted to say no with every fiber of her being, but her love for Vanessa and her family was too grand.

She said, "I'll protect them like they were my own

kids." As she walked away, she said, "Good night, Vanessa. Take care."

"Good night, Alicia."

Vanessa watched her until she turned the corner and vanished from her line of sight in the carport. She closed the front door, secured all of the locks and checked them twice, then went to the bottom of the stairs and looked up at the second floor. The hallway upstairs, like the rest of the home except for the foyer, was dark. The creaking had stopped, too.

She went down the hall next to the staircase. At the end of the hall, there was a set of bifold doors with wooden blinds. To her left, an archway led to a dining room. The archway to her right opened up to a living room. While leaving the lights off, she peeked through the archways to ensure her kids weren't snooping around.

The rooms were empty.

She opened the bifold doors, then tugged on a pull cord light switch hanging from the ceiling. The dim yellow light illuminated the cramped storage closet. Coats hung from a rod, cleaning supplies filled a bin on the floor, and there was a vacuum cleaner in the corner. She got down to her knees and crawled under the coats. She grabbed a thick rubber glove from the bin and slipped it over her right hand, which she then used to pull a floorboard up in the back of the closet.

Under the floorboard, there was a pile of sealed envelopes. Each envelope was filled with different amounts of cash from her different jobs. Her cross-border smuggling jobs paid the most. She took another envelope out of her tote bag and thumbed through the cash inside of it. Her count didn't matter much, though. As an underling, she knew she had to accept whatever the cartel paid her.

Payment disputes against cartels weren't sent to lawyers and courtrooms. They were sent to sadistic hitmen and makeshift graves.

Vanessa licked the seal, closed the envelope, then tossed it in the hole with the others. She got to her feet, then stepped on the loose floorboard a couple of times to secure it. She turned around and reached the pull cord light switch, but she froze before she could touch it. She found Lucía standing in the hallway behind her.

The girl was wearing sky-blue pajamas. She stared at her mother with tired but inquisitive eyes.

"*Oye, cariño. ¿Qué haces despierta tan tarde?*" Vanessa asked.

'Hey, darling. What are you doing up so late?'

Lucía shrugged and said, "*Nada.*"

'Nothing.'

Vanessa said, "*Oh. ¿Entonces cómo fue la escuela?*" It translated to: 'Oh. Then how was school?' Switching to English, she tittered to lighten the mood and said, "I heard you're learning English. Are you having fun?"

Lucía looked down at her bare feet and said, "*Es domingo.*"

'It's Sunday...'

"*Domingo,*" Vanessa repeated. "*Entonces, ¿cómo fue tu...*"

Before Vanessa could finish asking about her weekend, Lucía started sniffling and shuddering. Vanessa hurried to her and hugged her.

"*¿Qué pasa?*" she asked in a soothing tone.

'What's wrong?'

Going from sniffling to bawling, Lucía said, "*Tengo miedo.*"

'I'm scared.'

"*¿De qué, mija?*"

'Of what, honey?'

"*Los niños en la escuela dijeron que eres narco,*" Lucía explained in tears. "*¡Dijeron que te vas a morir!*"

'The kids at school said you're a cartel member. They said you're going to die.'

Lucía's words hit Vanessa like bullets, killing her inside. Anger was her first response. She wanted to ask for her classmates' names so she could confront their parents. Fear followed her fury. She had tried to hide her criminal career to protect herself from other cartels and the authorities. She looked over Lucía's shoulder at the front door, wondering if someone was watching her family. Then sadness replaced her fear as she listened to her daughter's weeping.

She hugged her tight and said, "*Están mintiendo. Estoy bien, Lucía. Estamos a salvo. ¿Me oyes?*"

'They're lying. I'm fine, Lucía. We're safe. You hear me?'

"*¿Eres... un narco?*" Lucía asked, toning her crying down to some sniffles.

'Are you... a narco?'

Vanessa said, "*No, no soy un...*"

Her voice petered out mid-sentence. She could already see the doubt in her daughter's eyes. It broke her heart to lie to her. She felt like she was betraying her trust and straining their relationship. At the same time, telling her the truth would have had the same consequences. So, she decided to continue the conversation in English. It was easier to lie in a foreign language.

She said, "I told you before, *mija*. I'm working at a farm. Do you remember that word? *Una granja*, Lucía. My boss is a very kind man from the United States. He's paying me a lot of money to take care of his farm. Maybe... Your friends are confused. Maybe they heard about a different farm. A 'bad' farm."

Speaking slowly, Lucía asked, "Are... you... lying?"

"Believe me, *mija*. Trust me. I'm working hard for us—for you, for your little brother. And please don't talk about these things with anyone. Don't ever talk about *cárteles* and *narcos*. You don't have to worry about that. It's not part of your life. Just... You're still a girl. Please don't think about death. Be happy, *cariño*."

Lucía kept sniffling while avoiding eye contact with her mother. She didn't believe her words, and it was difficult to be happy while growing up in a war zone. It was harder to be happy while surrounded by rumors of her mother's impending death. The fact was, cartel violence *was* part of her life. The shooting outside of her school had opened her eyes and the gossip from her peers opened her ears.

Vanessa kissed her forehead, then carried her upstairs to her bedroom, which she shared with Joaquín. A nightstand separated the two twin-sized beds in the room. Across from the beds, a television sat atop a nine-drawer dresser. A Nintendo Switch was hooked up to the TV with a stack of video game cases next to it. There was a desk in the corner so the kids could complete their homework with some comfort. Dirty laundry—mostly Joaquín's—was littered on the floor.

Joaquín was sitting up in bed with his eyes barely open. He was wearing a black t-shirt with the character Goku from the anime/manga series *Dragon Ball* on it.

"*¿Y tú qué haces despierto?*" Vanessa asked her son as she laid Lucía down on her bed.

'And what are you doing awake?'

Swaying as he fought a bout of drowsiness, Joaquín responded, "*¿Qué pasó?*"

'What happened?'

"*No es nada, mijo. Vuelve a dormir.*"

'It's nothing, my dear. Go back to sleep.'

Joaquín rubbed his eyes with his knuckles and yawned, then he lay his head on his pillow. He faced his sister's bed and watched his family. Sleepiness and curiosity played a game of tug-of-war for his consciousness.

As she tucked Lucía into bed, Vanessa whispered, "Everything is going to be okay, baby. In a few months, we'll be in America. I'll take you to Disneyland and Universal Studios and... and anywhere you want to go."

"*Disneylandia,*" Joaquín murmured, referring to the theme park in Spanish.

Lucía asked, "Why?"

"Why what?"

"Why are we leaving? Is it because you're a..."

Lucía glanced over at her brother, then looked at her mother, cupped her hand over her lips, and mouthed: '*Narco?*'

Vanessa caressed Lucía's forehead and said, "Because it's dangerous here. Because I want you to be happy."

"I am happy with you, ma."

Vanessa said, "And because I want you to grow up with *big* dreams and I want you to be able to follow those dreams. I love Mexico, but... we can't stay here anymore. Mexico is changing. It's... It's on fire. Burning. Going to explode." She opened her hand and made an explosion sound effect with her mouth. She smiled uncertainly and asked, "Do you understand what I mean?"

"*Creo que sí,*" Lucía said.

'I think so.'

"We're going to leave before Mexico explodes, *mija*. You won't have to be scared anymore. I promise."

With concern written on her face, Lucía nodded. Although the shooting outside of her school rattled her, she feared cartel violence less than her mother did.

Vanessa made the sign of the cross over Lucía's upper body and recited the blessing in Spanish: "*En el nombre del Padre, del Hijo y del Espíritu Santo. Amén.*" She kissed her daughter's forehead, then said, "*Te amo. Duerme bien.*"

'I love you. Sleep well.'

She went over to her son's bed. He was already asleep. A smile touched her lips as she noticed the smirk on his face. The talk of Disneyland made him happy. She blessed him with a quiet sign of the cross prayer, kissed his forehead, told him she loved him, then made sure his body was covered by his blanket.

She stopped at the doorway and gazed into the dark bedroom. Watching her children, she questioned her abilities as a mother and her unstable sense of morality. And once again, she told herself that she didn't have many other options.

She had long crossed the point of no return.

10

HAZARDS OF THE JOB

"¿*Eres Vanessa?*" the woman asked after opening the passenger door of the black SUV.

'You're Vanessa?'

From the driver's seat, Vanessa examined the young woman. She was wearing a white crop top with a low neckline, black leggings, and a pair of black Doc Martens steel-toed work boots. All of her clothing was skintight. A purse hung from her arm as she held the door open. Vanessa's eyes went to the rearview mirror, then she looked over the woman's shoulder. There was a restaurant behind her. She could see the patrons eating breakfast—pancakes, huevos rancheros, chilaquiles, chorizo and eggs—but she didn't spot any familiar faces.

"*Sí,*" she said. "¿*Y Caleb?*"

'Yes. And Caleb?'

The woman climbed into the passenger seat and slammed the door behind her. She opened her purse and pulled out a compact handgun. She checked the double stack magazine. It was loaded with fifteen cartridges of .40 S&W ammunition. Despite its small size, the pistol packed a heavy punch.

She put it back in her purse and said, "*Maneja.*"

'Drive.'

Vanessa was expecting to meet her, so she wasn't frightened by the firearm or bothered by her attitude. She was, however, concerned about Caleb's absence. She started driving to their destination.

She asked, "*¿Tú eres Yolanda? ¿Yolanda Torres?*"

'You are Yolanda? Yolanda Torres?'

The woman said, "*Usualmente, se pregunta eso antes de empezar a manejar. Pero sí. Yo soy La Muñeca de la Muerte.*"

'Usually, you ask that before you start driving. But yeah. I'm the Doll of Death.'

'*La Muñeca de la Muerte,*' which translated to 'the Doll of Death,' was Yolanda's nickname. She often went by the shortened version '*La Muñeca,*' which meant 'The Doll.' She was known for her pretty face, curvy body, and cold heart.

Vanessa said, "*Mucho gusto.*"

It was a casual way of saying: 'It's nice to meet you.' Uninterested, Yolanda nodded without looking her way.

Stopping the car at a red light, Vanessa asked, "*Entonces, ¿te llevo a La Casa Rosa?*"

'So, I'm taking you to La Casa Rosa?'

"*Ya conoces la misión,*" Yolanda said.

'You already know the mission.'

Vanessa kept driving forward. She could tell Yolanda wasn't in a talkative mood. Her new partner was correct, though. They both knew their assignment.

Vanessa was supposed to drive Yolanda to a bar called La Casa Rosa. Like Enrique's Bar, La Casa Rosa also operated as a brothel. Thanks to an arrangement made between the bar and Rafael's cartel, Yolanda had received permission to enter the establishment and act like a prostitute in order to assassinate a customer—a governor's brother who was known to frequent the brothel around lunch time. During the assassination, Vanessa was supposed to wait at the bar while their reinforcements set up shop in the neighborhood in case anything went wrong.

But the mission had changed. Someone was missing. *Caleb.*

Vanessa had only participated in trafficking jobs. This was her first time assisting in an assassination. So, in order to make her comfortable, Caleb was scheduled to ride along and supervise.

"*Perdóname, pero... ¿Dónde está Caleb?*" she asked while taking a right turn onto a cobblestone road.

'Sorry, but... Where's Caleb?'

"*Cómo jodes,*" Yolanda hissed. It was a vulgar way of saying: 'You're annoying me.' She scowled at Vanessa and said, "*Olvídate de ese maldito gringo. Nadie ha visto ni oído nada de él en días. Y tampoco estará siempre aquí para protegerte, perra. Concéntrate en la misión. Si tú jodes esto, ellos te van a joder a ti.*"

'Forget about that fucking American. Nobody's seen or heard a thing from him in days. And he won't always be here to protect you either, bitch. Focus on the job. If you fuck this up, they're going to fuck you up.'

Vanessa said, "*Perdó–*"

Mid-apology, Yolanda continued, "*¿Crees que puedes follar tu camino hacia la cima? ¿Crees que eres especial? Escucha, este es mi mundo. No eres mi jefe. No te metas conmigo.*"

'You think you can fuck your way to the top? You think you're special? Listen, this is my world. You're not my boss. Don't fuck with me.'

Vanessa had been warned about Yolanda's bad temper prior to receiving the assignment. She was going to try to apologize to her again, but she didn't want to worsen their relationship. So, she bit her lower lip, nodded in agreement, and kept driving. During the rest of the twenty-minute drive, she thought only of Caleb.

La Casa Rosa, a pink two-story building, was located between another bar and a nightclub. There was a hostel and some restaurants across the street. The district was most active at night.

Vanessa parked the SUV behind a dumpster in the alley next to the building. She wanted to review their mission before they got started, but before she could say a word, Yolanda hopped out of the vehicle. Vanessa checked the pistol in her tote bag—locked and loaded —then she got out of the SUV and hurried behind the assassin.

In front of the bar, Yolanda spoke to the bouncer about the arrangement. Vanessa felt vulnerable out there. The music in the bar and from the neighboring club clashed in the street, voices and instruments over-lapping to create a song of chaos. She glanced over at the restaurants across the street, then she ran her eyes over the hostel's windows.

It looked like a regular day, but she couldn't shake the feeling that she was being watched. The hair at the nape of her neck prickled and goosebumps rashed out across her shoulders and arms.

"*Oye,*" Yolanda said angrily as she tugged on Vanessa's shoulder. "*Vámonos.*"

'Hey. Let's go.'

She pulled Vanessa into La Casa Rosa. The place was small. The bar was to the left of the entrance, tables were crammed together in the middle, and booths hugged the wall to the right. The circular stairs at the end of the tavern led up to the rooms on the second floor. The room was lit up with pink and green neon lights.

Two older men—both looking like they were in their late sixties—sat at opposite ends of the bar, drinking beer while watching a soccer game on a TV behind the female bartender. Three men sat at a table in the middle of the room, roughhousing and cackling. A couple sat at one booth, and three men and a woman sat at another. It was a slow day.

Yolanda and Vanessa went to the bar. Vanessa sat on a stool while Yolanda asked the bartender about her 'client.' The bartender pointed her to the stairs and told her a room number.

Yolanda leaned close to Vanessa and whispered into her ear: "*Ya vuelvo. Dame cinco minutos.*"

'I'll be right back. Give me five minutes.'

Vanessa watched her as she strutted to the stairs. Yolanda ignored the catcalling from the men at the table.

"*¿Puedo traerte algo?*" the bartender asked.

'Can I get you anything?'

Vanessa said, "*Pues... Agua, por favor.*"

'Well... Water, please.'

The bartender brought her a glass of water. Despite the chatter and laughter around her, Vanessa felt a sense of danger lurking around every corner of the room. She didn't trust the bartender, the other customers, or Yolanda. She found herself wishing for

Caleb's company. Her throat tightening with anxiety, she took a big swig of water.

A minute passed.

She looked up at the ceiling and thought about the job. Smuggling contraband had already taken a toll on her conscience. The mere idea of aiding in a murder killed her inside. She had tried to talk her way out of it, but Rafael's lieutenants wouldn't allow it. She found some comfort in knowing she didn't have to pull the trigger and Caleb was going to join her. But she was alone now.

Another minute passed.

She felt like she had been sitting there for two hours. Leg bouncing and arms shaking, she guzzled the rest of her drink.

She beckoned to the bartender and said, "*Otra agua, por favor.*"

'Another water, please.'

As the bartender took her glass, Vanessa heard a faint popping sound. It came in a rapid burst—*pop-pop-pop-pop*. She looked at the speakers in the corners of the room, wondering if it was some sort of connection issue. Then she heard another burst. It was coming from outside, but it was closer and louder —*bang-bang-bang-bang!*

La policía, she told herself.

'The police.'

Gunfire erupted upstairs. It was coming from two different handguns. The exchange ended after ten seconds. The couple in the booth ran out through the front door while one of the elderly men at the bar hustled over to the men's restroom near the stairs. Then there was more gunfire from outside.

Vanessa stood from her stool. She took two steps towards the stairs, then one towards the front door. Her training told her to support Yolanda while her fears tried to pull her to the exit.

The other elderly man put some money on the bar, put on his baseball cap, then hurried out through the front entrance. The bartender, voice shrill with concern, called out to the bouncer three times. When he didn't respond, she grabbed the landline phone next to the cash register and called her boss.

Yolanda came stumbling down the stairs. Halfway down, she leaned against the handrail and shot up at the second floor. As she took another step down, someone shot back at her four times. Three bullets zipped past her, and one struck her right shoulder. Her feet tangled, sending her plummeting to the floor.

She landed face-first at the bottom of the stairs with her legs sprawled across the first few steps. The pistol slipped out of her hand and landed a few feet away from her.

"Yo–Yolanda," Vanessa stuttered.

The bartender and the remaining customers dropped to the floor and took cover under the tables. The men cursed and the women screamed.

"*¡Pinche puta!*" a man shouted as he limped down the stairs.

'Fucking bitch!'

The man was dressed in business attire—a white dress shirt, black slacks, dress shoes. There was a large, fresh, *growing* bloodstain at the center of his shirt. He had been shot somewhere in his abdomen. Woozy from the loss of blood, he struggled to reload his handgun as he went down the stairs.

Vanessa had seen pictures and videos of the governor's brother. This man was taller and burlier than their target.

This man was an imposter.

Vanessa took the pistol out of her tote bag and ran forward. Holding it in both hands, she pointed it at the stairs, lowered her head, and blindly squeezed the trigger just as the man finished sliding a new magazine into his handgun. She shot her pistol ten times before she noticed there was no return fire.

She looked up and gasped. The man was leaning back against the handrail. With his finger hooked around its trigger guard, his handgun hung upside down, swinging from side to side like a pirate ship attraction at an amusement park. He had been shot three times in the chest and once in the neck. The other bullets hit the wall behind him.

Blood soaked the front of his shirt while avoiding his sleeves, so it looked like he was wearing a red vest. He opened and closed his mouth like a stranded fish gasping for air. Only short, sharp whistling and bubbling noises came out of his throat, though. Dead, he started to slide down but stopped in a crouching stance. Arms hooked over the handrail, he couldn't go any lower.

Vanessa was paralyzed with fear and shock. She replayed the shooting in her head, watching it over and over as if it were her favorite scene from a movie. And she saw herself pulling the trigger from outside of her body, as if she were a cameraman floating through the bar. Although it had been a part of her life since she was a teenager, she had never contributed to the cycle of violence.

"*¡Vete!*" Yolanda screamed from the floor.

'Go!'

Vanessa snapped out of her guilt-induced daze. She ran up to her partner and tried to lift her from the floor. Yolanda screamed and pushed her away.

"*¡Para! ¡Para!*" she yelled.

'Stop! Stop!'

Speaking rapidly, Vanessa asked, "*¿Qué pasa? Tenemos que irnos. ¡Apúrate!*"

'What's wrong? We have to go. Hurry!'

Yolanda crawled forward until her legs were off the stairs. Face dewed with cold sweat, she rolled over and pointed at her right leg. Although it was difficult to see due to her black leggings and the lighting in the bar, there was a gunshot wound on her thigh. The bullet went through a quadricep muscle and came to a stop in one of her hamstrings.

"*Lárgate de aquí,*" Yolanda said. "*No dejes que te agarren.*"

'Get the hell out of here. Don't let them catch you.'

Vanessa stammered, "N-No, Yo–Yolanda–"

"*¡Lárgate, pendeja!*" Yolanda barked.

'Get out, idiot!'

Vanessa staggered away from her. She gazed at her downed partner, impressed by her sacrifice. Yolanda cared more about getting Vanessa out alive than herself. The assassin dragged herself to her pistol and checked her ammunition. The sound of gunfire came from every direction, some gunshots louder than others.

Vanessa ran off. She exited La Casa Rosa through the front entrance. The bouncer was gone. Across the street, diners took cover under tables and behind counters in the restaurants. The windows at the hostel were all closed with their curtains drawn. Cries for help, bursts of automatic gunfire, and the sound of skidding tires echoed through the streets.

The quiet area had transformed into a war zone in a matter of minutes.

Vanessa ran into the alleyway. Upon reaching the dumpster in front of her SUV, she saw two men running towards her in the alley. Both men wore bulletproof vests and carried assault rifles. Vanessa couldn't tell if they were on her side or if they were part of a rival cartel or if they were cops. She took a few more steps towards the SUV.

She was about to wave at them when one of the men stopped, crouched, and aimed his weapon at her. She ducked and ran back with her hand behind her head, as if that would stop a bullet from penetrating her skull. She heard bullets hit the SUV, the dumpster, the wall next to her, and the ground beneath her feet.

She made it around the corner, but quickly lost her footing. She dropped to her knees *hard* on the sidewalk. Pain radiated down to her ankles and up to her hips from her busted kneecaps. She picked herself up, took a few steps forward, then fell again in front of the bar. Fighting through the pain, she lurched across the street.

"*¡Ayúdenme!*" she cried as she approached one of the restaurants.

'Help me!'

She pushed, pulled, and pushed again on the door's handle, but to no avail. The entrance was locked. Through the glass door, she could see employees moving restlessly in the kitchen and customers hiding under tables.

"*¡Déjenme entrar! ¡Ayúdenme!*" she yelled.

'Let me in! Help me!'

Her pleas for help went ignored. She ran towards the neighboring café. Before she could reach the entrance, she saw two black pickup trucks speeding towards La Casa Rosa. Fitted with .50 caliber machine guns and metal plates for extra protection, they were known as *technicals*—improvised fighting vehicles. She recognized the trucks from Rafael's fleet.

"*¡Ayúdenme!*" she screamed for help as she ran into the street and waved her arms at the technicals. The truck in front slowed down as it reached the club next to La Casa Rosa. Vanessa repeated, "*¡Ayúdenme!*"

A thunderous *boom* roared through the street. A second later, a rocket-propelled grenade hit the vehicle from above. The truck exploded into a ball of fire about ten meters away from Vanessa, the ground vibrating and storefront windows shattering all around her. The hot shockwave hit her like a punch to her entire body, launching her back and knocking the wind out of her.

Vanessa writhed on the cobblestone road while a whirlwind of dirt, dust, sparks, blood, and glass fragments blew through the street. Severed limbs and organs rained down like large hailstones. The wrecked truck kept burning. The other technical stopped behind it. The passengers shot up at the roof of the club next to La Casa Rosa.

Out of breath, Vanessa rolled onto her stomach and crawled under a sedan parked in front of the café. Her ears were ringing, but she could still hear the bullets whizzing past her. So, she covered her ears with her hands and sobbed. Some bullets struck the road and others hit the parked sedan. She heard the diners screaming in fear and the cartel members cursing at each other.

She saw a man running backwards down the street, moving away from the burning truck while shooting an assault rifle at the club. Someone shot back at him, hitting him multiple times in the chest and abdomen. He collapsed in the middle of the street. Despite his injuries, he continued fidgeting. He wanted to continue fighting.

"*Dios, protéjame,*" Vanessa whined.

'God, protect me.'

The shooting slowed as she began to apologize for her sins. The incapacitated man on the road stopped moving and there was no one else in sight. She moved her hands away from her ears. She could still hear some ringing as well as more gunfire coming from another block in the area. Sparks of hope flickered in her eyes upon hearing the emergency sirens in the distance.

She lay there and listened to the sirens for a minute, waiting for the perfect opportunity to run out. Then she heard the café door open behind her followed by a barrage of hurried footsteps. She convinced herself that she had a higher chance of surviving if she stuck with a group of civilians. She crawled out from under the sedan.

Her legs wobbled as she got to her feet. She leaned against the car and groaned. The concussive blast from the explosion gave her a pounding headache. A wave of nausea rushed through her, too.

"*E– Esperen,*" she said weakly.

'Wait.'

A man in a bulletproof vest and ski mask ran up to her from across the street. She didn't hear him coming due to the commotion. He threw a black sack over her head, then grabbed her from behind and carried her back to the alley. Kicking and screaming, Vanessa was thrown into a van. The driver peeled out and took a left, racing away from the firefight.

11

REMEMBER ME

VANESSA WAS DOWN ON HER KNEES WITH HER HANDS bound behind her back with zip ties. Her bare feet were bound together, too. Pinpricks of white light pierced the black sack over her head like stars in the night. Her sniveling was stifled by the strip of duct tape over her mouth. She could hear someone else whimpering nearby. She also heard people breathing around her. They exuded an eerie sense of acceptance —defeated in peace.

The people around her knew what was coming. And they knew there was nothing they could do to stop it.

I'm going to die, Vanessa had thought, and the thought had been recurring since she was dragged into that van outside of La Casa Rosa hours earlier.

From Vanessa's left, footsteps approached the group. She heard some men speaking, but she couldn't make out their words over the sound of rustling sacks. She started panting as the footsteps closed in on her, tears and mucus running down her face and wetting the tape over her mouth. She rocked back and forth while shaking her head. *No, no, no,* she tried to scream, but only a long moan came out.

The sack was pulled off her head. She caught a glimpse of a man's lower body—a diamond-encrusted belt buckle with a horse on it, jeans, and cowboy boots. The guy moved to her right and took the sack off another hostage's head, then he moved onto the next one. All of the hostages—eight to Vanessa's left, six to her right—were lined up with about a yard of space between them. She recognized some of them from Rafael's cartel. Others appeared to be civilians caught in the crossfire.

Their captors walked in front of them and behind them. One of them used a camcorder to record the hostages in high definition. Some of the captors had action cameras attached to their bulletproof vests, too.

To Vanessa's left, Yolanda stood on her knees with her shoulders slumped forward and her back curved, looking like the number '2.' She was lethargic from the loss of blood and the pain from her untreated gunshot wounds. She had to fight to stop herself from falling over. But she didn't show any fear in the face of death. Her brow was furrowed in anger while her breathing was slow and calm. She wasn't going to give her captors any satisfaction.

Behind the hostages, there was an airplane hangar. The bifold hangar door was open, but they couldn't see much inside of it since the lights were off. There were no planes in sight. There was another building next to the hangar. A tall chain-link fence with razor wire at the top surrounded the property. At regular intervals, lampposts with LEDs lit up the perimeter with bright white light. The area looked like an old airfield that had been converted into a prison.

The lights and cameras frightened Vanessa. They made a loud, bold statement for the captors: '*We don't hide in the darkness. Come and watch the show.*' Showmanship was part of the culture. They were making real-life horror movies to instill fear—unadulterated, *debilitating* fear—into the country.

From the end of the line to Vanessa's left, a man shouted, "*¡Escuchen!*"

'Listen up!'

The captured cartel members kept staring forward. Vanessa and the civilians looked to their left. They saw Gustavo Rivera standing there. Unlike the other captors, he wasn't wearing a bulletproof vest—only a striped polo shirt under a windbreaker, jeans, boots, and a cap. He could have passed as one of the civilians in the group of hostages.

Gustavo said, "*Me llamo Gustavo Rivera. Soy el Empalador. Soy tu Dios esta noche. Cuando rezáis, me rezáis a mí. Y responderé a tus oraciones con la vida o la muerte. Todo lo que quiero es información. Estoy buscando a Rafael Vásquez. Dame lo que quiero y te daré lo que quieres. Es fácil, ¿no? Pero si me mientes... te mostraré una visión del infierno antes de mandarte allí. Y recuerden, todos han sido inyectados con un cóctel de drogas. Te prometo que no sentirás nada más que agonía y angustia si no cooperas. Te lo prometo.*"

'My name is Gustavo Rivera. I am the Impaler. I am your God tonight. When you pray, you pray to me. And I will answer your prayers with life or death. All I want is information. I'm looking for Rafael Vàsquez. Give me what I want and I'll give you what you want. Simple, no? But if you lie to me... I'll show you a glimpse of hell before I send you down there. And remember, you've all been injected with a cocktail of drugs. I promise you'll feel nothing but agony and heartbreak if you don't cooperate. I promise.'

He walked up to the first hostage—a bald man in his mid-thirties. He yanked the strip of tape off his mouth, letting it spiral to the soil under them. Ricardo Rivera, Gustavo's cousin, walked up behind the hostage and pressed the razor edge of his machete against the side of the man's neck. Another cartel member in a ski mask stood by, pointing a rifle at the bald man.

Towering over the hostage, Gustavo asked, "*¿Cómo te llamas y quién es tu patrón?*"

'What's your name and who's your boss?'

With a blank stare, the hostage said, "*No voy a decir nada.*"

'I'm not saying a thing.'

"*¿Estás seguro?*" Gustavo asked. It translated to: 'Are you sure?' The hostage stayed quiet. Gustavo slapped him lightly on the side of his head and said, "*Qué lástima. Pues, vamos a ver si esto te hace cambiar de opinión.*"

'What a pity. Well, we'll see if this changes your mind.'

He looked to his right, put two fingers in his mouth, and whistled. A black pickup truck with a camper cap emerged from behind the building next to the hangar. *Dancing Queen* by ABBA came out of the truck as it rolled over to the hostages slowly. Ignacio Tapia, a lanky man with short black hair and a trimmed beard, was driving the vehicle. He parked behind Gustavo.

Gustavo looked at the driver and said, "*Bájale, güey.*"

'Turn it down, man.'

Ignacio gave him a thumbs-up, then lowered the volume until it was barely audible over the hostages' panicked breathing. He hopped out of the truck and made his way to the back of it. Some movement was visible through the camper cap's tinted windows. He popped open the tailgate and flung the rear window up.

"*Ven aquí,*" he said as he reached into the cargo bed. "*¡Tú! ¡Ven aquí!*"

'Come here. You! Come here!'

Sniffling and whining came out of the truck.

While Ignacio fumbled about, Gustavo stared

down at the bald hostage and asked, "*¿Crees que soy tonto? ¿Crees que no sé quién eres? Eres la perra de Rafa, Arturo Chávez.*"

'You think I'm dumb? You think I don't know you already? You're Rafa's bitch, Arturo Chávez.'

The hostage brought his gaze up to Gustavo's eyes, his breathing accelerating. His reaction revealed the truth: Gustavo was correct.

Gustavo said, "*Y él... Este es tu hijo, Esteban.*"

'And him... This is your son, Esteban.'

Ignacio carried thirteen-year-old Esteban out of the truck. The boy's hands were bound behind his back with zip ties. Ignacio pushed him towards Gustavo, then closed the tailgate and the window. Esteban was swaying and sniveling, dizzy and scared. He had a similar mix of drugs flowing through him, albeit at a smaller dosage to avoid an overdose. Gustavo grabbed the boy's head and pulled him closer to him.

"*¡No lo toques, cabrón!*" Arturo barked.

'Don't touch him, asshole!'

"*Mira a tu papá, Esteban,*" Gustavo said with a smirk. It translated to: 'Look at your dad, Esteban.' He pushed him in front of him, then rested his hands on the boy's shoulders. He said, "*Estás aquí–*"

"*¡Que no lo toques, hijo de puta!*"

"*–gracias a él.*"

Gustavo had said: 'You're here thanks to him.' And Arturo had interrupted with: 'I said don't touch him, son of a bitch!' Arturo's yelling only agitated his son, though.

Still smiling, Gustavo said, "*Escúchame, Arturo. Esta es tu última oportunidad. Háblame de Rafa... o sufrir.*"

'Listen to me, Arturo. This is your last chance. Tell me about Rafa... or suffer.'

Shuddering, Esteban cried, "*Papá, ¿qué está pasando?*"

'Dad, what's happening?'

Arturo was a hardened criminal, an unfaithful husband, and a distant parent. He had tortured and murdered more people than he could remember. And he never showed a shred a remorse for his crimes. Yet, he still loved and valued his family. Despite his cheating and abuse, he was loyal to them.

He looked his son in the eye and said, "*Hijo, no tengas miedo. Cierra los ojos y reza. Todo va a estar bien. Confía en mí.*"

'Son, don't be scared. Close your eyes and pray. It's going to be okay. Trust me.'

Gustavo sighed, then said, "*Agárralo. Y con fuerza.*"

'Grab him. And tightly.'

"*¡Vete a la verga, güey!*" Arturo shouted.

'*Vete a la verga*' was vulgar slang for 'go fuck yourself' or 'go to hell.'

Ricardo crouched and grabbed Arturo in a rear naked choke. Gustavo did the same to Esteban. With his free hand, he snapped his fingers at Ignacio. Ignacio pulled a hunting knife out of a sheath attached to his waistband and handed it to his boss. Gustavo used the knife to tear Esteban's shirt vertically down the middle with one slice, revealing the boy's skinny torso. At the same time, the blade nicked his chest and upper abdomen.

Esteban's bare feet zigzagged across the soil as he wrestled with his captor. He said the same two words over and over: '*No*' and '*papá.*' Arturo lunged forward and screamed, but Ricardo kept pulling him back.

Vanessa watched in utter terror from the middle of the line. As a mother, she wanted to scream at them through the tape over her mouth. But, like everyone else, she saw the movement in the back of the truck. If her kids were in there, she didn't want to risk their lives with a useless outburst. As selfish as it made her feel, at the end of the day, her children were more important to her than anyone else's kids.

Gustavo tightened his grip on the boy's neck. He pressed the sharp edge of the blade against his chest at a downward angle. It was parallel to his clavicle, right under the protuberant bone. The blade dimpled his skin before piercing it. Tiny beads of blood oozed out and cascaded across the right side of his chest. The drugs in his system kept him conscious, but the concoction couldn't block all of the pain. The boy wailed and flailed in Gustavo's clutches.

Gustavo rotated his wrist, wedging the blade under Esteban's muscle. Then he pushed it downward while moving it with a sawing motion. The beads turned into roaring rivers of blood as the blade traveled under the strips of pectoral muscle. The blood raced across his torso and soaked the waistband of his shorts.

Esteban's eyes, big and bloodshot, bulged from his eye sockets as he shrieked. His scream reverberated through the empty desert like a gunshot. And when he ran out of breath ten seconds later, his scream kept echoing and he started panting and whining. His knees clapped, then his legs gave out. His left foot slithered out in front of him while the right foot slid back and hit Gustavo's boot.

Gustavo hoisted him up by tightening his grip on his neck. He kept sawing until the blade was under Esteban's nipple. He released the boy's neck and took a knee behind him, laying the boy down against his leg. Esteban's eyes rolled back and his eyelids fluttered, but he was still conscious. He felt everything.

"*¡Rafael te va a matar, pinche cabrón!*" Arturo yelled, face wet with tears. "*¡Estás muerto! ¡Muerto, hijo de puta!*"

'Rafael is going to kill you, you fucking bastard! You're dead! Dead, you son of a bitch!'

Gustavo grabbed the flap of Esteban's partially detached muscle in his left hand, then he tilted the blade and sawed outward. The boy's flesh made a loud *crinkling* sound as Gustavo ripped it off his chest. He threw the chunk of muscle at Arturo's knees, as if he were offering it to a rabid dog.

Arturo cursed at him again, but his words went ignored. Vanessa felt his pain, though. She had heard parents cry like him at funerals for their murdered children.

The right side of Esteban's rib cage was exposed. Remaining bits of severed muscle covered some of the bones. Gustavo thrust the blade into the cartilage between each rib. Then, with the butt of the knife's handle, he hammered away at the bones. Ignacio joined in and kicked Esteban's chest with his heavy boot. The boy convulsed and groaned, his bones cracking and crunching.

The men made a large hole in his rib cage. They could see his lung inflating and deflating in his chest cavity.

Ignacio forced a hand through the hole and grabbed the boy's lung. Wet and squishy, it slipped out of his hands. He grabbed it again and tugged on it until part of it protruded from the manmade opening on Esteban's chest. He was about to stab it when Gustavo pushed him away.

The leader said, "*No. güey. Agarra la bomba.*"

'No, man. Grab the bomb.'

Ignacio ran back to the pickup truck and opened the passenger door. He dug through a duffel bag on the passenger seat for a few seconds, then came back to Gustavo with a brick of C-4 in his hand. Gustavo took the explosive. He held it up to show it to the boy's father, then he pushed it into Esteban's chest cavity.

He pointed at Arturo and said, "*Tráelo.*"

'Bring him.'

Gustavo carried Esteban into the truck. He sat in the driver's seat with the boy laying on his lap. Ricardo and Ignacio carried Arturo into the truck through the passenger door. Ignacio sat between Arturo and Gustavo. Arturo was combative, so Ignacio pinned his head against the passenger window while Gustavo drove. Ricardo stayed behind to keep an eye on the rest of the hostages.

Vanessa watched as the truck drove towards a tree about fifty meters in front of her. Her legs trembled with an urge to give chase. Although she had stopped watching the boy's torture, she heard Gustavo's words: '*Agarra la bomba.*' Even though she had no idea if the rival cartel knew about her children, she was worried her kids were being held hostage close to an explosive.

She could see Gustavo and Ignacio carrying Arturo and Esteban out of the truck. Arturo continued putting up a fight, but he was quickly overpowered. The boy was barely conscious—barely alive. The captives were forced to sit on their asses with their backs against the tree, then they were tied to the trunk.

Gustavo and Ignacio got back in the truck. The truck returned to the hangar with Ignacio behind the wheel this time. He parked next to the line of hostages.

As he got out of the truck, Gustavo said, "*Sube el volumen.*"

'Turn it up.'

Ignacio turned up the volume on the truck's radio. *I*

Will Survive by Gloria Gaynor was playing mid-song. The music drowned out Arturo's screams.

Gustavo said, "*No, no, güey. Juega a Las Weather Girls.*"

'No, no, man. Play the Weather Girls.'

He mixed Spanish and English while saying the group's name.

Ignacio chortled and said, "*Sí, patrón.*"

'Yes, boss.'

Gustavo approached the line of hostages. He held a wireless detonator in his right hand, his thumb on a metal toggle switch. *It's Raining Men* by The Weather Girls started playing from the truck's speakers.

"*Miren,*" Gustavo said. "*Si no hablan, te mando al infierno en pedazos.*"

'Look. If you don't talk, I'll send you to hell in pieces.'

And just as the song reached its chorus, Gustavo flipped the detonator's switch. The C-4 in Esteban's chest exploded. The deafening detonation echoed for miles. There was a flash of red. A huge cloud of dirt whirled upward, and the tree fell over. Butchered human remains flew through the air—severed limbs, mutilated organs, chunks of muscle, strips of skin. The boy was beheaded during the explosion. Meanwhile, the right side of his father's head was blown off. After the explosion stopped echoing, the remaining survivors could hear the victims' blood plopping on the soil like big raindrops.

Vanessa fell into a state of paralyzing aghast. She had never seen such a level of cruelty with her own eyes before. A few of the other captives wept, but most of them were surprisingly still and unafraid. Yolanda looked like she was just waiting for Gustavo to finish. There was no hope or fear in her.

Gustavo threw the detonator at Ignacio, then he whistled at Ricardo. Ricardo handed him his machete, then he drew a handgun from his waistband and continued watching the hostages. Machete in hand, Gustavo turned his attention to the next man in line. The guy had a mullet and beard. Dried blood and soot were caked on his cheeks.

"*Y tú...*" Gustavo said. He peeled the tape off the hostage's mouth and asked, "*Tú eres Eduardo, ¿no?*"

'And you... You are Eduardo, no?'

Gustavo was correct. The man's name was Eduardo, but he remained quiet in defiance. It wasn't his first rodeo, so he knew how it was going to go down. All of the hostages were going to die whether they cooperated or not.

Gustavo asked, "*Eduardo, amigo, ¿dónde está tu patrón?*" It translated to: 'Eduardo, my friend, where's your boss?' The hostage responded with a sneer and a huff. Gustavo clicked his tongue, then said, "*En pedazos, entonces.*"

'In pieces, then.'

He grabbed the top of Eduardo's head, then swung the machete at his left ear, severing it with one chop.

The machete cut through the hostage's white t-shirt and sliced into his trapezius muscle as well. A blood-stain rapidly spread across the chest and sleeve of his shirt. The severed ear fell to the ground next to him.

Eduardo groaned through his gritted teeth, his face scrunched up in pain. Gustavo planted his boot on the hostage's right shoulder, forcing him to sit on his heels. With one tug, he pulled the machete out of him. Blood dripped from the blade.

"*¿Dónde está Rafael Vásquez?*" Gustavo asked, raising his voice while maintaining an image of self-control.

'Where is Rafael Vàsquez?'

He gave him ten seconds to answer, and he received ten seconds of panting in return.

Gustavo beckoned to Ricardo and said, "*Agárralo.*"

'Hold him.'

Ricardo crouched behind Eduardo and grabbed him in a rear naked chokehold. Gustavo pressed the razor edge of the machete against Eduardo's hairline and started sawing. Blood ran down the victim's face in a crimson waterfall. The blade slid *under* his scalp. It made a hair-raising screeching noise each time it scraped his skull. More blood sprayed out and hit Ricardo's face.

Trying to bottle his pain, Eduardo cycled between yelps and groans. He knew the footage of his death was going to be distributed on the internet. His body—his physical self—was going to die, but his name was going to live on. He was sure of it. So, he wasn't going to tarnish his reputation by crying, snitching, or begging.

Gustavo grabbed a fistful of Eduardo's hair and pulled on the loose flap of scalp. He could see some patches of skull through the mutilated connective tissue. He severed the flap of scalp with the machete, removing the top part of the hostage's mullet. He only had a bush of hair sticking out from the back of his head now.

His entire head was covered in blood. It entered his eye sockets and coated his eyeballs, turning his vision red. It looked like he was suffering from a subconjunctival hemorrhage.

Gustavo tossed the severed scalp aside, pointed the machete at Eduardo, and said, "*La última oportunidad, güey. ¿Dónde está?*"

'Last chance, asshole. Where is he?'

Eduardo felt the breeze on his exposed skull. It brought a little smile to his face. He looked up at Gustavo, but he could only see a faint outline of him through the blood in his eyes. He shook his head.

"*Está bien,*" Gustavo said.

'Fine then.'

Ricardo unwrapped his arms from around the hostage's neck, then grabbed the hair at the back of his head to stop him from falling. He took a large knife out of his waistband and used its serrated blade to saw into the back of Eduardo's neck. Meanwhile, Gustavo swung his machete at Eduardo's throat. The blade split his Adam's apple in two and punctured his voice box.

Eyes shut and jaw clenched, Eduardo's face twisted into a bloody knot of agony. His cheeks fluttered as he grunted. A cracking sound came out of his mouth, like shards of glass crunching under a pair of boots. He had ground his teeth so hard that some of the enamel broke. Awful, inhuman gurgling sounds came out of the wounds on his neck.

Gustavo swung the machete at his throat. again. The blade ripped through muscles, veins, and tubes with ease. Blood jetted out of Eduardo's severed jugulars. The hostage next to him—a man with grizzled hair in his forties—winced and grimaced as some blood hit the sleeve of his jacket. Ricardo kept cutting into the muscles and bones at the nape of the victim's neck.

With Gustavo's third swing at his neck, Eduardo fell over. His legs moved back and forth, as if he were walking while lying on his side, and his restrained hands flapped behind his back.

The men carried on with the beheading, cutting away at Eduardo's neck from every angle. The gurgling sounds turned into a hissing noise, like pressurized air leaking out of a hole on a tire. Eduardo stopped moving after thirty more seconds of hacking and sawing, but the noise continued to come out of his carved-up neck.

After another thirty seconds, Eduardo's head was

completely removed. The men rolled him onto his back, then placed his head on his chest, as if it were a trophy on a shelf.

Face and hands drenched in blood, Gustavo marched along the line of hostages and shouted, "*¡No estoy jugando! ¡Habla o muere! ¡Deja este lugar por donde viniste o vete al infierno en pedazos! ¡Te prometo que aún no has visto lo peor!*"

'I'm not playing! Talk or die! Leave this place the way you came or go to hell in pieces! I promise you haven't seen the worst yet!'

He stopped towards the center of the line and studied his hostages. The man next to Eduardo appeared hardened, so he assumed he wasn't going to get much out of him. Since he was unsuccessful with the men in the group, he focused on the women in front of him. A smile played around the corners of his mouth as he recognized Yolanda. Then he squinted at Vanessa.

He pointed at her and asked, "*¿Quién es ella?*"

'Who is she?'

"*La mujer de El Ken,*" Ricardo said as he walked behind the hostages.

'El Ken's woman.'

Vanessa whimpered upon hearing Caleb's nickname come out of the cartel member's mouth: *El Ken*. Caleb had told her that he received the title because of his Caucasian features. While working at Enrique's Bar, she heard he was given the nickname by his favorite prostitute at the time, a woman who went by the name of *Dulce*, which translated to 'candy' or 'sweet.' She ended up being beheaded with a chainsaw for stealing 3,000 pesos from a drug dealer.

"El Ken," Gustavo repeated, chuckling. He walked over to the women. He crouched in front of them and, in English, he said, "Vanessa Ramirez. You're Rafa's new girl. I hear you speak English well. You studied hard in school, no? And you work hard, too. You used to have what they call 'honest work' over at Chuy's Studio. Then you had to do some 'dirty work' at Enrique's Bar, but you did it for good reason, *mija*. You had to feed little Lucía and Joaquín somehow, no?"

Vanessa had been staring at the ground during Gustavo's speech. Upon hearing her children's names, she lifted her head slowly and made eye contact with her captor. Although there was a small smile on his face, she didn't see anything in his eyes. The windows to his soul revealed a frightening emptiness. It was like there was nothing inside of him—a killer operating on autopilot.

She looked over at the truck, then back at Gustavo. The horrific truth—the truth she had tried to reject— dawned on her: Her kids were in grave danger.

Gustavo continued, "But I never thought I'd see a young woman like you in a place like this or working for a guy like Rafa. Look at the people around you. You're surrounded by killers. And wherever there are killers, there is death. Look at the girl next to you?

She's your partner, no? Yolanda '*La Muñeca de la Muerte*' Torres. Death is in her name, and you're working with her. And what do you know about her? Where she's from? Where she's been? What she's done and what she's going to do? No, sorry, what she *wanted* to do? You don't have to say anything because I already know the answer: *Nothing*. You don't know anything about her."

Vanessa cried and nodded. He was right. She didn't know much about her partner. Most importantly, she wanted him to believe she didn't know anything about Rafael's business so he would spare her.

Gustavo looked at Yolanda and said, "You know, this girl speaks English, too. Maybe she's, uh... How do they say...? *Rusty*. Yeah, maybe her English is a little rusty, but she speaks it, too. She's American. Mexican American. Born and raised in California. Her dad, Juanito, was born over here in Mexico with the rest of us. He used to smuggle drugs for Rafa's old boss. He was good at it, too. Never got caught. Made it big and moved to the US but kept working. This girl, Yolanda, came over here for vacation with her family when she was small. She came for... for *concursos de belleza*, too. She loved it here, and Mexico loved her."

'*Concursos de belleza*' translated to 'beauty pageants.'

Yolanda shot a fierce look at him while Gustavo's gaze remained cold. Vanessa felt selfish for hoping he would spare her and take out his aggression on Yolanda.

"But Yolanda is a... *una traviesa*," Gustavo said. The Spanish translated to: 'A naughty girl' or 'a mischievous girl.' He continued, "When she got older, she got into some trouble. Rafa helped her out. He saved her life. So, like you, Vanessa, she started working for him. But, unlike you, I heard Rafa fucks her sometimes. He didn't save her because he liked her personality. He just wanted to park his dick in her ass. You know, I would have done the same."

The man chuckled. Yolanda said something to him. Although her voice was smothered by the tape over her mouth, her message was clear: 'Fuck you.'

Gustavo said, "They call you a 'doll.' You know what I used to do to my sister's dolls when I was a boy? I used to melt them with my lighter. I used to feed them to dogs. I cut their heads and arms and legs off, then I put them back together with glue. But I put everything in the wrong places. A leg where the arm used to be. A head on the chest. Sometimes, I mixed pieces from other dolls together. That's what I'm going to do to you, Yolanda. I'm going to burn you and cut you up, then I'm going to put you back together. I'm going to turn you into one of my sister's dolls. Then I'm going to feed you to my dogs."

Yolanda repeated herself, but this time, her voice was unintelligible.

"But first," Gustavo said as he directed his attention to Vanessa. "You're going to tell me about Rafa."

Vanessa's eyes widened until her eyelids seemed to

disappear. She wagged her head and leaned away as Gustavo reached for her face. The back of her head hit Ricardo's knee. She looked back and found him standing behind her with a bloody knife in his hand. As she looked forward, Gustavo took the tape off her mouth.

Distraught, she stammered, "N–N–No, I–I–"

"Calm down," Gustavo said.

"–don–don't know anything. Plee–Please don't hurt me. I–I–"

"*Cálmate,*" Gustavo interrupted, repeating his demand in Spanish. "Breathe, *mija.* Just breathe and listen."

Vanessa breathed in deeply, then exhaled shakily. Tears began to fill her eyes. She looked at Yolanda, then at the hostage to her right, then at Ricardo, and then back at Gustavo.

The cartel leader said, "You already know what happens if you don't talk, but I want to give you some information to help you make a... *wise* decision. Do you know why I know so much about you?"

Vanessa assumed, like Rafael, he had connections to corrupt politicians and police who had access to her records. She didn't want to make any assumptions around the killers, though, so she stayed quiet.

"*El Ken,*" Gustavo said. He let the revelation sink in for a few seconds, observing the emotional pain and shock in his hostage's eyes. Then he said, "Caleb Carter told us all about you. When we caught him, he—like they say in those American movies—'sang like a bird.' And we didn't have to touch him. He told us all about you. I know you're doing this to get Lucía and Joaquín out of here."

"Lu–Lucía," Vanessa stuttered. "Joaquín..."

"Caleb told us about your job with Yolanda, too. He helped set it up for us. That's how we knew where to find you. And he said Yolanda and you knew more about Rafa than anyone else."

"He lied. I don't... I wasn't... *He lied*. He's a *liar*."

"Anger is good, Vanessa. You should feel very angry at Caleb and Rafael. Caleb betrayed you and Rafael would do the same. And Yolanda? She would kill you if we told her to fight you for her freedom. Fuck them. You don't have to follow their rules. You don't have to die like these *pinches cabrónes*. Tell me what you know about Rafa and his business. Help me and I will help you."

'*Pinches cabrónes*' meant something along the lines of 'fucking bastards.'

Vanessa was ready to tell him everything she knew to save herself and her children. She thought about all of her discussions with Caleb and cast her mind back to her meeting with Rafael. Her jaw dangled open. Her mouth moved as if she were speaking, but she found she had nothing to say. The truth was: She didn't know anything about Rafael's location or his business. She did as she was told, and she didn't ask questions because she didn't want to know the answers. She protected her conscience through ignorance.

She said, "I–I'm sorry, but Caleb lied to you. I met Rafael in an office, but they covered my eyes and ears on the way there and–and... and on the way out. I don't know where he lives. *Por Dios te lo juro.*"

The Spanish translated to: 'I swear to God.'

Gustavo stroked his mustache and said, "That's not what I want to hear. If you keep lying to me, you're going to make me do something I don't want to do."

"But I'm telling the truth. Please believe me. I would never..."

Her voice faded upon hearing footsteps behind her. Glancing back, she saw David Carrillo—Gustavo's pudgy underling—and Gabriel Martinez—a burly guy with buzz cut hair and a goatee—standing next to Ricardo.

Speaking faster at a higher pitch, Vanessa said, "I would never put my kids in danger by lying to you. They're more important to me than Rafael or Caleb or Yolanda or anyone here. I'm telling you the truth, o–okay? Ask me anything and I'll tell you the truth."

"Where is Rafael Vàsquez?" Gustavo asked.

"*¡No lo sé!*" Vanessa cried, on the brink of a panic attack. "*¡Te lo juro, no lo sé!*"

'I don't know! I swear to you, I don't know!'

Gustavo's hand moved down to his chin where he started to caress his stubble. He examined Vanessa's behavior. Her fear and desperation made her untrustworthy. In the face of death, desperate people were willing to say anything to survive.

He stood up and said, "You don't belong here. You weren't built for this business. But here you are. What am I going to do with you?"

Vanessa said, "I'll tell you anything else. I can tell you... about Caleb. I can tell you a–about Rafael's other men. Like... Like Diego. Diego Ruiz. I met him in Nuevo Progreso. He–He's important. Diego and Caleb, they can give you more information. They know more than me." She bowed, forehead planted in the mud, and said, "Please believe me. Please don't hurt me or my family. Please, please, please. I'm begging."

"The *gringo* is already ours. I don't need him. I need Rafael. And if you can't tell me about him, I don't need you."

"I don't know anything. I only saw his–"

"*Pégale.*"

'Hit her.'

"No!" Vanessa screamed as she raised her head from the ground.

Ricardo kicked her upper back, sending her back down to the mud. He stomped on her again as she attempted to get up. David and Gabriel joined in on the stomping. Their boots *thudded* and *thumped* across her body. She screamed and wiggled on the ground, but she couldn't escape them. Unable to protect herself due to her restrained arms, she rolled onto her side, curled up into a ball, and hid her face behind her knees.

Ricardo punted her upper back. Every hostage heard the *crack* of one of her ribs. David stomped on her side, just below her armpit. Another rib cracked. Hindered by the pain from her broken ribs, Vanessa's bloodcurdling scream was reduced to a whimper. The slightest breath ignited a flare of agony in her chest. David interrupted the pain in her rib cage by knocking the wind out of her with a kick to her lower abdomen.

Gabriel stomped her lower body. On her right leg, he fractured her right ankle and cracked her kneecap.

Yolanda watched the beating with mixed emotions. A part of her believed Vanessa deserved it for her willingness to sell out her peers. She believed in the code of the streets. But a small part of her agreed with something Gustavo had said: Vanessa didn't belong there. Despite her work with the cartel, she wasn't one of them. There was a red, beating heart in Vanessa's chest and warm blood flowing through her veins.

Ricardo kicked the back of Vanessa's head. The tip of his boot left a two-inch gash on her scalp. Her body unfurled as she blacked out. She awoke three seconds later as David punted her stomach. She gasped for air and writhed on the ground, unable to draw a satisfying breath. Her ears rang and her stomach knotted up.

David stepped on her neck, pushing the back of her head into the mud while suffocating her. Vanessa swung her head around, but she couldn't slip out from under him. She fought for air, but to no avail. She felt the other men's boots colliding with her ribs and legs. Although she was still conscious, her mind darkened and her eyes began to roll back.

David took his boot off her neck and let her breathe before she could pass out. She pulled her head out of the mud. It felt heavier than before. As she rolled back onto her side, David kicked her right between the eyes, splitting the bridge of her nose wide open. The lacrimal bones facing her eyes broke as well.

Dazed, Vanessa fell back and groaned sluggishly. Blood ran out of her nostrils, dripped from the wound at the back of her head, and trickled out of her eye sockets. She couldn't think about anything except her pain. Everything ached and stung.

Ricardo rolled her onto her stomach. He thrust his knife into her lower back. The blade pierced the muscle about a centimeter away from her lumbar spine. The hot pain from the stabbing reinvigorated her. She raised her head from the mud and shrieked.

"*¡Oye!*" Gustavo shouted. "*¿Qué haces, güey? Tranquilo.*"

'Hey! What are you doing, asshole? Slow down.'

Ricardo pulled the knife out of her, causing her to grunt and whine, then he stepped back and raised his hands, as if to say: *Oops.* He had planned on ripping her spine out from the bottom to the top while she was still alive.

Gustavo put his fingers in his mouth and whistled

at the truck. Ignacio reversed it over to him, then jumped out and approached his boss. Gustavo said something to him, but Vanessa couldn't hear it over her hoarse gasping and the mud in her ears. She could only detect some feeble, childish whimpers coming from the truck.

"*Mi... Mis hijos,*" she murmured.

'My... My babies.'

Gustavo beckoned to his men, then he climbed into the driver's seat of the truck. The men surrounded Vanessa. Due to the damage to her eye sockets, she was seeing double, so she saw six figures standing over her. Ricardo grabbed one of her arms and Ignacio grabbed the other. They carried her into the truck's cab. She wasn't seen as a threat, so they sat her next to their boss. Ricardo sat on her other side with his arm over her shoulders. Ignacio and David rode in the back.

Vanessa faded in and out of consciousness as the truck rolled away from the hangar. It made it difficult for her to keep track of the time and their trip. But she only heard one song playing through the speakers —*You Make My Dreams* by Hall & Oates—during the drive, so she figured they couldn't have gone far. The truck stopped in front of a small pond. There was a tree next to the body of dark, filthy water.

Ricardo dragged Vanessa out of the truck. He lay her down on her stomach between the front of the vehicle and the pond. She heard overlapping voices and suppressed cries behind her. Gustavo walked in front of her. He stared at the pond for a long moment, as if hypnotized by the water.

He said, "I let Caleb live because he worked with me. Because he is valuable. I can do the same for you, *mija*. We can end this right now. Take you to a hospital. Pay you for your troubles. Get you out of Mexico with our *coyotes*. Just tell me where Rafa is hiding. Stop protecting these people. They're not your friends. They let this happen to you. So, tell me the truth and let me get revenge for you."

Out of breath, Vanessa said, "Gus–Gustavo, I don't... know anything. I swear to God... I swear on my babies... I don't know. That's the truth."

"Ah, well, we'll see about that."

There was a struggle in the truck—thudding, squeaking, crying. Then the childish whimpering got clearer. Footsteps moved around the vehicle.

From Vanessa's left, Alicia was pushed into the truck's headlights. She lost her footing and landed on her knees. The woman was naked with her hands restrained in front of her with zip ties. Her ankles were bound, too. To Vanessa's right, Ignacio forced Lucía and Joaquín—dressed in their pajamas—to their knees. They all had duct tape over their mouths. And they were all hysterical and pale with fear. David leaned against the front of the truck and munched on a *Gansito*—a Mexican snack cake— he had been saving in the vehicle's glove compartment.

Ricardo walked into the truck's headlights with a

fire axe. Alicia clasped her hands in front of her chest, looked up at him, and pleaded unintelligibly.

"No, no, no, no, no," Vanessa said. "Gustavo, I–"

Ricardo swung the axe at Alicia's neck. It tore into her throat, silencing her in an instant. Arcs of blood droplets sprayed out in every direction from under the axe's bit.

Vanessa shouted, "No!"

Alicia almost fell back as Ricardo pulled the axe out of her, but Gustavo pushed her forward with his foot. Just as Alicia raised her hands to her neck in an attempt to stop the bleeding, Ricardo swung the axe at her again. Both of her pinky fingers were severed. On her left hand, her ring finger was chopped off while her middle finger was left barely attached. The axe stopped in her neck again. The force from the blow made her head bob like an inflatable punching bag. She collapsed with the axe stuck in her throat.

"*Alicia, ¡perdóname! ¡Lo siento mucho!*" Vanessa cried. "*Es todo... mi culpa. Todo... Todo... Lo siento.*"

'Alicia, forgive me! I'm so sorry! It's all... my fault. Everything... Everything... I'm sorry.'

Ricardo stepped on Alicia's chest and pulled the axe out of her. Alicia's hands, mutilated and shaking, moved back up to her throat in an instinctive effort to protect herself. Ricardo kicked her hands aside, swung the axe overhead, then brought it down with all of his might. The third blow killed her.

But death wasn't enough for them. Fear was the

strongest currency in Mexico. In addition to cash payments, fear bought political influence, obedience, and silence. They had to send a message of terror with each murder to support their goals.

Ricardo kept chopping away at Alicia's mangled neck. He was unperturbed by the gore, treating her flesh as if it were a log of wood meant for a fireplace.

With brown and red streaks of tears across her cheeks, Vanessa looked at her children and said, "*No miren. Cierren los ojos, mis hijos. Todo va a... a...*"

'Don't look. Close your eyes, my kids. Everything is going...'

She wanted to tell them everything was going to be okay, but she couldn't bring herself to lie to them again. She was convinced they were all going to die soon. She didn't want the last thing she said to them to be another lie.

She said, "*Lo siento por mentirte, por todo...*"

'I'm sorry for lying to you, for everything...'

She stopped as hissing and spluttering sounds came out of Alicia's neck. Alicia's head rolled from side to side, attached to her body only by some strands of muscle and her cervical vertebrae. Her blood turned the dirt under her maroon.

Vanessa brought her tearful gaze back to her children. She smiled a little—a fake one to comfort her kids—and said, "*Lo siento por todo lo que he hecho. Te quiero con todo mi corazón. Nos veremos en el paraíso. Te lo prometo.*"

'I'm sorry for everything I've done. I love you with all my heart. We'll see each other in heaven. I promise.'

Lucía and Joaquín responded with more choked cries. Arms outstretched in front of him, Joaquín shimmied forward on his knees. Despite the tape over his mouth, Vanessa could make out his words: '*¡Mamá! ¡Mamá! ¡Mamá!*' Ignacio grabbed the back of his shirt and yanked him back. He slapped the back of the boy's head, making him wail harder.

"*¡No lo toques!*" Vanessa yelled as she looked daggers at him.

'Don't touch him!'

Ignacio huffed, then said, "*Cállate la boca, puta.*"

'Shut your mouth, whore.'

Gritting her teeth through the pain, Vanessa rocked her shoulders and hips to lift her ass from the ground. As she was about to raise her upper body, David stomped on her back and pinned her down. He threw the snack cake's wrapper to the ground and sucked the chocolate off his fingers.

Squirming under his boot, Vanessa shouted, "*¡Suéltame, marrano!*"

'Let go of me, you pig!'

Ricardo finished beheading Alicia. He grabbed her severed head by the hair and raised it above him. Her blonde hair looked like it was dip-dyed red by her blood.

"*Dios mío, no,*" Vanessa whimpered, awed by her friend's gruesome death.

'My God, no.'

Ricardo threw the head into the pond. After a big splash, it floated in the water like a beach ball. Gustavo snapped his fingers at Ignacio. Ignacio dragged the kids to him. Upon seeing their dead babysitter—a woman they regarded as family—Lucía and Joaquín shut their eyes, huddled together, and wept.

"No, no, please," Vanessa said, her voice gravelly from all of her screaming and crying. "They're kids, Gustavo. The–They're babies. They're *my* babies."

Gustavo put his hands on their heads and said, "I know. And this is your last chance to save them. Where is Rafa?"

"He's... He... I–I can take you to him. Take me to Nuevo Progreso and... and I'll take you from there."

"You said you couldn't see or hear."

"I could see a little," she said, lying to buy some time.

Gustavo cocked his head to the side and squinted an eye at her. He asked, "Which way did you go after leaving Nuevo Progreso?"

"South."

"South, hmm? You went south from the border? So, you're saying you went into Mexico. Rafael is south of the border, somewhere in Mexico. That's what you're saying? Come on, *mija*, that doesn't help anybody. It doesn't help *you* at all."

"I don't know every road or every town, but I can

show you the way. Let them go and take me... Even if he kills me, I'll take you to his home."

Gustavo narrowed both of his eyes now as he considered Vanessa's offer. He looked at Ricardo. His cousin lifted a shoulder in a half-shrug. Cold sweat dribbled across Vanessa's hot face. She stared at her captor with hopeless, pleading eyes. He was her God for the night, and she could only hope he believed her. Gustavo looked down at the kids sobbing at his feet. He smiled and ruffled their hair.

He said, "*Los hijos pagan por los pecados de su madre.*"

'The kids pay for their mother's sins.'

Gustavo hooked his arms around them and heaved them off the ground. He carried them into the pond. Vanessa screamed and lunged forward, but she couldn't slide out from under David's foot. She caught one final glimpse at her children's pallid, frightened faces before Gustavo dunked their heads in the water.

"*¡Para! ¡No pueden respirar!*" Vanessa cried. It translated to: 'Stop! They can't breathe!' She managed to wiggle a couple of inches forward before David placed more pressure on her back. She said, "*¡Por favor! ¡Por favor, para! ¡No lo hagas! ¡Te lo pido!*"

'Please! Please stop! Don't do this! I'm begging you!'

The water splashed as the kids flapped their restrained limbs in a panic. Unable to hold their breath, water quickly filled their lungs and deprived them of oxygen.

"*¡No, no, mis hijos!*" Vanessa yelled. "*¡Mis hijos!*"

'No, no, my children! My children!'

She buried her face in the mud and sobbed. She heard Gustavo's voice but couldn't understand his words. David grabbed a fistful of her hair and lifted her head.

"*Sí, sí, así,*" Gustavo said. It meant: 'Yes, yes, like that.' He locked eyes with Vanessa and said, "I want you to watch this, *mija*. Watch me so you'll never forget my name. I'll haunt you even in hell."

"*Mis hijos,*" Vanessa repeated weakly.

A bloody tear trickled out of her left eye as Joaquín stopped moving. He lasted forty-five seconds underwater. Then a red teardrop came out of Vanessa's right eye as Lucía became motionless twenty seconds later. She remembered her children having breath-holding contests at home when they were bored. Joaquín never won a single game.

Gustavo held their lifeless bodies under water for another minute. Then he waddled out of the pond, leaving them floating facedown behind him.

He squatted in front of Vanessa and asked, "What's your favorite song? I'll play it for you. I'll let you die with some comfort."

Vanessa lay stock-still, frowning at the pond. She took a trip down memory lane, picturing all of the good times she had with her children.

Gustavo nodded at David and said, "*Escoge para ella.*"

'Choose for her.'

While David went into the truck, Gustavo took a knee on Vanessa's upper back. He took a table knife out of his pocket. It was his favorite tool for beheadings because it took longer to kill people with it. And the longer it took, the more pain his victims felt.

"Tell your kids I said hello," he said.

He cut into the left side of Vanessa's neck just as music started playing from the truck's speakers—*Wake Me Up Before You Go-Go* by Wham! Vanessa's face twitched from the pain, but she didn't resist him. She sought a violent death. She told herself that she deserved it. She wanted to be punished on earth so she could be reunited with her children in heaven. Drops of blood crawled out of the wound at first. Her bleeding accelerated with each slice into her neck.

Just as the blade touched her external jugular, a crashing sound interrupted the beheading. The chain-link fence around the property rattled loudly, then there was another crashing sound. Technicals barreled through the fence. Gunfire from automatic firearms roared through the desert, the muzzle flashes lighting up the night.

David ran to the front of the truck and shouted, "*¡Son los soldados de Rafa!*"

'It's Rafa's soldiers.'

Gustavo pulled the knife away from Vanessa's throat, leaned close to her ear, and said, "*Recuérdame.*"

'Remember me.'

The men got into the truck and sped back to the

hangar. Ignacio and Ricardo killed the remaining hostages—two young women, a boy, and a girl—in the back of the truck by slitting their throats while Ricardo hung out the passenger window and fired an automatic rifle at the technicals.

Vanessa squirmed her way to the edge of the pond. Her bloody tears plopped in the dark water. Mumbling in Spanish, she begged her kids to get out of the water, to swim towards her, *to breathe*. She spoke to her children as if they were playing dead. Overcome with grief, she cried harder. She began to cough and retch, strings of saliva hanging from her mouth. Her emotional suffering was worse than her physical pain.

She didn't hear the truck stop next to the pond or the sound of doors slamming or the approaching footsteps. Three men in military uniforms and ski masks, armed with rifles, surrounded her.

One of the men said, "*Espera. Está con nosotros.*"

'Wait. She's with us.'

PART II

12

THE BIRTH OF A GHOST

Vanessa's eyes fluttered open to a blur of white and blue. She shut them and grimaced upon feeling a throbbing pain in her eye sockets. The pain radiated through her head, worse than the most debilitating migraine. Eyelids twitching, she forced her eyes open again. Her vision improved slightly, but she was still seeing double.

She saw herself laying on a bed under a white sheet. An IV line ran into her right arm at the crook of her elbow. A woman in white stood in front of some blue counters on the other side of the room, rummaging through some drawers. The door to Vanessa's left was wide open while the window to her right was closed. The room was bright from the sunshine and the fluorescent lighting.

Faint beeping, clicking, and hissing noises came into her room from down the hall. There were some groans, too. She recognized the place's atmosphere. Even with the brightest lights, hospitals were always bleak and cheerless. She looked at the bed to her left. She could only see the foot of it. She stretched her arm out and pulled the cubicle curtain back. To her dismay, the other bed was empty. She closed her eyes and whimpered.

The woman in white—a middle-aged nurse—gasped. She rushed to the patient's side and checked her vital signs.

She said, "*Ten cuidado. No te muevas. Regreso en un momento, mija.*"

'Be careful. Don't move. I'll be back in a moment, dear.'

She hurried out of the room. Vanessa's crying aggravated her broken eye sockets and, in turn, exacerbated her terrible headache. Yet, her physical pain didn't bother her as much as her grief.

Two minutes later, the nurse returned with a doctor. The man wore a long white coat with a plaid shirt underneath, black slacks, and dress shoes. There was more grizzled hair on his jaw than around the bald spot at the center of his head. His shiny blue irises summoned up memories of Caleb's eyes in Vanessa's mind. The nurse closed the door behind them while the doctor went to the patient's side.

He checked her vital signs and examined the state of her injuries, checking for any abnormalities or infections. The wounds on her neck, lower back, and scalp were stitched. The gash on her nose had been cleaned and sealed with surgical tape. Her eyelids, the bony ridge above her eyes, and her cheekbones were bruised purple and black. The dark bruises made it look like she was a cliché bandit wearing a domino mask. On her neck, there was another large bruise resembling a shoeprint.

The doctor dragged a stool to the side of the bed and took a seat. He said, "Vanessa, I'm Dr. Jack Farmer. Don't let the name fool you, okay? I've never worked a day of my life on a farm. I'm a real doctor."

He snickered and nodded, as if to say: *Funny, right?* But Vanessa didn't laugh. She looked at the empty bed to her left and sniffled.

Jack coughed to clear his throat, then he said, "Your employer tells me you speak English. But if you have any trouble understanding me, if you need any clarification at all, let me know and we'll bring a translator. Okay?" Vanessa stayed silent. The doctor said, "Okay. So, let's start with the basics. How are you feeling?"

The question bothered her because the answer was obvious. Racked with guilt, she felt nothing but torment and self-hatred. Her upper lip curled back in a sneer of anger.

Jack coughed again, this time into his fist, then he said, "I'm sorry. I understand you're in a lot of pain. For the sake of your health, though, I must ask: What do you remember?"

Yet again, Vanessa did not respond. She continued

staring at the neighboring bed, occasionally sniffling and grunting. Jack looked at the nurse standing at the foot of the bed. The nurse frowned and shrugged.

The doctor said, "I'm going to take a look at your eyes, okay?"

He walked over to the other side of the bed, bent over, and shone a light at her eyes. Her pupils shrank. He took note of the crusty blood at the corners of her eyes. After turning off his small flashlight, Vanessa kept looking right through him. Jack went to the foot of the bed and whispered something to his nurse. She jotted some notes down on a clipboard while the doctor returned to his stool.

The man said, "You're safe now, Vanessa. This facility is owned and protected by your employer. I apologize for my joke earlier, but I want you to know that I am a licensed physician in the United States. I am here to give you the best care possible while keeping you out of the 'system.' Your wellbeing is my only concern, so please don't hesitate to talk to me. Now, I want to go over a couple of items with you. If you'd like to do this some other time, just say so or shake your head or... or shoo me away. Don't worry, you won't hurt my feelings."

Vanessa stayed still. She didn't care about the doctor or her health. She only wanted to know about her children.

Taking her silence as permission to continue, Jack said, "You arrived about three days ago. You've been on some very strong anesthetics, so you've been resting for a while now. You're expected to make a full recovery. The lacerations, the bruises, and the broken bones... They'll all heal with time and rest. However, I am concerned about your eyes. You seem to have developed a case of haemolacria. Do you know what that means?" After another moment of silence, the doctor said, "It's a condition that causes a person to shed tears of... well, of blood. I believe this may be due to the fractures in your eye sockets, but I can't be entirely sure without further testing. Regardless, because of those fractures, I need you to refrain from blowing your nose and sneezing. I know that's not exactly an easy thing to ask of you, but I'll prescribe a nasal decongestant spray to help you out. Do you understand?"

There was another period of silence. Then Vanessa responded with a slight, almost imperceptible nod.

"Excellent," Jack said. "Our nurse here, *Señora Gómez*, will review some of the smaller details with you. But before I go... I have been asked to tell you about your children."

Vanessa turned her head and finally made eye contact with him. Her face twitched as she breathed through her nose. Shuddering all over, she nodded at him, as if to say: *Go on*.

Jack said, "I'm sorry to inform you of this, but... Lucía and Joaquín could not be resuscitated." Vanessa exhaled sharply, drops of spittle spraying out from between her clenched teeth. The doctor said, "Their remains were taken by your employer. He says that they are in good hands and are being treated with the utmost respect. He is prepared to have them buried *properly*. He wanted me to make sure I emphasized that. Is there any message you'd like me to send him?"

She wanted to scream something like: '*Tell him to keep his dirty hands off my children!*' But she was so angry—so frustrated, *so devastated*—that she couldn't speak. She looked away. She imagined her son and daughter sitting on the empty bed next to her. A bloody tear oozed out of her eye. It ran down her temple, wetting her hair and the white pillow under her head.

Jack patted her shoulder gently and said, "I am truly sorry for your loss. Don't hesitate to call for me if you need anything. I'm here for you, Vanessa."

Vanessa refused to acknowledge him. He whispered something into the nurse's ear, then walked out of the room. The nurse approached Vanessa and wiped her face. While doing so, she spoke about Vanessa's loss and offered a prayer for her and her family. Vanessa ignored her, too. Prayers couldn't reverse time or resurrect the dead. She thought only about her children, revenge, and self-punishment.

Another bloody tear crawled down her face.

Vanessa sat on a wooden deck chair at the facility's rooftop terrace, staring up at the clouds in the sky. After the bruises and fractures on her legs had improved, the nurses had talked her into getting out of her room for some brief exercise and fresh air. Despite listening to their advice, she didn't say a word to anyone.

The bruises on her face and neck had faded. Only some light green marks lingered. The stitches and surgical tape across her body were removed as she healed. She still felt some pain from her cracked ribs, though.

Her nurse, Gómez, sat in a deck chair next to her, knitting a colorful cap. The pager clipped to her coat pocket went off. She pressed a button to silence the notification, then she excused herself and jogged to the stairs behind them.

Vanessa didn't acknowledge the beeper or her departure. She stayed behind on the rooftop terrace by herself, staring up at the sky. She tilted her head and narrowed her eyes. A smile pulled the left side of her mouth up. She saw her children in the clouds— portraits of them standing next to each other, smiling with their arms around one another.

She dragged her feet over to the railing at the edge of the rooftop. Her smile grew as she saw a heart-shaped cloud above her kids. She felt like they were calling to her. She looked down at the small town below her. She didn't recognize it. There were only a few buildings in the area taller than the four-story cartel hospital. Beyond the city limits, she saw a sea of trees.

She leaned forward and peeked over the rail. The thought of jumping to her death crept into her mind. She leaned back, then forward, then back, and then forward again. She got closer and closer to hurling herself off the roof.

Before she could jump, a man asked, "*¿Qué haces?*"

'What are you doing?'

Vanessa stopped swinging back and forth. She stared down at the narrow road below as the man approached her. From the corner of her eye, she saw him lean forward with his elbows on the railing. She looked at him. It was Diego Ruiz.

Staring down at the town, he asked, "How's it going? They treating you right here?" Vanessa didn't respond. Diego said, "They better be. Rafael paid a lot of money to build this place. It's supposed to keep us out of civilian hospitals and out of prison. But you wanna know why he really built it? A couple of years ago, one of our top guys—a 'capo,' y'know?—had a kidney problem. He was pissing *a lot* of blood. He didn't clean the toilets after using 'em either, so they were always red. Didn't matter how many times he flushed. He got his blood all over the floors and walls, too. Real nasty shit. But he didn't want to go to a hospital. He thought he was going to get arrested. So, Rafael built this place for him and the rest of us. We're not good people, Vani. I'm not going to pretend like we're saints, but Rafael... The man has a heart. He takes care of his own."

Vanessa heard every word, but she didn't understand the purpose of his speech. *Am I supposed to be grateful?* she wondered. *Does he want me to thank him for saving me but not my children?*

Diego pivoted to his right to face her, leaning with one elbow on the railing. He sighed and shook his head, displeased with her silence.

He said, "I spoke to Dr. Farmer. He says you're doing good. Says you should be fully recovered soon. He also said that you haven't said a word in three weeks. He said... Shit, what was it? He, uh... Yeah, he said you went 'mute' because of some 'psychological trauma.' I get it. What those fuckers did to you and your family... That's the type of shit you can't forget or forgive. I know it probably doesn't mean shit to you, but... I'm sorry for how it went down."

Vanessa looked at him. His apology sounded sincere. Her mouth cracked open as she was about to accept it, but then she thought about the night of the massacre. Before the death of her children, she had offered to sell Diego out to Gustavo. She wondered if anyone else had survived the slaughter and if they had told him about her betrayal.

Diego said, "Look, I'm here because Rafael wants to see you. He has something to say that you'll want to hear. Something to show you that you'll want to see.

And it's... urgent. So, I can carry you out of here or you can walk out of here. The easy way or the hard way, what do you wanna do?"

Vanessa suspected they were going to interrogate, torture, and execute her for offering Gustavo information about Rafael's cartel. *La Muñeca de la Muerte*, she thought. *If she's alive, she told them everything.* She looked over the guardrail again. She wanted to die, but she didn't want to kill herself. She feared suicide would have damned her to hell, keeping her away from her children in heaven.

She sought punishment and death—and cartels specialized in torture and murder. The pieces fell perfectly into place. She was ready to be reunited with her family. She blew a kiss at the clouds, then nodded at Diego and walked away from the railing.

"The car's parked in the back," Diego said as he followed behind her. "You need a wheelchair or something?"

13

FOR FAMILY

Vanessa sat in the passenger seat of Diego's sedan without a sack, blindfold, or earplugs blocking her sight and hearing. In the rearview mirror, she could see they were being followed by an armored SUV and a technical. They had been driving for three hours, traveling from a lush forest to a barren desert.

She believed the cartel stopped caring about what she saw and heard because she was going to be executed. A dead witness was a quiet witness. She had said too much before and she had seen too much now. Even she knew she couldn't be trusted with any valuable information concerning Rafael's cartel. Death was inevitable.

"You good?" Diego asked from the driver's seat. "You need some water or something? Or a bathroom break?"

Vanessa stared out the passenger window, watching the desert scroll past. She took note of Diego's casual, friendly attitude. *What is he planning?* she thought.

Diego said, "I guess you're good then. Just let me know if you need me to stop. We're almost there anyway."

About thirty minutes later, the sedan rolled to a stop in front of a gate—the only entrance into the compound. The SUV and technical stopped behind the sedan.

A concrete wall surrounded the property. Surveillance cameras at regular 50-meter intervals monitored the makeshift border. Armed with automatic rifles, men in desert camouflage uniforms and ski masks also patrolled the perimeter. On the other side of the gate, in a security booth near the entrance, one of the armed guards recognized the convoy. He opened the gate for them.

Diego drove forward slowly with the other vehicles following his lead. Vanessa saw a villa with a beige exterior ahead. It was a lavish place, but she was unimpressed. Without her family, wealth meant nothing to her. She had no interest in being rich and lonely, no interest in leaving Mexico by herself, no interest in living on without her kids. They parked in the driveway.

Diego helped Vanessa out of the car, then with his arm hooked around hers, he escorted her into the building. They were greeted by a young maid in the foyer. They went up a flight of stairs, then down a hall to their right. They ended up in a small home office. Like the rest of the home, the room had eggshell-white walls and Spanish Mission Red tile flooring.

There was a large desk at one end of the room—a leather office chair on one side and two armchairs on the other. Behind it, there were some file cabinets. Bookcases covered the parallel wall.

"Sit," Diego said. "He'll be here in a second."

Vanessa approached the desk. She stopped between the two armchairs. The office sparked memories of Caleb. She hadn't thought of him since the night of the massacre. *You watch my back, I watch yours,* she heard him say in her head.

Diego walked up to her and asked, "What's wrong? Just sit and–"

Knocking on the door interrupted him. They looked back and found Rafael standing in the doorway, wiping something off his palms with a handkerchief. A man in a military uniform stood in the hallway behind him. Rafael tucked the handkerchief in his pocket and entered the office. There was a moment of silence as he looked Vanessa up and down. He stretched his arms out with his palms up, shook his head, and frowned.

"What did they do to you, *mija?*" he said.

Vanessa furrowed her brow, baffled by the sorrow and remorse in his voice. His sympathy for her felt genuine. They treated her like a younger sibling. Her eyes darted to Diego, then back to Rafael. Kindness without ulterior motives was rare in her world. She couldn't shake off her paranoia.

Rafael asked, "Are you thirsty, Vani? Hungry?"

Vanessa remained quiet.

"She doesn't talk anymore," Diego said. "The trauma, remember?"

"Right, right," Rafael said. He gestured at an armchair and said, "*Pues, siéntate. Mi casa es tu casa.*"

The Spanish translated to: 'Well, sit. My house is your house.'

Rafael sat in the leather office chair. As he got comfortable, he beckoned to his guest again. Hesitant but unafraid, Vanessa sat in the armchair to her right. Diego remained standing with his arms crossed.

The leader said, "All of the people here are pure-blooded *Mexicanos*. Some of them speak a little bit of English but none are fluent. Not like you or Diego or me. So, since I don't know if we've gotten rid of every traitor yet, we'll do this in English. Call me paranoid, but I don't want to give anyone a chance to betray us again." He bit his lip and nodded as if he were listening to someone, then he said, "I'm sorry about this... tragedy, Vanessa. Children shouldn't be part of our wars. I've said that from the beginning. They're not responsible for our sins. They're not born to be our soldiers. Your little Lucía and Joaquín..."

Upon hearing their names, Vanessa gave him a death stare that said something along the lines of: 'Watch your mouth, motherfucker.' Rafael recognized her rage. He had seen it in other grieving people before. He had seen it in himself, in fact. Grief and anger went hand in hand.

He said, "You did not contact me to make arrangements, so I had to bury them for you. We couldn't keep them in... 'storage' for much longer. They're in a graveyard in your hometown. You can rest assured that we took great care of their bodies. I can have one of my men take you to them anytime."

Vanessa became angrier, but she directed her fury at herself. During her time at the cartel's hospital, she had been given multiple opportunities to make funeral arrangements for her children. But she refused to speak. She had retreated to the darkest corners of her mind, hiding from her problems. She despised herself for abandoning her children.

Rafael said, "I know how you feel, Vanessa. I've lost people, too. Family and friends. People I loved."

Vanessa leaned forward and sneered at him. She looked like she wanted to jump over the desk and pounce on him. Her shoulders rose with each heavy breath.

"What?" Rafael asked. "Hmm? You don't think a man like me can love? You think I can't grieve like you?"

He nodded at Diego, commanding him without saying a word. Diego said something to the guard in the hallway, then shut the door.

Rafael said, "I've heard all about what happened to you and your family. I'll tell you, Vanessa, it could have been a lot worse. They could have taken their heads in front of you. They did that to your friend, Alicia Cortes, no? We buried her body, too, you know. They could have made *you* kill her and your children. And— you know this now but maybe you didn't then—they would have killed you afterward anyway. Even with their blood on your hands, even if you told them everything they wanted to know and did everything they asked you to do, they would have taken your head off and left your body impaled in public."

He paused for a moment. Like Vanessa, there was fire in his eyes. *Diego was right*, she thought. *He has a heart*.

Rafael resumed, "You don't get to my position without hurting *a lot* of people. And sometimes, you end up in situations where you have to—*you must*— hurt the people you love to survive and thrive. I learned that when my younger brother, Javier, broke away from us and tried to start his own cartel. I gave him many chances to come back. I called for peace, and he responded with bullets. He killed my men and tried to kill me. He left me no choice but to... to show him why I'm *El Decapitador*. So, I took his head. And I think it hurt me more than it hurt him."

His eyes dimmed with the last two sentences, the fire extinguished by a storm of melancholy. Yet, he didn't seem capable of crying.

"But I'm not telling you this to say I've suffered more than you," he said. "Grief is grief. It's not a competition."

"*Mátame*," Vanessa rasped with her head down.

'Kill me.'

Rafael leaned forward and asked, "*¿Qué?*"

'What?'

Vanessa looked at him and, switching to English, she said, "Kill me."

Rafael huffed, then he chuckled. He said, "I didn't bring you here to kill you, *mija*. I want to talk to you. I want to... *give* you something."

"What?"

"It's like I was saying earlier: I know what happened that night. Yolanda survived the attack. She told us what you said to Gustavo Rivera. About Diego. About Nuevo Progreso. About my home. It hurt us to hear that."

Stony-faced, Vanessa leaned closer to him and said, "Then give me death."

The men looked at each other. Diego was befuddled by her desire to die. Rafael understood her, though.

He smiled at her and said, "You remind me of my *hermanita*, Vanessa." '*Hermanita*' meant 'little sister.' He walked around the desk, then he sat on it with one foot hovering over the floor. He continued, "Her name was Leticia. We called her Letty. She was hardheaded like you. Determined, you know? If you told her she couldn't do something, she'd tell you she already did it. You look a lot like her, too, but... No. You're older than her now."

The room fell silent. Vanessa had one question on her mind, but she refrained from asking it: *How did she die?*

Rafael said, "When I was coming up, before I became the *big* boss, I used to run some territory down south. I won't pretend like my hands are clean now, but back then... *back then*, Vani, I was a monster. I had to be. The business was all about violence and fear. It still is. So, to send a message, I would drive around with my *sicarios*—my assassins—and point at people on the street. Just like this." He pointed a finger gun at Diego, then at her. He pretended to shoot her, then said, "I pointed at people that I thought were working for other cartels or the police... or people who I thought were related to my enemies. I had them kidnapped... and beheaded. I put their heads on spikes and put them on my rivals' front lawns. If they didn't have front lawns, I threw the heads through their windows. If they were cops or were related to cops, we'd leave their headless bodies in vans in front of police stations. That's how I got my title and that's how I became king. I didn't become *El Decapitador* by cutting the heads off chickens."

Vanessa asked, "What happened to her? To Letty?"

"You already know how this story ends, don't you?"

"*¿Qué pasó con ella?*"

'What happened to her?'

Rafael scrunched up half his face and said, "One day I heard a small gang was using a laundromat to sell drugs. We watched the place, but we didn't find them. I wanted information, so I pointed at the woman who was working there. My men took her to a mechanic's garage where we interrogated her. She didn't give us anything, so we took everything from her. We cut off her head and we left it on her mailbox. Her body... We put it in the trunk of her car and left it in her driveway. It turned out that a small gang wasn't operating from that laundromat. Actually, it had been purchased by that woman's brother. And that woman's brother is a man named..."

"Gustavo Rivera," Vanessa said it at the same time as Rafael.

"*El Empalador,*" Rafael said, nodding. "The Impaler. Ever since then, Gustavo and I have been stuck in this... this cycle of violence. He killed Letty. He... He..."

Rafael began to shudder. Fear and shame brought a series of big, noticeable spasms to his face. He rubbed his mouth to try to hide his twitching. Images of Letty's corpse flashed in his mind. She had been hogtied, skewered with a long spit—in through her anus, out through her mouth—and roasted like a pig. She was left in the back of a food truck at a busy plaza, still skewered with an apple in her mouth. A message was painted on the side of the truck with Letty's blood. It read: '*Un regalo para El Decapitador.*' It translated to: 'A gift for The Decapitator.'

Rafael went to a mini fridge behind the desk. He grabbed a bottle of water and took a swig—and then another.

Scowling, he said, "He killed my sister. That's all you have to know about that right now. Ever since then, Gustavo's been hunting me while I've been hunting him. He kills one of mine, I kill one of his. His boss lets him run wild as long as he gets the job done. And right now, the job is to weaken or extermi-nate me. At the end of the day, our conflict, Vanessa, goes beyond territory, power, money, and product. This is about family. And you do *anything* for family. Right?"

Vanessa sat there with a confused look on her face. She never expected to see a man like Rafael show such intense emotion. Their grief, raw and untreated, connected them. She agreed with him, too. She had always been willing to do anything for her children. But she didn't feel any pity for him. Although she held herself and Gustavo responsible for the deaths of Lucía and Joaquín, she placed some of the blame on Rafael, too. He started the cycle of violence by killing Gustavo's sister after all.

After a few more sips of water and some deep breathing, Rafael recomposed himself. He walked back to the other side of the desk and smiled wanly at Vanessa.

He said, "You really do look like her."

"Is that why you don't want to kill me? Because you can't kill a ghost?"

"No, no," Rafael said as he sat in the armchair next to Vanessa. "I was hurt to hear about your betrayal, but I understand why you did it. *And* I understand that you didn't really say anything. Before today, you didn't know where any of my compounds were located. You said Diego's name, but you don't really know anything about his work. You lied to Gustavo. You know who *didn't* lie to him? You know who the *real* traitor is? *Caleb Carter.*"

Vanessa clenched her fists and gritted her teeth. She remembered hearing his name during the massacre. Gustavo had claimed Caleb helped organize their capture. She had been stuck in a state of denial ever since. Instead of accepting the truth, she looked at the other possibilities: Gustavo lied, Caleb was already dead, there was a misunderstanding. Since Caleb wasn't at the scene of the massacre, she didn't connect him to it. Now, she saw him as the puppet master.

"Where is he?" she asked. "Take me to him. Ta– Take me to him and I–I'll... I'll kill him!"

"*Tranquila,*" Rafael said in a gentle tone, raising his hands from the seat's armrests. It meant: 'Calm down.' He said, "Caleb ran back to the US before you were attacked. He is hiding in a cozy gated community, pretending like nothing ever happened down here. We have our eyes on him, but we can't touch him yet. Sure, we could have had him shot a long time ago—we have soldiers up there who would be happy to kill a snitch like him for free—but we don't want him to take the easy way out. I want him to suffer. I want him to feel *real* fear and *real* pain. Just like you did."

"Good. That's what I want, too."

"And that's what I wanted to hear. Vanessa, *mija,* I want to give you the opportunity to exact your revenge. I want you to kill Caleb Carter."

Vanessa was sick of the business and tired of life. The offer reinvigorated her, though. She wanted to be punished as much as she wanted to punish her attackers. She couldn't rest in peace without avenging her children. As a religious person, she had some doubts. But as far as she knew, unlike suicide, murder wasn't an unforgivable sin. *Good people have to kill bad people all the time,* she rationalized.

"I'll do it," she said. "Take me to him and I'll kill him."

Rafael said, "Before you get to Caleb, you have to prove that you're still part of my family and you have to prove you're capable of getting the job done. You can't get cold feet at his doorstep. He thinks he's in hiding right now. If he survives the assassination or if he even gets a bad feeling, he'll go to the police and work out a deal to get into protective custody. It'll be a lot harder to touch him then."

"So, what do you want me to do?"

"Kill."

"Who? Because I won't kill any innocent people. I won't kill any kids either."

Rafael asked, "How about the men who killed your children?"

14

THE INITIATION

ACCOMPANIED BY DIEGO AND AN ARMED GUARD, RAFAEL led Vanessa to the back of the villa. Past the courtyard, a large pool, and some artificial lawns, they stepped into a swathe of desert. Through the heat haze rising from the ground, they could see more guards patrolling the border around the property in the distance.

In the middle of the villa's backyard, they went down a short flight of stairs leading to a blast door. Diego helped Rafael open it while the guard kept watch from the top of the stairs. As soon as the door cracked open, an indistinct voice seeped out. They entered a corridor with reinforced concrete walls, dimly lit by wall sconces at regular intervals.

"This is supposed to be a bomb shelter," Rafael said. "But the government's not dropping bombs on us–"

"*Yet,*" Diego chimed in from behind.

"–so we use it for business whenever necessary."

They went through another steel door—which was lighter than the blast door—then made their way down another hallway. The indistinct voice got clearer. A man was screaming. There were three steel doors at the end of the hall—to the left, right, and straight ahead. Rafael opened the door in the middle.

"*¡Pinche puta!*"

'Fucking whore!'

The man's insult echoed through the bunker. It died out at the stairs outside beyond the blast door.

The room had a curved ceiling. Shelves with nonperishable goods and other emergency supplies were pushed up against the walls to the left and right. Towers of cardboard boxes and plastic bins stood in the corners of the room. To the right there was a desk with a laptop and some notebooks as well as an entertainment center with a flatscreen television. On the left, there was a workbench. The room reeked of sweat, feces, and urine.

At the opposite end of the room from the entrance, Gabriel Martinez was locked into a sturdy wooden pillory, head and hands secured in its frame's holes. The pillory's horizontal post was lowered, forcing him to stand on his knees on the hard concrete. The black and purple bruises on his knees made it look like he was wearing kneepads, but he was completely naked.

He couldn't stand or twist his legs or tip the pillory over since it was fastened into place.

His face was covered in thick, bruised lumps. He could barely see through his swollen eyes. Fresh blood was smeared on his lips and chin. All of his incisor teeth had been pried from his gums. His dislodged teeth were scattered on the floor around his knees. More blood leaked out of his busted nose and the tiny cuts on his inflated lips. Droplets of it fell from his face and landed in a puddle of bloody urine under him.

Yolanda and a guard in a ski mask stood in front of the prisoner. Yolanda held a pair of pliers in her right hand, one of Gabriel's dislodged teeth between its jaws.

"*Mira quién es,*" she said as she limped towards Vanessa.

'Look who it is.'

Rafael stepped between them, raised one hand, and said, "English, Yolanda."

He looked at the guard to remind her of their precautions. His most trusted men were protecting him, but Caleb reminded him that trust wasn't perpetual. If caught under the wrong circumstances, his men could flip on him. Except for the higher-ups of his organization, he decided to keep his people in the dark until Caleb was eliminated.

Yolanda shrugged and said, "I just wanted to welcome the *rat* home."

Vanessa ignored the insult and walked past them.

She looked at the prisoner. Despite his injuries, she recognized him from the night of the massacre.

Yolanda stepped to her side and asked, "You remember him?" Vanessa nodded. Yolanda put a cigarette in her mouth, lit it, and took a drag. She said, "He's one of Gustavo's boys. Young, stupid, and slow. We caught him that night after it all went down. His 'friends' left him behind. He's been here since then. Like, a month now, I think. Been here waiting for you."

"For me?" Vanessa said.

Gabriel yelled, "*Chinga tu–*"

Mid-insult, Yolanda jabbed the cigarette's red-hot cherry at the prisoner's forehead. He heard his skin sizzling over his own screaming. Feathers of smoke rose from his face. She rotated the cigarette while pushing down on it, then she let the crushed cancer stick fall to the floor. The circular wound at the center of his forehead glowed like a ruby.

"*¡Suéltenme ya!*" Gabriel cried.

'Let me go now!'

Yolanda threw another cigarette in her mouth and lit it. Gabriel's sobbing and begging piqued Vanessa's curiosity. She had never seen a cartel member beg for mercy before.

"How old is he?" she asked.

"Twenty," Yolanda replied.

"He's a... a kid."

"A kid? This 'kid' was going to beat you to death. This 'kid' helped Gustavo find your family. This 'kid' would have killed your kids if Gustavo asked him to. He wasn't begging them to go easy on you when they were kicking the shit out of you, was he? He didn't say shit when they killed your friend, did he? He didn't stop Gustavo when he drowned–"

"*No hables de mis hijos,*" Vanessa snapped.

'Don't talk about my children.'

Yolanda blew a cloud of smoke at her face and said, "I like it when you're angry. But you should be angry at him. Not me."

She took another puff on her cigarette, then thrust the hot cherry at Gabriel's cheek. The pillory rattled as he screamed and convulsed. Due to his frantic movements, the cigarette slid across his cheekbone, leaving a horizontal burn mark on his face. Yolanda grabbed the back of his head, shoved the crushed cigarette in his mouth, then slapped him. He kept sobbing while cursing in Spanish.

"Motherfucker has a hard head," she muttered, waving her hand as if she had just touched a hot pan.

Rafael walked up to the women and said, "Hurt him, Vanessa. Show me that I can trust you with this job."

Vanessa stared down at the prisoner. In Spanish, he begged her not to hurt him, voice strained from weeks of crying. To her dismay, she found herself pitying him. She started to second-guess herself. *Maybe it isn't him*, she thought. *Maybe I just want him to be one of them. Maybe I'm sick and evil like them.* Despite the questions revolving in her mind, she remembered seeing him standing behind her before her torture began on the night of the massacre.

She asked, "Can I have a gun?"

"¡No! ¡No, por favor, no! ¡No me mates!" Gabriel yelled.

'No! No, please, no! Don't kill me!'

Rafael said, "No guns, *mija*. The traitor must suffer. If I wanted him shot, he'd be dead already. Hurt him. *Torture him.*"

"Let me take care of it," Yolanda said. "I can finish them all."

"Not now, you can't. You won't fully recover from those gunshot wounds for a few more weeks."

"I can do it with a limp. No problem."

Rafael said, "You wouldn't make it past the border, but..." He pointed at Vanessa before continuing, "But she can. Vanessa, you'll never be able to finish the job if you can't even kill one of the men who murdered your friend and your children. You have to make them pay for what they did. You still think it's wrong, no? Well, sometimes you have to be wrong to make things right."

Vanessa nodded in agreement. She was already starting to question if she could face Caleb. She didn't love him, but they were close. She cared about him, and she believed he cared about her. Despite all of the betrayal and carnage she had experienced, she continued to see the good in people. Tragedy broke her heart into a dozen pieces, but warm blood still flowed through her veins. She knew what she had to do.

To exact her revenge, she had to kill the last humane part of her. She had to become one of them.

Yolanda pointed her to the workbench and said, "Pick something."

Vanessa hobbled over to it and ran her eyes over the tools on the tabletop—knives, screwdrivers, hammers, box cutters, lighters, a machete, a handsaw, an ice pick. A pickaxe was leaning against the workbench. There were more tools in the drawers, too. Most of it was covered in blood already. Her shaky hand hovered over the tools as she considered all of her options. She took the rusty chef's knife, believing it was the easiest to wield.

As she walked back to the pillory, Gabriel said, "*No, no. No... No lo hagas. Ta–También tengo una familia, señorita. Por favor, déjame ver a mi mamá una vez más. Sólo... Sólo una vez más. Lo siento por lo que hice. Lo siento mucho.*"

'No, no. Don't... Don't do it. I have a family, too, ma'am. Please let me see my mom one more time. Just... Just one more time. I'm sorry for what I did. I'm so sorry.'

As the prisoner continued begging, Rafael patted Vanessa's shoulder and said, "He's trying to trick you, Vani. He knows why he's here and he remembers you. He knows family is your weakness. He abandoned his mother years ago when he dropped out of school and joined Gustavo's gang. She disowned him when she found out, but he still drops by once a year to flaunt his money. He gives her cash and electronics and furniture she does not want, then he leaves. Don't let him fool you."

Vanessa found it hard to believe. The prisoner's fear felt authentic. It stirred memories of her own hopeless begging during the night of the massacre. *They didn't care about me, so why should I care about them?* she thought. She bent over and held the rusty blade up to Gabriel's neck. The pillory clattered and banged as the prisoner jerked his head back. He spoke faster, his words jumbled together and unintelligible.

"What are you doing?" Yolanda asked. "Don't start with the neck or he'll die too fast. You have time now. Make him feel pain. Make him feel what you felt."

Vanessa knew true pain, but she didn't know how to inflict it. Again, she thought about the torture she witnessed during the massacre. She grabbed the prisoner's right ear, pulled it away from his head, then sawed into it at the base. Gabriel howled as the blade tore through the cartilage. Blood poured out of the wound. Two streams ran down to his neck—one from behind his ear, the other from the front. Some blood entered his ear canal, too, its warmth spreading through the right side of his skull.

Grinding her teeth, Vanessa pushed and pulled on the knife with all her strength. The ear looked thin and flimsy to her, so she was surprised by its durability. The human body was stronger than she imagined. Cartels and terrorist groups perfected the art of dismemberment, making it look like flesh was made of butter. The dull blade didn't help either. It kept getting stuck on its way down, so she had to wiggle it every which way to loosen the cartilage. And Gabriel's screaming made it hard for her to focus.

"*¡Mierda!*" she yelled as she dropped the knife.

'Shit!'

Gabriel's ear dangled from his head, barely attached by his earlobe. The blood reached the pillory, soaking into the wooden frame in dark stripes. Yolanda rolled her eyes, then picked up the knife. She grabbed the top of the prisoner's head and chopped at his ear. The rusty blade cut into his scalp and cheek. She pulled the knife back while tugging on his ear, finishing the job with one slice.

She let the severed ear fall to the floor, then she went to work on his left ear. She sawed into it while pulling on it, blood squirting from the wound. It only took her ten seconds to amputate his other ear. It landed on the floor next to his dislodged teeth.

Gooey strings of saliva mixed with blood hanging from his mouth, Gabriel whined, "*Chinga a... tu madre... puta.*"

'Fuck... your mother... bitch.'

"You're too weak for this," Yolanda said.

She turned and pointed the knife at Vanessa. She was about to continue scolding her, but she was taken aback by the bloody tears on Vanessa's face. She dropped the knife.

In a quiet, awed voice, Yolanda asked, "*¿Qué te pasa?*"

'What's happening to you?'

"She's fine," Rafael said as he dabbed Vanessa's cheeks with a handkerchief. "Finish him, Yolanda. Teach her how to kill like you."

Yolanda nodded slowly. She kept an eye on Vanessa as she walked past her. She looked like she was questioning her vision, wondering if she was standing in a room with a ghost. She went to the workbench. While looking through the tools, she took an occasional peek over at Vanessa. She opened a drawer and retrieved a cordless power drill. With a squeeze of the trigger, the tool buzzed as its bulky drill bit spun.

She returned to the pillory and said, "If you're going to torture someone, you have to make sure they won't get away from you. You have to, um... *cripple* them so they won't run or fight back. If I have time to play, I usually start by breaking their hands and feet with a hammer. Their elbows and knees, too. I make sure I break *every* bone. That way, if they do get away, at least they won't use their hands or feet for a very long time, and they'll never forget me." She looked at the guard in the room and said, "*Levántalo.*"

'Raise him.'

The guard turned a crank on the side of the pillory, causing the horizontal board to rise. Gabriel gagged as he felt some pressure on his neck. He was forced to stand on his feet. He felt some relief on his bruised knees, but he couldn't feel the cold, wet floor under his soles. His feet had gone numb. Only a tingling sensation lingered in his feet and lower legs.

"Watch," Yolanda said to Vanessa.

She squatted next to the pillory. The prisoner screamed, but his cries were just background noise now, like the hum of a room fan. She grabbed his clammy thigh in one hand to stop his leg from flopping around. She squeezed the trigger and thrust the drill at the side of his knee. Blood spurted out as the drill bit entered his leg. It showered Yolanda's face. She spit it out and kept pushing the drill.

The drill bit went through the ligaments, cartilage, and bones without a hitch. It continued spinning as it came out the other side of his knee. A drizzle of blood flew towards the spectators. Vanessa took two steps back while the others remained motionless.

Yolanda turned off the drill. There was only the sound of Gabriel's wheezing and the sound of blood plopping in a puddle in the room. The assassin flicked a switch to turn on the drill's reverse function, then she squeezed the trigger and pulled on the tool. The prisoner started screaming and thrashing again. The drill bit exited his leg through the entry wound. Thin strands of meat—which could have been shredded skin, fibrous muscle, or even veins—hung from both sides of his knee.

Rafael said, "We'll provide you with the drugs to keep him conscious, just like this poor fool."

A cocktail of drugs, Vanessa thought. *Just like the one Gustavo put in me.* She wasn't sure what disgusted her more: The idea of becoming like Gustavo or the sadistic torture occurring in front of her.

Yolanda made her way to the prisoner's other leg. He cursed at her and tried to jerk away, but he couldn't escape. With another flick of the switch, she put the drill in its forward function and thrust it at Gabriel's kneecap. Vanessa winced upon hearing the *crunch* of his bone—the patella—over his screaming and the drill. The drill bit came out through the pit at the back of his knee. She put it in reverse and yanked it out.

Gabriel was left groaning and whining. His legs wobbled violently, feet gliding through the puddle of blood and piss under him.

Yolanda stood up and said, "When they're crippled, you can do whatever you want to them. If you don't have any weapons, use anything you can get your hands on. You see a lamp? Use the light bulb. You see a pillow? Put the pillowcase over his head and choke him with it. You can even use food. Beat 'em with a can of beans or stab 'em with a chicken bone. And if you can't think of anything..." She pointed the drill at his genitals, causing him to swing his hips back and squeal. She snickered, then said, "Mess with their dick and balls. It's easy and it always works."

Rafael picked up the rusty chef's knife. He pointed

it at Gabriel's neck and said, "If you run out of time, kill your target quickly. Cut their throats from one ear to the other, but make sure it's deep. You have to cut the arteries, *mija*." He lowered the blade and pointed it at the prisoner's inner thighs. He said, "There are arteries in the legs, too. Cut them and they'll bleed out. You can also stab their hearts if you have a sharp knife. If you have a gun, shoot them in the head and chest twice. Twice *each,* okay? I've seen people get up after getting shot in the head one time but never after getting hit twice."

"I... understand," Vanessa said.

"*Bueno,*" Rafael responded. He beckoned to the guard and said, "*Prepáralo para el guiso.*"

'Good. Prepare him for the stew.'

He led Vanessa out of the room while the guard unshackled the prisoner. Gabriel fell out of the pillory, landing on his side. The guard grabbed one of his arms and Diego seized the other. They dragged Gabriel through the bunker, following Rafael's lead. Yolanda trailed behind them, ready to kill their captive if he managed to overpower the men. They all exited the bunker.

Outside, with the sun setting beyond the property's border, Vanessa watched as the men tightened an animal control pole's noose around Gabriel's neck. Then they lifted him from the ground and shoved his body into a gasoline barrel. The guard held him down with the animal control pole, stopping him from climbing out. They doused him in gasoline from a red can.

Standing over the barrel with a candle lighter in hand, Rafael said, "*Mírate ahora, imbécil. Escogiste el lado incorrecto. Tu patrón te dejó morir solo. Él se esconde, tú te mueres. Maldito cobarde, ¿eh? Pues así es la vida, ¿no? No podemos hacer nada ahora. Cocinemos.*"

'Look at yourself now, asshole. You picked the wrong side. Your boss left you to die alone. He's hiding, you're dying. Fucking coward, huh? Well, that's life, no? Nothing we can do now. Let's cook.'

Gabriel mumbled, "*Se–Señor V–Vásquez, por–*" Rafael lit the lighter and held the flame up against his prisoner's forehead. Upon feeling the heat, Gabriel recoiled and cried, "No!"

A second later, the gasoline ignited. A column of fire shot up from the barrel. The flames reached over their heads before appearing to retract back into the barrel moments later. Vanessa's eyes widened as she teetered away. Despite the flames lapping at his hand and face, Rafael didn't flinch. He only took one step back. The guard ducked to dodge the fire. Yolanda laughed at him. They acted like a bunch of friends standing around a bonfire.

Gabriel's body was consumed by the flames. He flailed in the barrel, causing it to sway in every direction. But he couldn't tip it over. The animal control pole pinned him and the barrel down. Gabriel's skin turned pink, then red, and then *red* and *swollen* and *blistered.* His blood, which had begun to puddle at the bottom of the barrel, sizzled from the extreme heat. As the fire ate away at the layers of his skin, he began to bleed from his shoulders and chest.

His vocabulary was reduced to one word. It was the first word he said as a baby and the last word he would say as a man: '*¡Mamá!*' And he said it repeatedly.

He stopped screaming after cooking for about three minutes. Only crackling, croaking, and clanging sounds came out of the barrel. The croaking came to an end after another minute. And a minute later, the clanging stopped. The fire was extinguished with two buckets of water. Then the guard tipped the barrel over with a kick.

Gabriel's corpse rolled out, plumes of smoke rising from his cooked flesh. Some areas of his body burned faster than others. Large patches of his torso were charred, black and crispy. Parts of his chest and abdomen looked like they had been skinned, revealing his pulpy pectoral muscles and the yellow layers of subcutaneous fat in his belly. His limbs were a mix of pinks and reds, skin peeling and blistering.

His head was swollen, dark red with black streaks all around. Without his ears, it looked like a large, round tomato with grill marks was propped up on his neck. His face was unrecognizable, a mass of red and black lines between lumps and blisters. His nose, once wide and long, was reduced to a nub with only one visible nostril. His eyes had melted, a gooey mixture of blood and vitreous gel glistening on his cheeks. It filled his eye sockets, too.

Vanessa gazed at the body with her hand over her mouth. Bloody tears came to her eyes as she caught a whiff of the meaty, coppery stench hanging over them. She put her other hand over her stomach and retched.

Rafael said, "*Córtale la cabeza y manda un mensaje.*"

'Cut his head off and send a message.'

The guard drew a machete from the sheath attached to his utility belt. He stood over the burnt corpse and chopped at the back of his neck.

Rafael turned to face Vanessa and said, "Come. Let's discuss…"

The stench disrupted Vanessa's other senses. Her hearing faded, she tasted rot in her mouth, and her vision went hazy. Arms crossed over her stomach, she lurched away from the group. Just a few meters away, she lost her balance and tumbled into a bush. On her hands and knees, she vomited.

15

THE PLAN

AFTER GABRIEL'S MURDER VANESSA WAS ALLOWED TO brush her teeth in a bathroom in the villa. She now sat at the edge of the pool with her feet in the water and a towel draped over her shoulders. There were small bloodstains on the towel from when she had dabbed the tears from her eyes. She gazed at her reflection in the pool water, thinking deeply about her desire for vengeance.

Rafael sat on a patio lounge chair behind her. Diego stood nearby while guards watched them from the villa's balconies above. Yolanda had left with Gabriel's corpse and head to send a message to their enemies. Although his primary target was Gustavo, Rafael wanted the entire country to know that he was ready to retaliate if anyone crossed him.

"How are you feeling?" Rafael asked.

Vanessa said, "*Vivo y libre.*"

'Alive and free.'

Rafael smiled upon hearing his catchphrase. His lips sank as Vanessa glanced back at him. For a second —*a millisecond*—she looked *exactly* like his deceased sister. As she pushed her hair behind her ear, the eerie resemblance disappeared.

"What's next?" Vanessa asked.

Rafael swiped at his nose, then said, "That depends on you, *mija*. What do you want to do?"

"I want revenge. I want to... kill Caleb."

"I'm not sure you're ready for that. You could barely cut off that man's ear and you threw up before it was all over. And you didn't even know him. Killing strangers is supposed to be easier than killing people you love. I know that from experience."

"I *don't* love Caleb. I never did. And I only threw up because of the smell. I've... I've never smelled anything like it before. These people... Caleb, Gustavo and his gang... They're not 'strangers.' They killed my babies. *They* deserve to die, and *I* deserve to kill them."

Rafael detected a trace of doubt in her angry voice. Doubt opened the door to hesitation and, in their line of work, hesitation often led to death.

He said, "Diego is going back to the States to handle some business soon. You can go with him, but I'm afraid you're not ready to finish the job."

"I told you, I–"

"Vani, I know you can kill him. Anyone can point a gun and squeeze a trigger. But you're not ready to *punish* him. You don't have the experience to make him suffer—to make an example out of him. And if you leave now, you'll miss your chance to kill the others while they're weak and separated. And that includes Gustavo, *mija*."

Vanessa looked at him, her eyes narrowed with curiosity. She got out of the water, then took a seat on the patio lounge chair next to his.

"You'd let me kill them?" she asked. "All of them?"

"As long as you take it as an opportunity to practice, sure."

"After what he did to your sister... I don't know. I guess I thought you would have wanted to kill Gustavo yourself."

"As long as it's one of my people who gets him, it doesn't matter. And you are one of my people, aren't you? You are part of my family, right?"

Rafael had asked for her loyalty before, but now he was asking for her total dedication to his criminal organization. Vanessa had already spent months working for the cartel, but she always told herself that it was only temporary. She never considered herself to be part of the 'family.' She looked up at the orange sky and thought about her children. Lucía had already expressed her disappointment in her mother when she heard the rumors about her criminal career. She knew it would have scared Joaquín, too.

But Vanessa was obsessed with vengeance. She

couldn't move on with her life until her attackers were brought to justice.

"*Sí, patrón,*" she said, the doubt purged from her voice.

'Yes, boss.'

"Good," Rafael replied. "Gustavo and his crew of *perras* scattered like cockroaches after we overpowered and outnumbered them. Since you've been in the hospital, our worthless government has been putting on a show of force. To groups like ours, that's all it is: *A show*. They want the public to think they're working so they're sending the military to get their hands dirty. They're targeting smaller groups—groups like Gustavo's. So, those *perras* are still laying low. They think they've been hiding, but we've had our eyes on them. We were planning on kidnapping them all at once and executing them for a video, just like they tried to do to you and Yolanda and the rest of my people. I think it would be better if you hunted them down one by one while making your way to the border."

'*Perras*' meant 'bitches.'

Vanessa said, "I've never... 'hunted' anyone before. I can kill them, I know I can because I've done it before, but I might need a little bit of help, especially if I can't use a gun."

"We'll help you find them and trap them. But once they're in your hands, it's up to you to finish them off. And you must make them suffer, Vani. You're part of my family now. Your actions reflect on me. The way you kill sends a message for both of us. Don't let that message be one of weakness."

"I understand."

"We'll go over the smaller details later, but I believe you'll be starting with a man named Ignacio Tapia. I'm sure you'll recognize him when you see him. He's the closest to us now. After you're done with him, you'll catch a bus or a taxi—don't worry, we'll arrange the transportation for you—to another town and you can start hunting your next target. We'll have you cross at Nuevo Progreso. On the other side, Diego will meet you and take you to Caleb's hometown."

Vanessa looked over at Diego. He gave her a nod, as if to say: *That's right*. She nodded back at him.

Rafael continued, "Once you're in the States, Diego will be your only friend, but he won't be able to get close to Caleb without raising any alarms. It'll be up to you to take him out."

"And what about Gustavo?" Vanessa asked. "Where is he?"

"Gustavo... He's a little smarter than his soldiers. He knows how to blend in, how to hide in plain sight. You've seen him. He dresses like a civilian, no? The last time I saw him, he looked like my mechanic. But don't worry, we've heard he's somewhere up north. So, you'll be able to get him right before you cross the border. Yolanda will track him down and hand him over to you before you get there. That girl is reliable. Be like her.

Now, do you have any questions? Or are you ready to get started?"

"I have a question, but I don't know if I can ask it."

Rafael chuckled, then said, "What? Are you afraid you're going to hurt my feelings? Ask me anything. Go ahead, we're family now."

"Why are you doing this for me? How can you trust me when I tried to betray you? What do you get out of all of this?"

"Well, that's actually three questions, *mija,*" Rafael said with another laugh. "Vanessa, we both get what we want: Revenge. And I trust you because you're the only person in this world who wants to see Caleb and Gustavo dead as much as me. Your eyes... They're like mine after my Letty was taken away from me. I didn't cry blood like you, but it felt like I did. I know you will get this done for me. *¿No es verdad?*"

The Spanish translated to: 'Isn't that right?'

Vanessa wasn't convinced by his smooth talk. Rafael didn't lie to her, but he didn't tell her the entire truth either. He was testing Vanessa by having her target Gustavo's soldiers first. If she failed—captured, killed, or disappeared—he planned on sending Yolanda to the United States to kill Caleb. His contingency plans made him a good leader, keeping him one step ahead of his competition.

Vanessa said, "I'm ready."

Rafael beckoned to Diego and said, "Get her some cell phones and cash. Give her a map to Gustavo's *perras* and some of our safe houses. And teach her how to use our special 'equipment.' She can take whatever she needs." He walked over to Vanessa, patted her forehead, and said, "*Buena suerte.*"

'Good luck.'

She felt some comfort from his gentle touch. She recalled her time in Caleb's arms. She learned comfort made people vulnerable. She wasn't going to let anyone betray her again, so she kept her guard up. *They're not my friends,* she told herself. She focused all of her energy on getting revenge. Murder was the only thing on her mind.

As Rafael walked away, Vanessa said, "*Gracias, patrón.*"

'Thank you, boss.'

16

THE FIRST TARGET

VANESSA SAT ON THE WINDOWSILL AND STARED AT THE
bar across the street. It was a joint called *La Cantina de
Catalina*, which translated to 'Catalina's Cantina.' The
red neon lights at the front of the bar illuminated half
her face while the darkness from the hotel room
behind her veiled the other side of her body.

From her room on the second floor, she could hear
the music, chatter, and laughter inside the bar. Two
burly bouncers stood at the entrance. Bar-hoppers and
drunkards loitered on the sidewalk and even on the
street. Drivers had to honk and swerve around them to
avoid hitting them. A pair of women—tourists from
the US—were in the alley next to the bar. One of them
was puking while the other called for a taxi. An older
Mexican man stood next to them, inviting them to his
home for a glass of water in English and Spanish and
Spanglish. He made kissing sounds and snapped his

fingers at them as if he were calling to a stray animal. They ignored him.

An SUV slowed to a stop in front of the bar. Three men hopped out and approached the bouncers. While they exchanged words, Vanessa looked down at the sheet of paper in her hand. It had information on her first target: *Ignacio Tapia*. From the picture printed on the sheet, she recognized him as the truck driver. He didn't hurt her children, but he brought them to Gustavo. He escorted them to their deaths. She saw him standing at the entrance of the bar now. The bouncers let him and his crew in, then the SUV rolled away—all according to plan.

The paper crumpled as she clenched her fist, then it flapped as her arm shook. Struck with a bout of dizziness, she closed her eyes and breathed deeply through her nose. She was sick with anger and doubt.

"*Para mis hijos,*" she murmured.

'For my babies.'

She went into the bathroom, turned on the sink, and drank tap water from her cupped hand. She splashed some on her face, too.

She looked at her reflection in the grimy mirror and said, "*Puedes hacerlo.*"

'You can do this.'

With a lighter she set the information sheet on fire. It burned to ashes in the sink. She grabbed the makeup cases from the counter and prepared for the next step in her plan.

Vanessa strutted across the street, smiling a fake smile. She had changed into a red lace-up crop top, tight jeans, and high heels. Makeup covered her lingering bruises and the scar on her neck. It was all part of her act. She had to blend in with the crowd so as not to arouse any suspicion from Ignacio's crew.

She greeted the bouncers, then she leaned in close to one of their ears and told them about Rafael's arrangement in a whisper. The bouncer checked her bag so he wouldn't look like he was giving her preferential treatment. He caught a glimpse of a wallet, some keys, a metal case, a meat tenderizer, and a utility knife. He acted like he saw nothing out of the ordinary, though.

Vanessa was permitted into *La Cantina de Catalina*. She went directly to the bar to the left and ordered a martini. She hoped the alcohol would help her get through the next phase of the plan. Instead of the bartender, an older man with buzz cut hair in a colorful button-up shirt brought her the drink.

"*¿Cómo estás, hermosa?*" he asked.

'How are you, beautiful?'

Vanessa replied, "*Estoy bien, gracias.*"

'I'm fine, thank you.'

"*Bueno, bueno. Me llamo Hugo,*" the man said. It translated to: 'Good, good. My name is Hugo.' Leaning closer to her and lowering his voice, he smirked and said, "*Seguro que has escuchado muchas cosas buenas sobre mí, ¿no?*"

'I'm sure you've heard a lot of good things about me, right?'

Vanessa recognized the name. She was told about him prior to embarking on her journey, but she didn't hear anything particularly *good* about him. He was a pimp. He managed the bar as well as others in the area. He made a deal with Rafael to help set up Ignacio in exchange for cash and protection.

"*Sí, claro,*" Vanessa said. "*Gracias por tu ayuda.*"

'Yes, of course. Thank you for your help.'

"*De nada, muñeca,*" Hugo responded with a wink. It translated to: 'You're welcome, doll.' He slid the drink closer to her and said, "*Sólo habla bien de nosotros con tu jefe. Eso es todo lo que quiero.*"

'Just put in a good word for us with your boss. That's all I want.'

Vanessa wanted to say something like: 'That's all you'll get' or 'I don't care.' She was tired of the sleazy pimp and she had no interest in his deal with Rafael. But she knew she needed him to proceed. So, she smiled and nodded at him.

Hugo said, "*Genial. El flaco está arriba con una de mis muchachas. Te avisaré cuando esté listo para ti. Disfruta tu bebida.*"

'Great. The skinny guy is upstairs with one of my girls. I'll let you know when he's ready for you. Enjoy your drink.'

Vanessa sipped on her martini while waiting at the bar. She was surrounded by dozens of people—as young as eighteen and as old as sixty. The atmosphere was electric and the patrons were mostly jovial.

She spotted Ignacio's partners sitting at a booth with four prostitutes. Each time one of the men downed a drink, one of the women persuaded them to order another. They were already drunk, getting loud and handsy. As she waited, a man approached Vanessa at the bar with a pick-up line. She respectfully declined his advances. Shortly afterward, another guy invited her to his booth. She declined his invitation as well.

Halfway through her martini, she heard someone speaking English behind her. She peeked over her shoulder and saw an American man flirting with a Mexican woman. He didn't look anything like Caleb— this guy had his black hair in a man bun—but he still reminded her of her former partner. His mere presence at the bar angered her. Although she knew it was unwarranted, she wanted to throw her drink at him and pull the woman away from him.

Just as she moved to get up, Hugo caught her attention with a short whistle. The pimp pointed at the ceiling, then held up three fingers. Vanessa got the message: 'He's ready on the third floor.' She polished off the rest of her drink, then headed to the stairs at the other end of the room. The music and chatter in the bar sounded clear on the second floor. On the third floor, the noise blended and faded into an unintelligible hum.

She ended up in a gloomy hallway, floorboards creaking without any movement and dirty wallpaper hanging from the walls. She heard faint moans and groans coming from the rooms to her left and right. A woman named Ana, one of Hugo's prostitutes, stood next to the third door on the right.

As Vanessa approached her, Ana asked, "*¿Buscas a Nacho?*"

'Are you looking for Nacho?'

Nacho was the short form of Ignacio. Vanessa nodded.

"*Está dormido. Usé el cloroformo como me dijeron,*" Ana said. "*No es mi culpa si ya está muerto, ¿entiendes?*"

'He's asleep. I used the chloroform like they told me to. It's not my fault if he's dead already, understand?'

Vanessa said, "*Te oigo. Está bien. Puedes irte.*"

'I hear you. It's fine. You can go.'

She reached for the doorknob, but Ana blocked her path. The prostitute stood in front of the door with her hands on its frame.

She said, "*Tengo familia. Mis niños significan el mundo para mí. No salgas de ese cuarto hasta que estás segura de que está muerto. Si él vive, mi familia muere. ¿Me oyes?*"

'I have a family. My boys mean the world to me. Don't leave that room until you're sure he's dead. If he lives, my family dies. You hear me?'

Vanessa understood her fear. Although they didn't share a resemblance, she saw a shade of herself in Ana.

She said, "*Ya está muerto. Te lo prometo.*"

'He's already dead. I promise.'

Ana looked ill, pale and sweaty. She had a bad feeling about the whole situation. She didn't want to be involved, but she wasn't given any options. She believed Vanessa, though. She hurried down the hall and exited the building through the fire escape to avoid being spotted by Ignacio's men.

Vanessa looked at the number on the door: 6. She entered the room and locked the door behind her.

———

Vanessa felt like she had stepped into the past. The room resembled the one she had worked in at Enrique's Bar. It was a red room with a shaggy carpet and peeling wallpaper. Like her old room it had a bed, nightstands, a sofa, a coffee table, and an entertainment center. This room had a mini fridge next to the sofa, though.

Ignacio lay spread-eagle on the bed, lips flapping as he snored. He was nude, beads of sweat shimmering across his skin. His limbs were handcuffed to the bedposts at the wrists and ankles. A moist rag, wet with chloroform, covered his nose. It wasn't difficult for Ana to restrain him. She just asked him if he wanted to play with handcuffs and he said yes.

Vanessa pinched the rag, as if she were afraid the chloroform was going to burn her skin, then tossed it aside. She gazed at Ignacio's face for a minute, standing in total silence. He was out cold. She put her bag down on the sofa and pulled the meat tenderizer out. She tapped his forehead with it.

Once...

Twice...

She stopped in the middle of the third swing, holding the tenderizer up to her shoulder. She stepped back and lowered the weapon slowly. Hand over her mouth, she took some short, quivery breaths. She was supposed to torture him, but she didn't know where to start. She was afraid he was going to awaken and scream if she didn't kill him with the first blow.

She put the tenderizer down and looked through her bag. Buried under her other tools, she found a roll of duct tape. She slapped Ignacio's arm. He didn't react to it. She poked the side of his head. He remained unconscious. She sat next to him and wrapped the duct tape over his mouth and around his head ten times over.

"Start by breaking their hands and feet," she murmured, repeating Yolanda's advice.

She grabbed his ankle and raised the tenderizer overhead. She paused for a few seconds, took a deep breath, then swung it down. The tenderizer hit his left foot with a loud *thud* and a muffled *crack*. His metatarsal bones shattered and a horizontal gash stretched across the top of his foot. His upper body rose from the bed in a violent recoil, but his eyes remained closed.

Vanessa swung the tenderizer at his foot again, breaking every toe except the little one. The toenails flew off his middle and long toes, too. The gash grew longer and wider. She could see the bloody muscle between his broken bones in the wound. He began to groan, handcuffs rattling as he moved restlessly.

Vanessa let go of his ankle and swung the tenderizer down at his foot. She crushed three of his toes, then the tenderizer slid across his foot. The tenderizer's teeth got caught in the gash, but it kept moving. It peeled the skin off the top of his foot, all the way up to his ankle. She jerked her head to the side after seeing more of his broken bones, stringy muscles, and ligaments.

Ignacio had finally awoken. Hot bolts of tremendous pain shot up his leg from his smashed foot, but he couldn't see what was happening. The vapors from the chloroform stung his eyes, leaving his vision blurred. He had a severe headache, too, but he couldn't tell if it was caused by the pain in his foot or something else.

Fearing she'd get cold feet if she stopped, Vanessa hurried to the other side of the bed. To Ignacio, she looked like a shadow darting across the room. She held his leg down at the shin and swung the tenderizer at his other foot five times in quick succession. The tenderizer's teeth left small puncture wounds on the top of his foot. Although it wasn't as bloody, she left more broken bones in his right foot than in the left.

Ignacio bounced on the bed and screamed as the shadow in his vision approached the headboard. He tried to jerk away, but he couldn't break free from the handcuffs. He didn't even remember putting the restraints on or his meeting with Ana. All he knew was that he was in a great deal of pain and he was terrified. There wasn't a clear thought in his head.

Vanessa swung the tenderizer at his right hand and hit his palm. With the second swing, she hit his ring, middle, and pointer fingers, bending them all back at a 90-degree angle. His knuckles *popped* and *crunched*. She missed the third swing and hit the bedpost, causing the wood to splinter. So, she held his arm down against the mattress and pounded his hand again.

The thug stopped screaming as his thumb was crushed. His broken thumb gyrated wildly, as if he were moving the joystick on a video game controller. Blood spurted out of the cut at the base of the finger. He stared at the ceiling and held his breath until he passed out twenty seconds later.

Vanessa moved to the other side of the bed. She hammered away at his left hand until every bone in his palm was broken. She put the tenderizer down on the coffee table and inspected the damage while catching her breath. His feet had swelled up. His left foot was a bloody mess while his right foot turned blue and red. His hands suffered from similar swelling and bruising.

Vanessa stayed vigilant, though. Ignacio wasn't capable of running away or using most weapons, but one good headbutt could knock her out and change everything. She took the metal case out of her bag and popped it open. The syringe inside had a clear liquid in its barrel. She injected it into his outer thigh.

Ignacio's eyes cracked open about thirty seconds later. He whined as he lifted his head from the pillow, jugulars bulging from his neck. He checked on his hands first, then he looked down at his feet. His extremities stung and ached, but he was now more concerned about his rapid heart rate. His heart was beating so fast that his sternum was starting to hurt. The tingling in his thigh worried him, too.

His eyes bugged out as he looked to his left. He saw Vanessa standing there, quiet and still. He mistook her for Ana. Furious, he lunged at her. The bedposts groaned and the handcuffs rattled. He fell back onto the bed and writhed as the pain in his hands and feet reignited. Whimpering, he glared at the woman. His anger turned into confusion as his vision cleared up. He didn't recognize his attacker.

Vanessa said, "*Te he inyectado con un... 'cóctel de drogas.' Vas a sentir todo. Todo, cabrón.*"

'I've injected you with a... 'cocktail of drugs.' You're going to feel everything. Everything, fucker.'

She took the utility knife out of her bag and

approached the side of the bed. Ignacio mumbled incoherently and, fighting through the pain, scooted to the opposite edge of the mattress. She crouched next to the bed and thumbed the utility knife's slider, slowly pushing the sharp blade out.

"*¿Me recuerdas?*" Vanessa asked. "*¿No? Claro que no. El asesinato es como... la comida para ti. No puedes recordar a quién mataste ayer como no puedes recordar lo que comiste para el desayuno.*"

'Do you remember me? No? Of course not. Murder is like... food to you. You can't remember who you killed yesterday just like you can't remember what you had for breakfast.'

She sliced his side with the blade, cutting him from his lower ribs to his hip. Blood spilled out of the thin but deep cut, mixing with his cold sweat and drenching the bedsheet. He moaned and drew back, but he could only move his torso another centimeter. The pressure on his left wrist and ankle aggravated his broken bones. His forearm and lower leg were throbbing.

"*Mataste a mis hijos,*" she said through her clenched teeth.

'You killed my children.'

Ignacio stammered and shook his head frantically. The chloroform addled his brain and twisted his tongue. He could only say one word clearly: "No! No! No!"

"*¿Cómo qué no?*" Vanessa said, sniffling. "*¿Crees que*

soy estúpida? ¿Crees que soy ciega? Te vi... Tú y Gustavo, tu patrón. Lo viste matar... a mis hijos... en el agua!"

'What do you mean no? Do you think I'm stupid? You think I'm blind? I saw you... You and Gustavo, your boss. You watched him kill... my kids... in the water!'

She lunged forward and attacked his abdomen with a flurry of slashes. He flopped and screamed with each slice. He felt the blade ripping through his abdominal muscles. With some slashes, she drove it just deep enough to nick his intestines. She left his abdomen with vertical and horizontal cuts as well as some Xs. His stomach looked like a tic-tac-toe board without any Os.

As he howled, she turned on the lamp on the nightstand and yelled, "*¡¿Me recuerdas ahora, hijo de puta?!*"

'Remember me now, motherfucker?!'

Ignacio's pupils expanded with fear. He didn't recognize her, though. Vanessa was partially correct. Ignacio couldn't remember the last person he had murdered, but he could remember his breakfast. Murder was like breathing to him. He needed to do it to survive. He was only scared now because of the bloody tears dripping from Vanessa's eyes. He felt like he was staring at a monster from his worst childhood nightmares.

Vanessa held the blade up to his neck. It cut him next to his Adam's apple. She considered cutting the lump out and feeding it to him, but she didn't want to kill him yet. Her eyes crawled over his body. She didn't think the blade was durable enough to strip the muscles from his chest. She skipped his abdomen since it was already mutilated. Her gaze settled on his hairy crotch.

She crawled onto the bed and straddled his legs, her knees next to his thighs. She grabbed the shaft of his flaccid dick and gave it a good tug.

Upon feeling her hand on his penis, Ignacio lifted his head from the pillow and glared at his crotch. He started thrusting his hips up and swinging his body from side to side. He couldn't knock her off, though.

Vanessa tightened her grip until her knuckles turned white. She held onto his dick as if it were a bull rope and Ignacio were a bull. She forced the tip of the blade into his urethra through the meatus, sending daggers of blazing pain through his cock. A droplet of blood seeped out of his urethra and streamed down to her thumb.

She thrust the knife deeper. The tip of the blade stuck out through the glans near the crown while the honed edge severed his frenulum. More blood streamed out, wetting the bottom and top of his shaft before reaching her fingers. Ignacio stopped screaming. His eyes spun in their sockets, and he breathed in short, panicked gasps.

Vanessa yelped as she unintentionally cut her thumb. She had successfully split his glans in half vertically down the middle. It opened up like a flower with two petals. Blood leapt out of it like spurts of semen. Since Ignacio stopped resisting, she released her grip on the shaft and kept sawing into his cock from within.

She cut his dick in half lengthwise. She left the flaps of mutilated penis attached to his crotch. A sudden spell of nausea stopped her from severing the pieces. She was ready to kill and hungry for vengeance, but the gore still sickened her. She dropped the knife and ran into the bathroom.

While she puked in the toilet, Ignacio fidgeted and whined in bed. He unleashed one awful groan after another. His eyes were glazed over and his chest barely moved with his short breaths. Pain circulated through every inch of his body as if it were traveling through his veins. He didn't want to move or even look down at himself, fearing it would only worsen his agony.

After washing her hands and face in the sink, Vanessa returned to the room. She was hoping to find Ignacio dead from a loss of blood or shock, but he clung to life. She looked at the door and thought about running. She tried to convince herself he would die soon without her anyway.

But she had to be sure he was dead—for Rafael, for Ana, for herself.

She grabbed the tenderizer from the coffee table and walked to the side of the bed. She held it over his face. He didn't react to it, his gaze as hollow as a corpse's.

"*Para mis hijos,*" she said.

'For my babies.'

She swung the tenderizer at his head as hard as possible—over and over and over. At first, its teeth ripped a chunk of skin off his brow. It hit the headboard with a splat. The tenderizer cracked his forehead, then shattered his cheekbone, then hit his forehead again. The supraorbital ridge over his left eye broke. His eyebrow sank *into* his eye socket. His brain was visible through a hole on his forehead.

She kept beating his face with the tenderizer, though. She crushed his nose, broke his teeth, and pulverized his other cheekbone. Through the hole on his forehead, she landed a direct hit on his brain. It made a *squishy* noise upon impact. Blood came out of every opening on his head—his eye sockets, his squashed nostrils, his mouth, his ear canals, the gashes on his face. She stopped after she caved the center of his face in.

The tenderizer was stuck in his skull, surrounded by flaps of loose skin, broken bones, and mushy brain. His eyes and nose were no longer visible under the tenderizer's head. Gooey ropes of dark blood—almost black—poured out of his collapsed eye sockets. His limbs shook and his fingers twitched, but his chest was still. He had stopped breathing after his forehead was cracked open.

Vanessa put her hand over her mouth and wobbled back. The nausea returned along with a bout of dizziness. She went back to the bathroom and washed Ignacio's blood off her. She scrubbed at the blood with soap and scalding water until her hands were red and numb. Staggering through the room, she grabbed her purse and the metal case. She left her weapons behind since crime scene cleanup was part of the deal with Hugo anyway.

She exited the room just as she started to find her bearings. To her utter relief, the hallway was empty and the moaning continued in the neighboring rooms. She hurried to the fire escape.

———

After the assassination, Vanessa returned to her hotel room across the street. She changed into something a little more inconspicuous and washed her hands again. She called a taxi to the hotel, then started packing all of her belongings in a suitcase and a backpack. While packing she peeked out at *La Cantina de Catalina*. She expected Ignacio's friends to discover his body and start shooting up the place before chasing after her.

The taxi arrived five minutes later.

She hopped in and directed the driver to the city's bus terminal. As they drove off, she took one final glance at the bar behind her. In the building, Ignacio's friends were inebriated at their booth and they planned on taking a prostitute—or two—to the rooms upstairs for some fun. They weren't going to find Ignacio's body. They couldn't even remember arriving with him.

At the station, Vanessa boarded an overnight bus with a prepaid first-class ticket. It was heading north, directly to her next target. Sitting at a window seat in an empty row, she pulled a folder out of her backpack. And from the folder, she retrieved another information sheet. It had a picture of Ricardo Rivera on it. He was Gustavo's cousin and, due to their familial relationship, he was expected to be surrounded by hitmen.

Rafael recommended a drive-by shooting outside of a nightclub as a means of assassination. He had scheduled a meeting between Vanessa and some of his men in the area to organize it. Vanessa had some doubts, but she didn't have time to hesitate. She was sure news of Ignacio's death was going to reach Ricardo and the other cartel members soon. She tore the paper to shreds, then let the pieces fly out the window as the bus cruised on a highway.

17

THE SECOND TARGET

"*No... No puedo hacerlo,*" Vanessa said, holding a cell phone to her ear. "*Es demasiado peligroso. Y no mato–*"

"*Oye,*" the man on the phone interrupted with a deep, monotone voice. "*La vieja está en la casa, ¿no? Entonces cuidado con lo que dices o habla en inglés.*"

Vanessa had said: 'I... I can't do this. It's too danger- ous. And I don't kill–'

And the man had interrupted with: 'Hey. The old lady is home, no? Then watch your mouth or speak English.'

Vanessa looked down at the floorboards. She was in a room that had been converted into a studio apart- ment on the second floor of a house. An old woman— senile but nosy—owned the home. She was downstairs watching a telenovela with the television blaring on what sounded like full volume. The woman knew the type of people who rented the unit upstairs. She didn't seem to care as long as she was paid, she was unharmed, and the room was left clean.

Vanessa cast her eyes down at the AK-47 on the bed in front of her. To her, it was a weapon meant for a battlefield, not a nightclub filled with civilians.

She said, "This gun is too... It's too much. I don't even know how to use it. I could miss him. I could kill the wrong person. And I *don't* kill innocent people. I said that from the beginning."

"*Vamos a ayudarte,*" the man replied. "*No te preocupes.*"

'We're going to help you. Don't worry about it.'

"I don't want your help. I don't want... *this.*"

The man said, "*Pues, es lo que quiere el patrón.*"

'Well, it's what the boss wants.'

"Tell him that I'm not doing it," Vanessa answered bluntly. "Tell him I'll do it my way."

She ended the call before he could respond. Listening to the creaking in the home and the cars outside, she wrapped the bed covers around the rifle to hide it. She sat on the windowsill, sunshine bathing her body. The home was located near an intersection. There was a busy Circle K convenience store in one corner and a Mexican restaurant in another. In the intersection, just off a curb and under a large umbrella, a woman stood behind a cart selling a variety of chips with an assortment of toppings—pork rinds, chili powders, salsas, salt, lime. The area was peaceful.

Vanessa searched a nightclub on her phone. Located downtown, it was a place called *Luces Rojas*, which translated to 'Red Lights.' Ricardo was known for visiting the nightclub every Friday night. Word on the street was he had been spending more time there since the night of the massacre. Rafael wanted Vanessa and his crew to gun him down outside of the club if the opportunity arose or to raid the club and shoot it up. Although it angered the government, collateral damage wasn't a serious issue for the cartels.

Vanessa inspected the club's website and investigated the area around it, searching for alternate entrances, escape routes, and security lapses. Due to the public nature of the nightclub, torture was out of the question. The assassination had to be quick and quiet. She had to get him while he was alone. *In a bathroom?* she thought. *Or if he goes out to smoke a cigarette in the alley?* The cell phone rang.

"*¿Sí?*" she answered.

'Yes?'

The line was silent. She heard some shuffling, then a sigh.

"*El patrón dice… buena suerte*" the man said. "*Si necesitas algo, dímelo ahora. O si no, estás por tu cuenta.*"

'The boss says… good luck. If you need anything, tell me now. Otherwise, you're on your own.'

Vanessa considered all of her options. She thought about asking for a pistol with a silencer like the ones she had seen in Hollywood action movies. But weapons weren't the problem. It was the location. *Luces Rojas* was just too public for her taste. If she wanted to catch him anywhere else, she needed a means of transportation.

She said, "A small car. A black one."

After another brief pause, the man said, "*Por supuesto.*"

'Sure thing.'

The call disconnected. Vanessa threw the phone at the bed and started getting ready for a night on the town.

Luces Rojas had a prominent glass wall exterior. Vibrant red lights ran down the sides of the building between its tinted windows in perfectly vertical, parallel lines. A brighter overhead sign with the club's name stuck out above the entrance. A ring of red light circled the building, illuminating the surrounding sidewalks. A line of customers stretched around the club, too, forced to wait by the bouncers at the entrance. In front of the club, a couple of men hung out on the side of the road smoking cigarettes.

Luces Rojas was surrounded by fancy restaurants and luxury stores. Pedestrians strolled down the sidewalks and cars filled the street. There was a sense of normality in the area.

Vanessa sat in the driver's seat of a small black

hatchback parked on the street. Across the intersection in front of her, she could see the club's entrance. She had been watching the building for an hour. She didn't see Ricardo or any of Gustavo's other men enter the club. She assumed they were already inside, but she kept a close eye on every male visitor lined up around the building anyway. She couldn't let him slip past her.

She leaned back and sank into her seat as a police car drove towards her. One of the cops in the vehicle looked in her direction, but the car kept moving. She held her breath as she watched it through the sideview mirror. She expected to see it stop and to hear a *whoop* from its siren. The police car vanished around a corner. She wrenched her gaze away from the mirror and brought it back to the nightclub.

She nibbled on her fingernails and bounced her leg rapidly. Her heart rate increased and a sheen of cold sweat glistened on her brow.

She considered entering the club, but she was worried she'd miss him while waiting in line. Wearing a hoodie and jeans, she wasn't exactly dressed for a party either. She was hoping he would step out and join the men in front of the club for a smoke. She imagined running him over, popping the door open, and shooting him twice in the head and twice in the chest from the comfort of her seat.

But Ricardo was nowhere in sight. She watched the clubbers come and go. Most of the surrounding stores started to close. About forty-five minutes later, the fancy restaurants followed suit.

Maybe he's not even inside, she thought.

She took the cell phone out of her hoodie pocket and accessed its call history. She had only called one person—the man with the monotone voice. She didn't catch his name, but she knew he worked for Rafael. She wanted to ask for his help or, at the very least, his advice. She hesitated, though.

From her experience, cartel members shot first and didn't bother to ask questions later. They would fire-bomb a busy building—*raze it to the ground*—to kill a fly.

She saw young adults waiting in line to enter the nightclub. Some of them looked younger than eighteen, baby-faced teenagers trying to sneak in with fake IDs. A bittersweet smile blossomed on her face as she thought about her slain children. She pictured them as teenagers and then as young adults.

These kids have parents, she told herself. *They don't deserve to die.*

She put the phone away and continued reminiscing about her children. Her face ached from all her smiling.

Fifteen minutes later, her lips drooped into a neutral expression and her eyes lit up. Ricardo walked out of the club with a gang of men, cackling and yelling and teetering drunkenly. They walked around the building. Vanessa peeled out of the parking space and raced against the traffic lights. She lost, so she had to stomp on the brakes and stop at the red light.

"Fuck!" she shouted as she slapped the steering wheel.

She leaned forward and stared unblinkingly at the club. The hatchback inched over the stop line, then onto the crosswalk. As soon as she saw the green glow of the traffic light from the corner of her eye, she stepped on the gas petal and sped forward. She slowed down as two armored SUVs—each blasting a different Spanish song—drove out of the parking lot next to the nightclub. Ricardo and the men were gone, so she was sure they were in the SUVs.

While following them, Vanessa retrieved a small pistol from her bag. Locked and loaded, she put it in her hoodie pocket. She took a small switchblade out next. With a push of a button, a sharp three-and-a-half-inch blade sprung out. She retracted it, then put the switchblade in her pants pocket.

She let another car squeeze between her hatchback and the SUVs so the cartel members wouldn't catch on. Next, she took a utility knife out of her bag. She inspected the blade, retracted it, then hid it in the shaft of her boot. With one eye on the road and one hand on the steering wheel, she reached into her bag for the fourth time. She felt the rubber grip of a steel claw hammer.

Before she could take it out, the SUVs pulled into the parking lot of a strip mall. They stopped in front of a Mexican restaurant between a convenience store and a closed smoke shop.

Vanessa parked in front of a Burger King at the outermost edge of the parking lot. It was open 24/7. She continued looking through her bag, although she had already decided to leave the hammer. It was too big for her pockets. To keep a semblance of innocence, she acted like she was searching for something—a wallet or a phone. She kept watching the SUVs, though.

Ricardo jumped out first. He had been sitting in the front passenger seat of one of the SUVs. But Vanessa's relief was short-lived, replaced with dread as the other doors opened. More cartel members exited the SUVs like clowns coming out of a clown car. She counted eleven. One of them dropped a beer bottle. It shattered between the vehicles. Another guy dropped his pistol. He quickly scooped it up and tucked it into the back of his waistband. They stumbled into the restaurant.

Outnumbered and outgunned, Vanessa couldn't kill them all. She was kicking herself for leaving the AK-47 at home. She couldn't get close to her target without exposing herself either. But she refused to leave without seeing Ricardo's blood. She decided to join them for a late-night supper.

———

The door chime announced Vanessa's arrival at the restaurant. There was a bar to the right and the kitchen was directly behind it. To her left, dining tables were cluttered together. Food menus and advertisements for local concerts, all old and tattered, were taped to the walls. Mariachi music played from a radio behind the bar. It sounded like it had been recorded with a tape recorder.

Ricardo and his gang sat at the dining tables, enjoying a fresh round of beer while waiting for their food. Vanessa smiled at the cook behind the bar. He invited her to sit anywhere. He didn't seem bothered by his cartel clientele. Vanessa squeezed between one of the cartel members and a stool. She went to a table at the back of the restaurant.

A young couple—no older than their mid-twenties—sat at the other table in the corner back there. They were stiff and quiet, leaving their meals half-eaten. The thugs scared the shit out of them. And fear stole their appetites as well as their ability to think rationally. All they had to do was pay for their food and walk out, but they looked like they were being held up at gunpoint.

Vanessa sat down. One of the cooks approached her. Although she wasn't hungry, she ordered a plate of *carne asada* tacos and a Coke. While waiting for her food, she fiddled with her phone and spied on the gang. They spoke about sports, money, women, and cars. When the conversation veered to the topic of guns, Ricardo flaunted his gold-plated pistol.

The staff brought them plates of tacos, quesadillas, and enchiladas as well as another round of beer.

Ruben Perez—a young guy with slicked back hair —caught Vanessa staring at them. She looked back at her phone. *Fuck, fuck, fuck,* she said to herself. Ruben wasn't drunk like most of the other gangsters. He had a buzz going on, but he controlled his drinking since he was driving that night. He didn't care about the law or the other drivers on the road, he just didn't want to get caught off guard by a rival cartel. He started glancing at Vanessa every once in a while.

The cook brought Vanessa her plate of tacos and her drink. He asked the couple about their meal. They said they were fine and began to eat again. As soon as the cook departed, they stopped eating and complained about each other's lack of action. The man wanted his girlfriend to ask for the bill while his girl- friend was waiting for *him* to lead her out of the restau- rant. After a thirty-second argument, they quieted down out of fear of bothering the cartel.

Vanessa acted natural. She ate a taco while flicking her finger across her cell phone's screen. She read the local news—Canadians murdered at a resort over a gang dispute; journalists killed with little consequence; piles of butchered bodies found here, there, and every- where. The silent civil war in Mexico raged on and on.

Laughing, Ricardo stood up and announced his urgent need to piss. He chugged the rest of his beer, then walked to the back of the restaurant. He didn't notice Vanessa or the couple as he walked past their tables. He walked down a short hallway leading to the restrooms—the men's room on the left, women's on the right.

Vanessa counted to sixty in her head, hoping the others wouldn't notice her following him if she waited for a minute. Due to a spike of anxiety, her count was fast, so she stood up about forty seconds after Ricardo passed by her. No one saw her hustle down the hallway. She opened the door to the women's restroom and glanced over her shoulder, then she juked across the hall and entered the men's room.

"*¿Quién es?*" Ricardo asked.

'Who is it?'

He stood in front of a urinal with his back to the entrance, swaying back and forth. He had spent a minute wrestling with his zipper. He finally pulled his dick out and started peeing. It immediately streamed down his fingers before ricocheting off the urinal and hitting his jeans.

Vanessa reached for the pistol in her hoodie pocket. *No,* she told herself as she touched its grip. *It's too loud.* She took the switchblade out of her pants pocket. With the press of a button, the blade shot out with a *click*. Ricardo didn't hear it over his moans of satisfaction and the splashing of his urine. She marched past the stalls to her left and sinks to her right, boots thudding on the grungy tile flooring.

As his urine slowed to a trickle, Ricardo said, "*Oye, tienes un poco–*"

In the middle of him asking for some cocaine,

Vanessa thrust the knife into his neck. It missed his
jugular and pierced his larynx. He felt like he was
punched and pinched on the neck at the same time.
He staggered away from the urinal, drops of piss
landing on his fingers and plummeting to the floor. He
took a short inhale, then, unable to scream, a gurgling
noise came out of his mouth. He crashed into the wall
next to him, shoulder first, and reached for his neck.
He only realized he had been stabbed after he touched
the switchblade's cold handle and felt his warm blood.

"*Eso es para mis hijos, cabrón,*" Vanessa snarled.

'That's for my kids, bastard.'

Ricardo turned to look at his attacker, eyes bulging
from his hot face. He didn't recognize her, though. He
was still in shock from the stabbing and oxygen depri-
vation. Keeping his left hand over his neck, middle and
ring fingers around the blade, he put his hand on his
holster and wrestled with its safety strap.

An expression of awe dawned on Vanessa's face. It
said something along the lines of: 'No fucking way.'
She jumped forward and grabbed his forearm. She
slammed it against the wall, then pressed her hip up
against his holster to block it. She bent over and pulled
the utility knife out of her boot. She drew the blade
and swung it at his flaccid penis without a second
thought. She sliced the shaft at the base, cutting
through half of it. A jet of blood jumped out of his
cock.

Ricardo produced a harsher, louder gurgling noise.

It reached the dining area, but it was drowned out by the music and laughter. As she swung the blade at his dick again, he pushed her back against a stall wall. The customers heard the *bang* from the hard collision, but they mistook it for outdoor noise. The utility knife slipped out of Vanessa's hand.

The thug grabbed a fistful of her hair and pulled her away from the stall. The powerful yank made her whole scalp sting. He stepped aside and swung her at the urinals. The pistol fell out of her hoodie pocket, clacking on the floor in the corner of the room. She slapped the wall to stop herself from face-planting on a urinal.

She turned around, then let herself fall to the floor, sloppily dodging an overhand punch. Ricardo's fist hit the tile wall instead, breaking his hand upon impact. He unleashed a ghastly gurgling scream, then started coughing. He tottered around, stepping every which way but barely moving in any direction, as if he were playing a game of *Dance Dance Revolution*.

Ruben heard the ruckus. He glanced at the hallway, then at Vanessa's table. Brow furrowed, he crept over to the back of the restaurant. He couldn't tell what was going on.

Kneeling on the restroom floor, Vanessa dug into her hoodie pocket and patted her stomach. She didn't realize she dropped the gun until she spotted it in the corner next to the urinal. And Ricardo saw it, too. She scrambled towards the pistol, sliding on the blood and piss on the floor. Before she could grab it, Ricardo kicked the back of her head. He kept his boot planted on her scalp, using the last bit of his energy to push her face up against the filthy, moist tiles.

Ricardo unbuckled his holster. He was too weak to get a decent grasp on the pistol's grip, though. Vanessa exerted all of her energy and swept his other leg out from under him. As he landed on his side, the butt of the knife's handle also hit the floor, sending the blade deeper into his throat. Vanessa pounced on him. She grabbed the sides of his head, then screamed as she thrust his face at the bottom of a urinal.

His skull *clanged* on the porcelain with each hit. The upper half of his face tore open in a mess of deep gashes—across his cheekbones, on the bridge of his nose, over his eyebrows, under his hairline. His blood dyed the disintegrating, discolored disinfectant cake red. Then the urinal cake, which looked like it hadn't been changed in months, slipped into his mouth as his jaw broke.

Vanessa heard the bathroom door crack open. Without looking back, she dove off Ricardo and grabbed her pistol from the corner of the room, then she crawled to the stalls.

"*¡Oye!*" Ruben shouted as he rushed into the room and took a pistol out of his waistband.

'Hey!'

From under one of the stall doors, laying on her stomach with both hands on her gun, Vanessa shot up at him. She squeezed the trigger five times. Two bullets struck his abdomen—one at the center, the other under the right side of his rib cage. A third bullet hit his right bicep under the short sleeve of his white shirt. The firm muscle burst like a water balloon, a fountain of blood spewing out of the crater on his arm. His bicep was decimated.

Ruben dropped his pistol as he fell back and screamed. He landed with his upper back against the door, unintentionally blocking it. He crossed his good arm over his shot abdomen and grabbed his other arm at the crook of his elbow. Vanessa crawled out from under the stall. As she stood up, she pointed her pistol at Ricardo. He was unresponsive. She walked up to Ruben and aimed her pistol at him, finger on the trigger. Bloody tears coursed down her cheeks.

"*Po–Po–Por favor,*" Ruben stammered.

'Pl–Pl–Please.'

The other gangsters in the dining area heard the shooting. Some of the men shrugged it off, too drunk to care. Two guys ran to the back of the restaurant with their pistols drawn. One of the men in the dining area pointed a revolver at the couple and another guy pointed his pistol at the cooks. The cartel members started asking questions in Spanish: 'What's happening? Who else is back there? Do you have something to do with this?'

The restroom door rattled a little. The gangsters

couldn't get it open because of Ruben's body, and Ruben couldn't move because of his gunshot wounds.

Vanessa didn't recognize Ruben from the night of the massacre, so she didn't feel compelled to kill him. She saw the fear in his eyes, too—the fear of death, *the fear of her bloody tears*.

"*Háblales de mí*," she said, voice quivering with adrenaline. "*Háblales de la mujer con lágrimas de sangre.*"

'Tell them about me. Tell them about the woman with bloody tears.'

She put her pistol in her hoodie pocket and went back to the urinals. She took the gold-plated handgun out of Ricardo's holster. It was heavier than hers. She stepped back, raised the golden pistol, then shot him twice in the back of the head and twice in the upper back at point-blank range. Streaks of blood and bits of brain were splattered on the cracked porcelain. More blood rushed down the grooves between the tiles under his torso. The gunfire—louder than that from her own pistol—left her ears ringing.

As she stepped aside, the urinal flushed automatically. Water washed the blood and pushed the brain tissue down to Ricardo's pulpy face.

Vanessa stood on her tiptoes and pistol-whipped one of the hopper windows above the urinals, then tucked Ricardo's handgun in her waistband. She leaned her shoulder against the wall and pressed her foot on the side of a urinal. She then shimmied her way up until she could reach the windowsill. She pulled herself through the broken window, landing on her side on top of a dumpster behind the strip mall.

She jumped off the dumpster and landed in an unsteady crouch in the alley. The sound of the thugs hollering and the door rattling followed her through the broken window. She thought about running back to her car near the Burger King, but she was afraid the other cartel members were already outside, piling into the SUVs to start hunting her. She only had two options: Fight or run.

She pulled the hood over her head and sprinted down the alley.

18

LA LLORONA

Vanessa ran through a residential neighborhood, zigzagging between the sidewalk and the road to avoid the light from the lampposts. While sprinting, she tapped her cell phone's touch screen, hoping to open her map app to find her way home. But the device didn't register most of her tapping. It wasn't until she was close to another lamppost that she noticed the blood on her hands. She slowed to a jog while gazing at her bloody thumb.

She wasn't sure if the blood belonged to her, Ricardo, or Ruben. An image of herself standing in a restroom—walls, ceiling, and floor red with blood—surrounded by mutilated bodies flashed in her mind. Disoriented by the vision and sickened by the violence, her jog turned into a lurch as she nearly lost her balance. She ran on her hands and feet for a few seconds, then straightened up and kept sprinting.

She didn't recognize the area. She was surrounded by colorful homes—red, blue, yellow, pink, white. She ran into the middle of an intersection and glanced around. She saw more of the same—more reds, more blues, more yellows. She went down the street to her right. Gunfire popped off in the distance.

Vanessa gasped and crouched between a pickup truck and a sedan parked on the road. She put her hand in her hoodie pocket and gripped her pistol, ready to pull it out and start shooting. The street was calm and quiet, though. In a crouch she walked onto the sidewalk. She continued moving, staying low to hide behind the vehicles parked on the street. After passing three houses, another crackle of gunfire stopped her in her tracks.

She hit the ground, laying prone next to a sedan. She looked at the car next to her, expecting a hail of bullets to rain down on it. Again, only silence followed the burst of gunfire. She grabbed fistfuls of her hair and grunted in frustration. She couldn't tell if the gunfire was coming from Ricardo's crew or if it was just part of the everyday violence plaguing her country or if it was just some drunks shooting for fun.

Vanessa got up to her feet. She took a few unsteady steps forward, then she dropped to her knees with her hands over her face.

"*¿Qué estoy haciendo?*" she whimpered. "*¿Qué me está pasando?*"

'What am I doing? What's happening to me?'

The burden on her conscience grew heavier. She despised the men who killed her children, but she felt some pity for Ruben. She wondered if he had kids—young and innocent—waiting for him at home. She was worried about the couple and the employees in the restaurant, too. She feared she put them in harm's way for her own selfish reasons. She thought about their families as well.

She pressed her hand over her mouth, gritted her teeth, and snorted upon hearing a purring engine behind her. She crawled under the sedan next to her. The purring got louder. It was accompanied by some indistinct voices.

From under the sedan, she saw two cheap technicals—lacking the large-caliber machine guns found in Rafael's fleet—cruise down the street. She couldn't make out their words, but she sensed some exasperation in the men's voices. Some of them were wearing sombreros and ballistic vests. All of them were armed with rifles. She didn't recognize them from the restaurant.

Vanessa stayed still until she couldn't hear the technicals. She washed the blood off her hands in the puddle of filthy water next to the curb, then she dried them on her hoodie. She managed to unlock her cell phone and search for the nearest bus terminal. She crawled out from under the sedan and ran up the street, retracing her steps back to the intersection. She took a right.

Her skin crawled as she felt eyes on her—countless eyes watching her from every angle. She didn't see anyone on the street, though. Then she noticed the silhouettes standing at the windows in the homes to her left and right. She saw human-shaped shadows standing at *every single window*. Another vision of murder flashed in her mind. She saw herself standing in Ana's room in *La Cantina de Catalina*. Ignacio's mutilated body and Gabriel's burnt corpse were on the bed. Death haunted her.

"*Se lo merecían,*" she hissed.

'They deserved it.'

She ran up a steep street, then sprinted across a park to get away from the houses. She slid on the wet grass, so she slowed to a brisk walk. On her way through the park, two teenagers called out to her from a basketball court. They were playing a game of one-on-one while listening to Spanish rap music. As she got closer to the basketball court, she could make sense of their words. They were catcalling her. Head down and arms crossed, she marched forward.

"*Oye, ¿ no me oyes?*" one of the teenagers asked.

'Hey, can't you hear me?'

Vanessa ignored him. The other teenager kept shooting the ball at the basket while laughing. His friend—a tall, bald seventeen-year-old named Rodrigo—jogged over to her.

"*Para, chula, para,*" he said. It translated to: 'Stop, cutie, stop.' Vanessa walked faster as he got closer. He said, "*Cálmate. Pareces cansada, hermosa. Ven aquí. Puedes sentarte en mi cara si quieres.*"

'Chill. You look tired, beautiful. Come here. You can sit on my face if you want.'

Rodrigo laughed as he grabbed her arm. Vanessa jerked away from him and pulled the pistol out of her hoodie pocket. It came naturally to her, drawing her weapon speedily like a gunslinger in a western movie. She pointed it at his face, the muzzle just a few inches away from his forehead. Although she wasn't sure how many cartridges were left in the magazine, her finger was on the trigger.

In an instant the teenager turned pale. He shut his big mouth, raised his hands in surrender, and walked backwards. Noticing the gun, his friend dashed to a backpack on the sidelines, leaving the basketball bouncing behind him. He opened the bag and rifled through it. At the bottom, under a binder and heaps of crumpled paper, he found a small revolver. He hesitated. It didn't belong to him, and he had never shot a gun before.

As Rodrigo reached the sidelines, the other teenager froze up. He wasn't scared of Vanessa's gun, though. Like his friend he was terrified of her bloody tears.

He said, "*Quién... ¿Quién eres?*"

'Who... Who are you?'

"*La Llorona,*" Vanessa blurted out.

'The Weeping Woman.'

Everyone in Mexico knew the legend of The Weeping Woman—a vengeful ghost who roamed around bodies of water in search of her children whom she drowned.

Vanessa said, "*No me chingues. Te mato como maté a los otros narcos. Las perras de El Empalador lloraron por sus madres. Puedo hacerte llorar a ti también.*"

'Don't fuck with me. I'll kill you like I killed the other cartel members. The Impaler's bitches cried for their mothers. I can make you cry, too.'

The two teenagers hadn't heard about Vanessa's recent assassinations, but they knew Gustavo's nickname. They were troublemakers, part of a local gang of small-time drug dealers and graffiti artists, but they knew better than to cross any of the cartels in Mexico. The music stopped playing from the speaker next to the backpack. The teenagers walked backwards across the basketball court.

Still pointing her pistol at them, Vanessa said, "*Vayan a sus casas y quédense allí. No salgan en la noche. Es muy peligroso. Esta es tu única advertencia. Vayan.*"

'Go home and stay there. Don't come out at night. It's very dangerous. This is your only warning. Go.'

She spoke to them as if she were their mother. They reminded her of her deceased son, Joaquín. They were what she feared Joaquín would become if he had lived and stayed in Mexico. The teenagers ran off. That night they told their families and friends about their encounter with The Weeping Woman at the park.

They mentioned her message about the cartel members she had killed. The story spread through social media like a viral challenge.

Vanessa proceeded to the bus terminal. She went into the women's restroom and locked herself in a stall. Sitting on the toilet, she sent a text message to the only number on her phone. The message read: *It's done. I'm going to America.* She waited ten minutes for a response, wiping her eyes and nose with toilet paper while contemplating her actions. No one answered her. She sent another text message: *I left the stuff at the woman's home. I'm going to the border. I'll cross at Reynosa. It's closer.*

She exited the stall and washed herself at the sink. She dabbed the stains on her clothes with paper towels soaked in warm water, too. At the ticket booth she purchased a first-class ticket to Reynosa—the largest city in the state of Tamaulipas. It was also on the Mexico-United States border. The plan was for her to cross in Nuevo Progreso, but she felt like she was running out of energy. She wasn't a killing machine.

While sitting at a bench in the terminal's waiting area, Vanessa's phone buzzed. She didn't recognize the number, and only Rafael's cartel knew about her phone.

"¿*Sí?*" she answered.

'Yes?'

The caller said, "In English."

Vanessa immediately put a face to the voice
—*Yolanda*.

She asked, "Why are you calling me?"

"I heard you're leaving Mexico."

"I am. I need you to ask our 'friend' to pick me up on the other side of Reynosa. It's not far from the original plan."

"I can do that," Yolanda replied.

Vanessa said, "Thank you. I should be there by–"

"But if you leave now, you'll miss your chance to get *him*."

They didn't mention any names during their phone calls to avoid eavesdroppers. The government was always listening. Many cartels developed counterintelligence divisions of their own to monitor phone calls and analyze wiretaps as well. Despite the lack of names, Vanessa knew who Yolanda was referencing. *Gustavo Rivera*, she thought.

She asked, "You found him? Really?"

"Yeah."

"And he's alive?"

"Yeah."

Vanessa clenched her fist and inhaled deeply through her nose. Gustavo's mere existence made her blood boil. She glanced around. She wanted to punch something or someone—*anything* or *anyone*. Only an elderly woman sat at another bench in the waiting area.

Yolanda continued, "You can cross in Reynosa. I'll

get your message to our 'friend' on the other side. Or you can meet me in Nuevo Progreso like we planned... and you can finish this job before you cross and finish the other one. Either way, it doesn't matter to me. I would be *happy* to take care of this motherfucker for you. What do you want to do?"

Face red and angry, Vanessa said, "Wait for me. I'll get a taxi in Reynosa. Keep him alive and don't tell him I'm coming. *He's mine.*"

19

CAPTURED

Grainy black-and-white footage played on the flatscreen television on top of a dresser, the low-quality video stretched out to fit the high-definition display. The soundless footage showed Gustavo at a casino, gambling at a craps table. In his trucker cap and windbreaker, he blended with his environment. It cut to a video of Gustavo eating *cabrito*—young goat on a spit—with a group of men at an upscale restaurant.

With the next cut the footage showed Gustavo in the restaurant, taking cover behind the dining table, which was now flipped over. A man lay next to him, only his spasming legs visible in the frame. Blood stained the surrounding floor, appearing as black streaks and puddles in the video. From behind the table Gustavo and his remaining men shot at someone off camera. They had been ambushed by Rafael's hitmen, led by Yolanda.

The video cut again. The next scene showed men in ski masks and military uniforms handcuffing Gustavo and the other survivors after the shootout. Out of ammunition, Gustavo and his men could only run or surrender. Gustavo knew when to admit defeat and he refused to show fear in front of his enemies. The video stopped on a frame of him looking up at the surveillance camera, as if he knew someone was going to watch the footage. Although blurry, he appeared to be smirking.

Vanessa and Yolanda stood between the TV and the foot of a double bed. They were inside of a motel room.

Yolanda unplugged a flash drive from a USB port on the side of the TV. The screen faded to black, then a message popped up regarding the lack of signal.

She turned off the TV and said, "We found him a week ago. We already knew he was in that area, but then we heard about a poor, 'average' guy betting big at casinos. That's how we knew it was him. We caught him three days ago. Maybe four. But don't get it twisted, it wasn't as easy as it looked. The fucker stayed in there for almost thirty minutes. He called more of his *perras* for help, but we were ready for them outside. We lost two *soldados*, but he lost everyone."

'*Soldados*' translated to 'soldiers.'

The walls in the room were decorated with bloody handprints and large blotches of blood. The carpet was covered in dark stains as well. Some of the furniture was out of place, looking as if someone had bumped into it without moving it back. The curtains had been yanked off the rod, balled up on the floor under the window. The stench of blood permeated the air. So pungent and so familiar, it was impossible to breathe without tasting it. A chainsaw, blade covered in blood and threads of human flesh caught in its chain, lay on the bed.

Unemotional, Vanessa peered into the bathroom. More blood—*gallons* of it—turned it into a red room. It was all over the walls, the floor, and even the ceiling. It puddled in the bathtub, coated the toilet, and ran down the cracked mirror. The shower curtain was bundled up and tossed into the corner of the room. Four severed human arms hung from the shower rod, bound to it by chains at the wrists. Headless and limbless, two human torsos—one flabby, one muscular—and four severed legs were piled up in the bathtub.

The heads were already removed from the property. Along with the severed heads of three other victims, they were impaled on spikes and placed on the side of a road near a school on the outskirts of town. The public display was meant to send a message reaffirming Rafael's grip on the region. He didn't need to leave a written message. Even without bodies, the heads spoke for him. And everyone in the country knew his modus operandi.

Vanessa asked, "Is he in there? Gustavo?"

"I told you I'd save him for you, didn't I?" Yolanda replied. "I kept my word. I always do."

"Where is he?"

"We made him watch us kill his friends here. We cut them to pieces with a chainsaw. Like that scene in Scarface, remember? Since I promised to hold him for you, I thought I'd fuck with his head, y'know? But that motherfucker... He has *cojones*. He didn't give a mad fuck. Didn't blink, didn't sweat, didn't cry. So, I sent him to a garage. We closed it up for the weekend and I have guys watching him all day and all night. It has a lot of space to 'play,' too."

'*Cojones*' was a vulgar word used to refer to a man's testicles.

Vanessa said, "Take me to him."

"Are you ready?" Yolanda asked. "I mean, are you *really* ready?"

"I said take me to him."

Yolanda walked forward until she stood toe to toe with her and said, "You better be sure you're ready for this. You're not walking out of there without finishing the job. And if you don't finish it, you're not walking out of there at all. And you better have a plan. If you give him the easy way out—a bullet to the head or any of that pussy shit—we're going to give *you* the hard way, Vani. This motherfucker killed a lot of my brothers and sisters. He doesn't deserve a quick death."

"I know what he deserves... and I'm going to give it

to him," Vanessa said with unwavering determination. "I have a plan. I just need you to get something for me before we go."

"And what's that?"

"Fire."

20

VENGEANCE

"So, you... you're the reason they cleaned me up," Gustavo said, laughing inwardly. He was standing on his knees at the back of the small garage, nude with his hands cuffed in front of him. He stopped laughing and, with his lip curled, he said, "They sprayed me with a hose outside like an animal. Too scared to get close to me. *Pinches maricones*."

'*Pinches maricones*' translated to 'fucking pussies.' Aside from being used to denote a coward in Mexico, '*maricones*' was also a derogatory term used to refer to homosexual men.

"*Cállate, güey,*" a man with a deep voice said from behind him.

'Shut up, asshole.'

Two guards stood to his left and right, between him and a workbench at the back of the garage. They wore ski masks and military uniforms, armed with assault rifles and protected by bulletproof vests.

Vanessa and Yolanda approached him, walking around the old sedan hoisted on the auto lift in the middle of the room. Screeching and clattering the garage door descended behind them. The sunshine vanished, leaving only bright white light from the bulbs at the back of the garage.

Vanessa stopped in front of Gustavo and ran her eyes over his naked body. He wasn't as intimidating as she remembered. Although he didn't show any fear, he looked vulnerable—exposed, *powerless.*

She asked, "So you remember me?"

"I remember killing your little ones," Gustavo said matter-of-factly.

"Yeah? And do you know what I'm going to do to you for that?"

"I got my injection already. I feel the drugs in my body. I know you're going to torture me. How? I'm not sure yet. But I can't wait to see what you've learned from us."

"If you know who I am and what I'm going to do to you, then why are you so... so *fucking* calm?" Vanessa asked, voice tightening and bloody tears welling in her eyes. "*¿Qué te pasa, hijo de puta?*"

'What's wrong with you, son of a bitch?'

Gustavo said, "I always knew it was going to end like this, *mija.* Murder and torture... It's part of the job. Part of our lives. We do it for money and we do it for fun. You've heard the saying, no? 'Live by the sword, die by the sword.' We take lives until it's our turn to be taken. That's the way it works." He chuckled, then said, "In *México*, if you're not dying from a heart disease, you're dying from a bullet to the heart or a ripped-out heart or... or a broken heart. Isn't that right, *mija?*"

Vanessa squatted in front of him and held his gaze. With a blink, the bloody tears spilled from her eyes.

"You're right and you're wrong," she said. "I died from a broken heart when you killed my babies, but there are more ways to kill a man. There are other things I can rip out and break."

"Then show me what you've learned. Show me what I made you."

"I'll show you, but first... first I want to show you something else."

Yolanda dropped a duffel bag next to her. Vanessa took Ricardo's gold-plated pistol out of it. She held it out in front of Gustavo.

"A gift from your *primo,*" Vanessa said.

'*Primo*' translated to 'cousin.' To the untrained eye, Gustavo seemed unbothered. Vanessa was well acquainted with grief and depression, though. She noticed a slight change in his eyes. His upper eyelids drooped a little, his pupils dilated, and his gaze became unfocused. It was a thousand-yard stare. She smiled, relishing in his misery.

She said, "He's waiting for you in hell. Say hello to him for me when you get there." She put the pistol back in the bag, rummaged through her supplies, then pulled a pair of side cutting pliers out. She said, "*Empezamos con los dedos. Agárralo.*"

'We'll start with the fingers. Grab him.'

The masked guards grabbed the prisoner's arms and dragged him to the workbench. One of the guards stayed behind him. To hoist him up he wrapped one arm around Gustavo's neck and the other around his chest. With a firm grip on his forearms, the other guard held the prisoner's hands down against the tabletop.

Vanessa placed Gustavo's right pinky between the pliers' jaws. One of the blades nicked him along the crease at the base of his finger. She gave him a moment to react—to insult her, to threaten her, to cry and beg and *apologize*. He just stared at his steady, dry hands, breathing calmly with his jaw clenched.

Vanessa squeezed the handles. Gustavo's first knuckle—the metacarpophalangeal joint—*popped*. A thread of blood lashed out of the cut like a whip. His whole arm started to shudder. The guards reinforced their grips on him. With a moist crunch, his pinky was cut off. It landed on the workbench, rolling from side to side like a pencil. More blood spewed out.

"*¿No vas a gritar?*" Vanessa asked.

'You're not going to scream?'

A series of facial spasms broke Gustavo's emotionless expression. He was breathing fast, close to panting. He kept his mouth shut, though.

Vanessa closed the pliers over his ring finger, right

at the base of it. His arm jerked back as fresh jolts of pain surged through his hand. But, since the blades were already deep in his finger, his movements only worsened his suffering. He couldn't break free from the guards either. Vanessa opened the pliers a bit, then squeezed the handles again, severing his ring finger. It landed next to the pinky.

Gustavo let out a heavy sigh, sending goops of mucus into his mustache. Veins stuck out of his forehead and beads of sweat raced down his face. He didn't cry, though.

Vanessa repeated the process on his middle finger. As she snipped away at it, more cracking and popping noises came out of his hand. The blades got stuck in it, leaving the finger dangling from a tendon. She twisted the pliers while squeezing the handles with both hands. Gustavo gasped as the last piece of tissue tore. Blood dripped from his exposed knuckles, plopping in the puddle on the workbench.

"*Puta... madre,*" he wheezed.

'Mother... fucker.'

"Breathe," Vanessa said. "Your cheeks are turning blue. You have to breathe or you'll faint. You're not going to faint already, are you? I thought you were stronger than that."

Gustavo snarled at her, frothy saliva spuming out from between his teeth with each breath. He tried to hide his pain with a show of rage.

Vanessa cut off his index finger with three snips,

then moved on to his thumb. She cut through the web of his thumb first. She couldn't find the right angle to reach his knuckle, so she adjusted her aim. Snipping and sawing at the same time, she cut into the lower half of his thumb—the lower phalange. She jiggled the pliers around to break the bone. It took her longer to amputate his thumb than all of his other fingers combined. When she finally severed it, only a short stump stuck out from the side of his hand.

"*Y ahora los otros,*" Yolanda said, smirking while watching the torture from behind the guards.

'And now the other ones.'

Starting with his other thumb, Vanessa went to work on his left hand. Growing tired, she used both hands to squeeze the handles each time. His tendons and ligaments crinkled while his knuckles popped and crunched. One by one, his detached fingers fell from his hand and splashed in the puddle of blood on the workbench. There was so much blood now that it started to spill over the edge.

After cutting off his pinky—his last finger— Vanessa dropped the pliers and studied his face. She was both fascinated and frustrated by his resilience.

Light in the head, Gustavo's legs were now limp. His head was whirling wildly, as if his cervical spine had been jellified. The guard behind him had trouble holding him up, arms gliding across his sweaty skin.

Gustavo's eyesight was blurred and unsteady, as if his eyeballs were loose in their sockets, jiggling around with each sway of his head. He tried to look at his palms, but he could only recognize his forearms. The blood on his hands blended with the blood on the workbench, creating a big red blotch in his vision. A disconcerting warmth spread through his arms and heated up his torso. He felt his body getting hotter and hotter—*and hotter*.

"Are you going to cry for me?" Vanessa asked. "Or should I pull your eyes out next?"

Gustavo panted for a moment, making a 'ha' sound with every inhale. He glanced in her direction and sniggered, delirious and amused. He was seeing triple.

Between breaths, he said, "You should have... have cut my fingers... piece... by... piece. This is..."

His face crumpled in a grimace of agony. Waves of pins and needles blasted through his hands from his knuckles to his wrists. Out of habit he tried to clench his fists to scratch his aching palms. It was hard for his mind to accept the fact that his fingers had been amputated. He felt like they were still there, like he could still move them if he tried hard enough. Tears dripped from his eyes, fusing with the sweat on his cheeks. But it wasn't the type of crying Vanessa sought. She wanted to hear an emotional bellow.

"This is... nothing, *mija,*" Gustavo said.

Yolanda said, "Vani, I told you he has *cojones*. Don't let him fuck with your head. Keep going. You got this."

Vanessa gestured to one of the guards and said, "*Dame tu machete y ponlo boca abajo en el suelo.*"

'Give me your machete and put him facedown on the floor.'

One guard unsheathed a machete and handed it to Vanessa. The other one threw Gustavo at the floor. The prisoner landed face-first. His head bounced on the hard floor, the *thud* of the impact echoing through the garage. Blood trickled out of his broken nose and lined his upper teeth, which were now cracked and loose in his gums. His forehead was redder than the rest of his face. He uttered a long, low groan while squirming around.

A guard stepped on Gustavo's lower back. The other planted his boot on the back of his head. They could hear the busted cartilage of his nose crunching. A fresh stream of blood rushed out from under his face.

Vanessa raised the machete overhead, stalled for a few seconds, then swung it down at Gustavo's left ankle. The blade severed his Achilles tendon and came to a stop halfway through his ankle, stuck under his fibula bone. Gustavo felt his heel cord shoot up into his lower leg in a flash of electrifying pain, as if a downed power line were jumping around *in* his leg. His mouth flew open, but he could only produce a thick, agonized moan.

"*¡Grita!*" Vanessa yelled.

'Scream!'

She stepped on his calf muscle and pulled on the machete. Her hand slipped off it and she stumbled back. She hurried back to him and stomped on his lower leg, causing him to bounce as his knee and mutilated ankle played a game of Ping-Pong with a ball of pain. With a strong grip on it, she tugged on the machete's handle again. She staggered as the blade slid out. The slit on his ankle grew into a deep, wide trench of flesh and bone as his foot, which was barely attached to his leg, shook involuntarily.

Vanessa shouted, "*¡Llora!*"

'Cry!'

She swung the machete at his other ankle. Due to his flailing, she missed his Achilles tendon and chopped his calf muscle instead. With the second swing, she cut the outer side of his lower leg. The top of the blade hit the floor.

"*Concéntrate, Vani,*" Yolanda said.

'Concentrate, Vani.'

Vanessa roared as she swung the machete down at Gustavo's right leg for the third time. Although it didn't go as deep, the blade ripped through his Achilles tendon. He was immobilized and rendered defenseless. He continued groaning and whimpering, twisting and turning under the guards' boots.

Vanessa stepped on his mangled ankle. A crippling jolt of pain sent him into convulsions. A smile teased the corners of her mouth as he screamed. But before it could reach a crescendo, he suppressed his screaming by grinding his teeth. It quickly faded into another long groan. Crumbs of bloody enamel fell out of his mouth as his teeth shattered. The pool of blood under his face rippled with his laborious breathing. Despite all of the pain, he remained conscious.

"Fucker!" Vanessa screamed. She pushed the guards aside and rolled Gustavo over. She straddled his chest, grasped his neck with both hands, and shouted, "Cry, you motherfucker!"

"Don't choke him out, *pendeja,*" Yolanda said. "Remember what we talked about. He has to pay."

'*Pendeja*' was a term meaning 'idiot' or 'dumbass.'

Although she didn't acknowledge her, Vanessa's hold on his neck slackened. She gazed into his narrowed eyes, tempted to crush his throat until she saw his life fade away. But she agreed with Yolanda. She wanted him to pay for his crimes—*suffer* for his sins. Tears of blood trickled out of her eyes.

She said, "You killed my babies. You took everything from me. How many people have you killed, Gustavo? How many kids—*¡niños!*—have you murdered? You can't even remember, can you? You're going to burn in hell for everything you've done. You know it already, but you won't cry about it. I'm hurting you, but you won't scream. You won't even... apologize."

"Did he... tell you... about my sister?" Gustavo rasped. "Did Rafa tell you he... he cut her head off?"

"That has nothing to do with me, *cabrón*. I didn't touch your sister! My *kids* had nothing to do with your sister or you or any of this!"

Gustavo grinned and gave voice to a hoarse laugh. It only lasted a few seconds before he started coughing. And each cough sounded wet and gurgly and harsh. His throat was filled with bloody mucus.

He said, "*No eres inocente, mija.*" It translated to: 'You're not innocent, darling.' He coughed again, then frowned and said, "Business... It was only business. He took my sister... so I took his. That's the life and you... you're part of this life. How many kilos of *cocaína*... and *heroína*... and *metanfetamina* did you take with you to the States with your '*novio,*' El Ken?"

He had listed three narcotics in Spanish—cocaine, heroin, and methamphetamine in that order—while '*novio*' translated to 'boyfriend.' Vanessa could already see the point he was trying to make. She was poisoning communities and tearing families apart by contributing to the sale of dangerous drugs.

Gustavo continued, "Ha... Ha–How many people have you killed? You have blood... on your hands." He laughed and coughed again, then said, "It's on your hands right now. You think you'll meet your kids in heaven... after everything you did? A sin is a sin, *mija*. If I go to hell... you're coming with me."

The bloody teardrops fell from Vanessa's jaw and landed on Gustavo's cheeks. She was hurt by his words because she agreed with him. She continued to believe in God and an afterlife, but she was certain she was never going to see her kids again. She had strayed too far from the righteous path, losing sight of the way to redemption.

Yolanda said, "Vanessa, want me to finish him?"

"No. He took my kids, so I have to take his. That's the life."

"His kids? What are you talking about?"

Vanessa stood up and said, "*Tráelo aquí.*"

'Bring him over here.'

The guards grabbed the prisoner's arms and lifted him from the floor. Gustavo shut his eyes and whimpered as they dragged him back to the workbench. His feet, barely attached to his limp legs by some soft tissue, swayed behind him. He heard Vanessa's voice, but it sounded distorted over the thrumming in his ears. He could only think about his pain anyway.

His eyes cracked open as he heard a screeching sound. He couldn't make anything out, so he closed his eyes again. His head tilted back and swung from side to side. He felt himself drifting away, close to finally falling unconscious. Then another screeching sound brought him back to reality. He flung his head forward and looked down at himself.

His eyes flew wide open, although his vision stayed blurred. His penis and scrotum hung between the jaws of a vise attached to the end of the workbench. The vise screeched again as Vanessa turned its crank handle. The jaws closed in on his genitals. He felt their cold metal as he inadvertently slapped them with his scrotum while his hips shook with fear.

With another turn of the crank, the jaws hugged his genitals. He felt like his testicles were being pinched ceaselessly, stabbed with someone's sharp fingernails from every angle. The workbench vibrated as he thrashed about.

He yelled, "*Tus hijos–*"

Before he could finish insulting her children, Vanessa turned the crank again. The veins in his dick and scrotum burst under the pressure. Under his skin, smudges of blood spread across the shaft of his penis. Some blood escaped the damaged veins on his scrotal sac through tiny holes, like sweat from pores.

Gustavo's howl of pain brought a smile to Vanessa's face. He screamed until he was out of breath, then he started hyperventilating. The guards cringed, but their grip on the prisoner never wavered. Meanwhile, Yolanda looked like a proud mother, beaming from ear to ear as she watched the torture.

Vanessa kept turning the crank. The back of Gustavo's scrotum ripped open, revealing one of his pink testicles. The soft tissue in his penis crinkled as it was flattened. Blood seeped out of his urethra. Excruciating pain rose into his abdomen. Then one of his testicles *popped*. Its tubular innards hung out of the hole on his scrotum like strings of ground beef.

Projectile vomit shot out of Gustavo's mouth. The thick brown puke hit the wall in front of him. Like his eyes, his head rolled back. The vise screeched once more, then his other testicle burst with a crunchy *pop*.

His head fell forward as he lost consciousness. Bloody urine sprayed from his constricted urethra. It drizzled on the puddle of blood under the workbench.

Vanessa examined the cadaverous pallor of Gustavo's face. He continued to amaze and annoy her with his tenacity. She didn't want to give him too much credit, though. *The drugs,* she told herself. *He's still alive because of the drugs.*

"*Sácalo,*" she instructed, spinning the crank handle in the opposite direction.

'Get him out.'

Gustavo's eyes fluttered open. He saw the silhouettes of three people in front of him. He spotted the outline of the sedan on the auto lift, too. He squeezed his eyes shut and groaned. His face stung, hot and tingly. The powerful stench of rubbing alcohol irritated his nose and eyes. He gagged as he leaned forward. He tried to look down at his neck, but he couldn't see anything.

He peeked over his shoulder. A guard stood behind him, holding an animal control pole with both hands. Despite the pain coursing through every part of his body, he could put two and two together: The pole's noose was around his neck. He looked down at himself. He was sitting on the floor.

His damaged vision, along with his tears, protected him from the grotesque sight of his crushed genitals. It looked pixelated, but he could still see the different shades of pink and red from his mutilated genitalia and blood. Although his genitals had gone numb, the pain lingered in his abdomen. He felt an urge to vomit again.

"You're awake," Vanessa said.

Gustavo raised his head slowly. He couldn't see the faces of the people in front of him. The person in the middle was now crouching. He could tell it was Vanessa. The other two were Yolanda and the second guard.

Vanessa said, "I put a gel on your face. No, all over your head. Even in your mouth and ears. The gel is, um... *inflamable.*" The Spanish translated to: 'Flammable.' She said, "I'm going to light your head on fire. I'm getting you ready for your first day in hell. But before I do that, I want to ask you one last time... Do you have anything to say to me?"

Sniffling and moaning between each word, Gustavo stuttered, "*Te–Te... veré... en–en... el infierno.*"

'I–I'll... see you... in–in... hell.'

Vanessa drew a deep breath, then nodded and said, "*Sin duda.*"

'Undoubtedly.'

Yolanda lit a propane torch with a lighter. It hissed loudly as a blue flame shot out of its brass tip. She handed the torch to Vanessa.

"You took my kids with water," she said. "I'll take you with fire."

She held the flame up to the gel glistening on Gustavo's chin. A sheet of blue fire covered his face like a mask. The flames spread onto his ears and through his hair, covering his entire head in seconds. He let out a short groan at first, as if he didn't realize what was happening, then he started to scream and squirm.

The guard behind him had to wrestle with the animal pole to stop it from slipping out of his hands.

Gustavo's swollen face turned dark red, skin blistering and peeling, and his hair crinkled as it burned. He raised his fingerless hands to his face to try to pat the fire out, but to no avail. And whenever the fire weakened, Vanessa held the torch to his face and reignited it. The stench of burnt flesh and hair—a sulfurous odor mixed with the scent of overcooked beef—filled the garage.

Gustavo lost his vision. His eyelids were burned off and the vitreous fluid in his eyeballs was boiling. There was fire *in* his ear canals. Over the hissing and popping, his own screaming sounded muffled to him, as if it were coming from someone else. His eardrums burst from the immense heat. Overpowering the guard, he fell to his side and flopped on the floor.

Vanessa kept lighting the gel with the torch, ensuring the fire wouldn't die out on its own. His head began to blacken. After a few minutes his violent convulsions weakened to some twitching. He ended up on his back, fingerless hands resting on his neck. The guards threw buckets of water at his head. Vanessa turned the torch off and handed it back to Yolanda.

Although the fire was extinguished, some of the

remaining gel on Gustavo's head had a blue glow to it —still hot, still cooking. His charred, scaly face was unrecognizable. Small patches of hair stuck out of his fleshy, scorched scalp. Parts of his skull were visible, too. His right eyeball had liquefied while the other looked blood-red and rubbery. His lips were gone, leaving his broken teeth exposed. A squishy pink substance oozed out of his ear canals. Meanwhile, his outer ears had burnt to a crisp and crumbled off his head.

Yolanda said, "Finish it. Make sure he's dead."

Vanessa stood up and stared down at Gustavo's face. His left eye appeared to be moving, but it didn't look like he was breathing. Satisfaction and self-disgust fought for control of her face. She smiled, frowned, and smiled again, all with bloody tears building up in her eyes. A voice in her head told her to run to the closest church and confess. Another part of her—the stronger part, *the vengeful part*—told her to keep going.

She stomped on Gustavo's face. His upper jaw—the maxilla—shattered and sank into his mouth. With the second stomp, the center of his face was pushed into his skull. His left eye was no longer visible. Except for his yellowish lower teeth, his head was red and black without any distinguishable facial features. Vanessa wiped her boot on the floor, flakes of charred skin dropping from the grooves on the sole.

She said, "*Manda un mensaje: La Llorona está mirando.*"

'Send a message: The Weeping Woman is watching.'

She wiped her boot again, then marched away. The guards stood in silent astonishment. They looked at Yolanda for direction. The garage door started rolling up.

"*Ya la has oído,*" Yolanda said. "*Corta su cabeza y manda el mensaje.*"

'You heard her. Cut off his head and send the message.'

She walked away following Vanessa's lead out of the garage. The guards took out their machetes and began chopping away at Gustavo's neck.

21

ESCAPE FROM MEXICO

Vanessa sat on the edge of a doctor's examination table. Yolanda leaned back against the wall next to the door, arms and legs crossed. She wore a backpack slung over one shoulder.

Jaime Alvarez, the doctor at the small clinic, was hired by Rafael to take care of Vanessa before her trip to the United States. He had just finished checking on the injuries she had sustained during her trek through Mexico. He also examined her case of haemolacria. He flushed her eyes and gave her antibiotic eye drops to stave off any infections. After completing the examination, he excused himself from the room and gave them some privacy.

Vanessa's eyes were glued to the floor. She thought about the times she took her kids to the doctor's office for their checkups. Lucía never minded going to the doctor's office. She liked answering the doctor's questions and practicing English with her. Joaquín, on the other hand, was shy and anxious around strangers. There were times when Vanessa had to bribe him with cheap toys and visits to his favorite restaurant to get him to visit the doctor without fussing.

"You wanna know something?" Yolanda asked, breaking the silence in the room.

And just like that, Vanessa's memories went from crystal clear to fuzzy and dark. She was brought back to the real world. She rubbed her temple and looked at her fellow assassin.

Yolanda continued, "I didn't think you were going to show up. I heard about what you did to Ricardo and Ignacio, but... I don't know. I guess I didn't think you had the heart to face Gustavo. I didn't expect you to fuck him up like that either. Like... *damn*, girl, you even taught me a couple of things today. I'm proud of you, y'know?"

Vanessa wasn't sure if she was supposed to smile and thank her. It didn't feel appropriate considering she was being praised for her *torture* skills. It wasn't like a family member was congratulating her for being a good mother. She wasn't interested in camaraderie, so she stayed quiet.

"But don't think you're off the hook yet," Yolanda said. "A snitch is a snitch. That's going to stay with you forever. But I don't see anything wrong with a snitch killing *another* snitch. Do what you did to Gustavo to Caleb. Nah, fuck that. Do him worse, Vani. He's the reason you're here right now. He's the reason you lost everything. He *deserves* worse."

Vanessa said, "I know. I'll take care of him."

"I never liked him. I had a feeling something was up with him. Like, I *knew* he was no good. I thought he was DEA or ICE, but no. He was worse. He was a fucking snake. And now he thinks he's safe up in the States. He thinks he can make money off us and walk away. Fuck that. You're going to bring hell to his doorstep. Right?"

"I said I'll take care of him."

"That doesn't mean shit to me. Say you're going to send him to hell like Gustavo. Say it."

Vanessa sensed the pure hatred in Yolanda's voice. She finally found something they shared in common, aside from their expertise in torture.

"I'll send him to hell," she said. She got off the examination table and walked up to Yolanda. She said, "I know what he did, and I know what I have to do. I'll make him suffer. I promise."

"Good. I wish I could go with you, but it wouldn't look right. They'd ask too many questions at the border if we crossed together, and they'd get suspicious or whatever if we crossed separately. I don't know if I could control myself if I saw him anyway. I'd cause a scene for sure. Whatever. I've got enough shit to do over here. I'm not done hunting yet."

"¿*El marrano?*"

'The pig?'

Yolanda said, "Yeah, him. We'll find him soon. When we do, we'll keep our eyes on him until you get back. Then we can pick him up when you're ready."

They were talking about David Carrillo, Gustavo's paunchy soldier. During the night of the massacre, he had stomped on Vanessa and held her down while Gustavo drowned her children. He was the last surviving member of Gustavo's personal entourage.

"*Gracias,*" Vanessa said, thanking her in Spanish.

"Yeah, yeah. Listen, after you cross, Diego can't pick you up right away. It wouldn't look good. You're gonna walk to a hotel in Progreso. Room's already booked under your name. It's a long walk, but you can relax after you get there. We've got your papers, some clothes, money, and a cell phone in this bag. The directions to the hotel are in the phone. You know how to use it. If you need anything else on the other side, Diego will get it for you. Get changed, wash your face, and put some makeup on. C'mon, you don't have all day."

Yolanda handed her the backpack. Vanessa opened it up and took out a fresh set of clothes. She washed herself at a sink before changing. Yolanda noticed the purple and green bruises scattered across her body as well as the scar on her neck and lower back. She never expected a woman like Vanessa—once a caring mother with a gentle soul—to survive her journey through Mexico's underworld.

Once their preparations were finished, they said their goodbyes to the clinic's staff and stepped outside.

Yolanda patted Vanessa's shoulder and said, "*Buena suerte.*"

'Good luck.'

"*Y a ti también,*" Vanessa said.

'And to you, too.'

The women split ways.

Vanessa walked to the Progreso International Bridge. Foot traffic was light while the road was swamped with vehicles. At the border checkpoint she met a familiar face: Hector Ortiz. Along with Caleb she encountered him during her first smuggling job. She saw him during two other jobs as well. They recognized each other, but Hector stuck to the script.

"*¿Hablas inglés?*" the border patrol agent asked.

'Speak English?'

Vanessa said, "Yes, sir."

"Papers."

Vanessa handed him her passport and Border Crossing Card. Unlike her previous visits to the border, she didn't feel any pressure. She smiled, reinforcing her semblance of friendliness.

While checking her paperwork, Hector asked, "Anything to declare?"

"No, sir."

"And what's the purpose of your visit today?"

"Pleasure."

Hector looked up at her, curious. The answer

struck him as odd. Although he dealt with thousands of travelers, he knew there was something different about her. He could see the faint scar on her neck under a coat of concealer.

"Where's your fiancé?" he asked.

Vanessa almost huffed. *Great memory,* she thought. She recalled telling the border patrol agents she was engaged to Caleb every time they crossed together. The mere idea of touching a man like Caleb made her sick now.

She said, "He's waiting for me."

"Where?"

"Progreso, Texas. He's taking me to his hometown, then we're going to get married in Las Vegas."

"You've been engaged for months and you're going to get married in Vegas?"

"Yes, sir. Just like in the movies."

Hector wasn't buying her story, but her paperwork checked out. A female border patrol agent joined him at the checkpoint. Together, they frisked Vanessa and searched her backpack.

Hector returned her paperwork and said, "Do you need any assistance, ma'am?"

He seemed to believe she was a victim of human trafficking. Vanessa's smile broadened. It was the first time a border patrol agent showed more concern for her safety than her immigration status.

She said, "No, thank you. May I go now?"

"Yeah. You're free to go."

Vanessa continued walking over the bridge. She saw a sign that read: BOUNDARY OF THE UNITED STATES OF AMERICA. She looked out at the Rio Grande below her, then looked behind her. Pictures of her children flickered in her mind like images on a damaged film reel. She risked everything to try to get them out of Mexico only to get them killed in the end. She considered jumping into the river and drowning herself. It seemed like the appropriate place to end her life.

But she wasn't finished yet. Her desire for vengeance fueled her will to live. She had to finish the job. She had to kill Caleb. She advanced over the bridge.

PART III

22

HELL'S ARRIVAL

THE MOTEL ROOM WAS SMALL BUT COMFORTABLE. THERE was an orange accent wall behind the queen-sized bed. The rest of the walls were white. A small coffee table stood in front of a corner chair. Across from the bed, a flatscreen television was mounted on the wall. The room didn't have much in the way of amenities—no dresser, no hair dryer, no refrigerator, no safe—but it did have complimentary HBO. An episode of *Silicon Valley* played on the TV.

Vanessa had just finished bathing. She sat in bed in a bathrobe, her hair wrapped in a towel. The clock on her cell phone read: 11:06 PM. After crossing the border, the walk to the motel took her an hour and a half. After checking in she spent the evening in her room, waiting for Diego or one of Rafael's other confidants to show up. She enjoyed the peace and quiet, but she was eager to finish the job.

She snatched the remote off the nightstand and flipped through the channels. None of the programs could hold her attention. But then she stopped on a commercial. She went back two channels to Adult Swim. An episode of *Dragon Ball Super* was airing. She leaned forward, cocked her head to the side, and squinted at the TV. She recognized the art style. She felt like she had seen the show before, but she couldn't put a name to it.

Then it hit her.

She recognized Goku, one of the series' main characters. Unless it was in the laundry or he was too lazy to change, Joaquín wore a t-shirt with Goku on it nearly every night. He admired the character. He told his sister and his mother and anyone who would listen that he wanted to become as strong as him when he grew older. He was drowned while wearing his favorite shirt. Rafael had agreed to store the children's clothes for Vanessa until she was ready to pick them up.

Vanessa smiled and sobbed as she watched the show, as if she were watching the most tragic comedy. Positive memories of her children flooded her mind.

"*Los extraño,*" she murmured.

'I miss you both.'

She flinched as someone knocked on her door. Pessimism flipped her smile into a frown. She was afraid the police had found her. She imagined an army of FBI, CIA, ICE, and DEA agents lined up in the hallway outside. Then she thought about Caleb. She wondered if he already knew about her visit to the United States. She expected him to put up a fight. She didn't have any weapons on her, though.

The visitor knocked again.

Vanessa slunk over to the foyer of the room. She opened the closet slowly so as not to make any noise. She took the clothing iron out and raised it over her shoulder, ready to swing it. Sidestepping, she approached the door. On her tiptoes, she peeked through the peephole. Diego stood in the hallway by himself. He knocked again. He said something, but it wasn't loud enough to enter the room.

"*Gracias a Dios,*" she whispered.

'Thank God.'

She turned the deadbolt and unhooked the door chain. Then she sighed, lowered the clothing iron, and opened the door.

"Vani," Diego said. He was going to say more, but his voice trailed off as he spotted the clothing iron in her hand. Over her head, he peered into the room and asked, "You good?"

"I'm fine."

"You look pale. What–"

"I'm fine," Vanessa interrupted, raising her voice. She stepped aside and asked, "Are you coming in or not?"

"You alone?"

"Who else would I be with?"

Diego strolled into the room. While Vanessa

secured all of the locks, he checked the closet and bathroom for any unexpected guests. He walked to the window and made sure it was closed, then he glanced at the bed.

"There's no one under there, but you can check if you want," Vanessa said.

Diego said, "No, I'm good. Just being cautious." He smiled at the TV as the commercial break ended. He asked, "You like this? I used to watch it when I was a kid."

Vanessa quickly changed the channel and lowered the volume. She didn't want Diego to taint her memories of Joaquín's favorite show with his own nostalgia. Diego was prone to violence like every other cartel member, but he wasn't heartless. He could read emotions, so he could see she was still grieving.

"Straight to business then," he said.

He walked over to the corner chair and took a seat. Vanessa tightened the knot on her bathrobe, made sure she wasn't exposing herself, then sat on the bed.

Diego asked, "How was the trip?"

"They asked more questions than usual, but it felt easier than before."

"Yeah? That's good. Sorry I couldn't pick you up. I had a meeting. Y'know, business doesn't stop just 'cause you're wiping out the competition. It just gets busier."

"I'm not interested in that part of the business anymore. I'm only here for Caleb. Is he ready for me?"

Diego puckered his lips and stroked his chin. He looked at the TV as if he were interested in the infomercial. It was advertising a pressure cooker and air fryer combo.

"I think that's the wrong question, Vani," he said. "We should be asking something like... Oh, I don't know, maybe: Are *you* ready for *him?*"

Eyes sharpening, Vanessa said, "What's that supposed to mean? You haven't heard about what I've done? Hmm? You didn't hear what happened to Gustavo?"

"I heard some–"

"I crushed his little *pelotas*. I burned his face. His head! His whole *fuckin'* head! I melted it! Then I broke his face. And I caught his 'friends,' too. I know there's one more out there, but I've done enough. I–I've... I've already shown what I can do. Don't tell me I'm not ready for Caleb. I wouldn't be here right now if I wasn't."

'*Pelotas*' literally translated to 'balls,' but it was also used as vulgar slang to refer to a man's testicles. Although he had heard rumblings about Vanessa's actions in Mexico, Diego was still surprised by her speech. He saw the murder in her eyes. He raised his hands to show her his palms, as if to say: 'Look, I come in peace.'

He gave her a moment to breathe, then said, "Listen, I've heard the stories, but I don't think you've seen the whole picture. What do you know about Caleb?"

Vanessa said, "He's a smuggler and a snake. He only cares about money. He told me something about... about his nephews and nieces. He said his money was theirs, but I know it was all bullshit now. He only cares about himself. He used me to get what he wanted, then he threw me and my family at those... those animals."

"It's a little more complicated than that."

"How?"

"I think you should see it for yourself. I mean, see *him*. But you can't touch him yet. No matter what, don't care how angry you get, you can *not* let him see us. He lives in a gated neighborhood. If we make any noise, his neighbors will call the police for sure. And if he sees us... we're probably not going to see him again for a very long time. Got it?"

Without any hesitation, Vanessa said, "I won't let him get away from me."

"All right. Get dressed and pack up," Diego replied as he stood from his seat. On his way to the foyer, he said, "We're going to California."

Vanessa leaned forward and repeated, "California?"

"Yeah. Wear something comfortable. It's gonna be a long drive."

23

THE TRUTH

THE DRIVE FROM PROGRESO, TEXAS, TO LOS ANGELES, California, took Diego and Vanessa two days. They spent a night at a hotel in El Paso, Texas, then took another twelve-hour drive to Los Angeles. They didn't act like a couple during any of their stops or say much during the entire trip. They were both focused on finishing the job for different reasons.

Diego was only doing what he was assigned to do. It was strictly business for him. Meanwhile, Vanessa's bloodlust came from an emotional place. Revenge was the only thing on her mind.

When they arrived in Los Angeles, they checked in to a hotel in the neighborhood of Los Feliz—which was located in the greater Hollywood area. They took a few hours to shower, rest, and eat in their room. After they finished their meals, they went on another hour-

and-a-half drive to their final destination in the neighboring San Bernadino County.

They stayed in Los Angeles to put some distance
between themselves and their target. They were
hoping to blend in with the tourists as well.

They ended up at a gated community in Rancho
Cucamonga. Diego stopped the unassuming silver
sedan at the front gate and punched a code into a
keypad. The code was given to his cartel by an
associate who worked at the company responsible for
the community's security. The gate rolled open and
they drove in.

Vanessa was impressed by the sheer affluence of
the community. The houses were large with well-kept
front lawns and spacious backyards. From the street,
pools and hot tubs were visible behind some of the
homes. The vehicles parked in the driveways and
streets looked like they were just driven off the lot, new
and clean. The neighborhood also offered gated access
to the walking trails surrounding the community's
brick partition.

Yet, after cruising down a few streets, it all started
to look the same to Vanessa. The houses were nothing
like the colorful homes in her hometown. Culture
shock hit her harder in California than it did in Texas.

They pulled over to the side of the road. The shade
from a tree shielded them from the sun. To their right
there was a large park with more recreational activities.

There was a tot lot, a barbecue area, a swimming pool, basketball and tennis courts, and a gym. Kids ran across a field playing with a Golden Retriever. A couple of families had a picnic near the barbecue area. No one noticed the silver sedan.

Fiddling with his cell phone in an attempt to act natural, Diego said, "Look at the house across the street. The big beige one."

Vanessa leaned forward and said, "They're all beige and big. Which one are you–"

"Don't move around so much," Diego interrupted. He sounded irritated, but he didn't take his eyes off his phone. He said, "It's the only one with a dark green roof. Just two houses in front of us."

Vanessa craned her neck to look. She saw the two-story house, but it didn't look like anything special. She looked out the window to her right as a pair of teenage girls walked past them on the sidewalk. They were looking at their phones with Bluetooth earbuds plugged in their ears, completely unaware of each other and their surroundings. One of them could have been snatched off the street by a child predator and the other one wouldn't have noticed until she reached her destination.

"I see it," Vanessa said. "It's Caleb's house?"

"That's right."

"Do you... Do you think he's home now?"

Diego said, "No. His car's usually parked in the

driveway. And it doesn't matter anyway. We don't need him to be home because we're not touching him today, right?" When there was no response, he pried his gaze away from his phone and directed it towards his companion. He repeated, "Right?"

Although she was unarmed, Vanessa was prepared to confront Caleb. It had been the only thing on her mind since Gustavo's execution. But she understood the consequences of failure.

"Right," she said. "I was just wondering."

Diego looked back at his phone and said, "I brought you here to show you the real Caleb. He works in real estate. Investing. Managing. That sort of thing. He launders money, too. For Americans. Mexicans. Canadians. He'll work with anyone. We should have seen it coming. Should have never trusted him."

"Yolanda said the same thing."

"This is supposed to be a–a–a... a way of life or whatever. We're in this until we die. That's the deal. People like Caleb—*pinches panochas*—act like they're down until shit really goes down. They get scared and run or rich and snitch. I was expecting him to tell the police everything if he ever got caught at the border. Didn't think Gustavo would catch him first. He was smart, though."

'*Pinches panochas*' was another vulgar way of saying 'fucking pussies.'

Vanessa asked, "Who? Caleb?"

Diego said, "Nah. I mean he's smart, too, but I'm talking about Gustavo. He saw something we didn't. We thought Caleb was going to try to get out sooner or later, but we didn't know he was going to go out like that. Gustavo saw that he was weak. Instead of going straight to the top, he was starting at the bottom. He worked all the way up to Caleb, and Caleb gave him everything he wanted. He even started laundering money for them. Yolanda was next on Gustavo's list. You weren't even on his radar. Shit, if you didn't go with Yolanda that day, you would have never ended up out there with her. And if Gustavo got what he wanted from Yolanda, he would have gone after me next. And you know what? I wouldn't have told him shit."

Vanessa felt a pang of disappointment. A tumor of regrets swelled in her mind. *If I didn't go with Yolanda that day, my kids would still be alive,* she told herself. *If I didn't waste time saving Yolanda, I could have escaped from that bar. If I didn't tell Caleb about my life, Gustavo wouldn't have used my babies to hurt me*. Her thoughts started to overlap until all she heard was: 'If I didn't... If I didn't... If I didn't...' The burden on her shoulders got heavier. Her anger towards Caleb increased, too.

"Why?" she asked.

"Huh?"

"If you all thought he was going to betray you, why was he working for you in the first place? Why did you let *me* work with him?"

"Because he was valuable. Rafael was going to use him until he had nothing left. And if he proved us wrong—if he stayed in his place, *if* he stayed loyal—we planned on letting him stay. No point in killing a good mule. But if we were right... we planned on killing him at the first sign of trouble. It's just too bad that he ran back home right after he betrayed us. Bet he thought Gustavo was going to wipe us out."

Vanessa said, "So, he's just been living here for... for what? Two months now? He hasn't heard anything about what's going on in Mexico? He hasn't thought about moving? You know where he lives. He can't be stupid enough to just be sitting there waiting for us."

"He never told us about this home," Diego responded, staring out the windshield. "He told us he lived in Texas. We found him out here in California on our own. And it's not easy for a guy like him to just pack up and leave."

"What? Why?"

Diego nodded and said, "See for yourself."

Vanessa saw a white SUV crawling down the street in front of her, moving well below the speed limit and still slowing as it neared. The driver was cautious —*very cautious*—around the park due to the kids in the area. He seemed like an upstanding citizen from his driving alone. The SUV turned into the driveway of the house with the dark green roof.

"Caleb?" Vanessa whispered with a quizzical look.

The SUV's driver door opened. A man got out. His

hair was messy but stylish and his beard thick but groomed. He was wearing sunglasses, a white t-shirt, and jeans. Even from afar Vanessa recognized him immediately. Facial tremors broke her expression of confusion, twisting her face into a grimace. Bloody tears wet her eyelashes like red mascara.

"*Caleb,*" she repeated in a growl.

Without thinking, her hand went to the door handle. She was about to pull it when the SUV's rear driver's side door opened. Caleb helped a boy jump out of the car. The kid looked to be about ten years old. He had wavy brown hair—much like Caleb's. Then a blonde woman emerged from the other side of the SUV. She held the boy's hand as they walked to the front porch with Caleb trailing behind them. They were smiling and giggling.

Vanessa released the door handle and whispered, "No."

"That's his family," Diego said.

"No."

"His wife, Leah, and–"

"No, no, no."

"–his son, Nathan."

The revelation sent Vanessa's mind into a tailspin. Thinking about her slain children and Caleb's son, she found herself revisiting the first four stages of grief: Denial, anger, bargaining, depression. Instead of reaching the final stage—acceptance—she entered a state of fear as she looked at the house. She didn't see

Nathan with his parents on the porch. She saw Lucía and Joaquín standing with Caleb and Leah.

The bloody tears ran down her face in multiple streams. She began gasping for air while clawing at her aching chest.

"Calm down," Diego said. "It's over if he sees us. Breathe, girl. Relax."

"Go," Vanessa whined, eyes shut tight as she hung her head. "Drive or I'll... I'll kill him. I'll pull his eyes out. I'll cut his throat with my fingernails. I'll crush his balls with my hands. Go or I'll do it. I'll kill him right now, I swear."

"They're already in the house. Give them a second to settle in. If they see us leave all of a sudden, Caleb will get spooked. Remember, he's smart. He doesn't know that we know about this place, but that doesn't mean he doesn't look over his shoulder."

Vanessa ground her teeth and continued sniveling. She kept her eyes shut and listened to the muffled laughter in the park. It sparked an image of Nathan laughing with his parents at a picnic in her mind. By killing Caleb, she would be destroying the boy's life. It hurt her to think about the families of her victims— past and future.

Violence had a ripple effect. It touched the lives of everyone close to the epicenter. It could burden loved ones with grief and infect witnesses with survivor's guilt. As a victim Vanessa knew this terrible truth for most of her life. She tried to bury it at the back of her mind as she slaughtered her attackers, but guilt was difficult to kill.

She sighed as she felt the car move. Diego made a U-turn and drove slowly through the community, leaving Caleb and his family oblivious of the horrors lurking outside of their home.

24

ANGELS FOR ANGELS

AFTER THE VISIT TO CALEB'S NEIGHBORHOOD, VANESSA and Diego took a silent drive back to their hotel. In their room Vanessa sat on a sofa and stared vacantly at the bottle of water in her hand. With Caleb's family on her mind, she thought back to the night of the massacre. She saw flashbacks to the deaths of Arturo and his thirteen-year-old son Esteban. From her first-hand experience, she knew family wasn't off limits for the cartels. As a matter of fact, the murder of family members seemed to be encouraged in the competition to be the most feared. She was convinced Caleb's family was in danger.

Diego watched her from the bathroom doorway, leaning against the frame with his arms crossed. An atmosphere of unease hung over the quiet room.

"You wanna go back to Mexico?" Diego asked.

Complete silence followed. He said, "You can go back. I can take care of Caleb by myself. It's nothing."

More silence.

He walked over to the sofa and sat next to her. She didn't acknowledge him until he took the bottle out of her hand. She looked at him with a deer-in-the-head-lights expression, as if she had just run into a fugitive serial killer. Upon finding her bearings, she scooted away from him and leaned over the armrest with her fingertips against her forehead.

Diego asked, "What do you wanna do? You wanna go home or what?"

The silence continued.

He muttered indistinctly as he pulled his cell phone out of his pocket. He flicked and tapped his way to his contact list.

Vanessa said, "Without my babies, I don't have a home." Thumb hovering over a CALL prompt on his phone, Diego turned his head slowly and stared at her. Vanessa said, "I want to kill Caleb. I want him to pay just like Gustavo did. No, I want it to be worse. I want to... cut him into... Damn it, I don't know what I want to do yet, but I know I want him to feel pain."

"Good. That's why you're here. We'll take him and his family out soon. I've got a place–"

"No," Vanessa interrupted. "I told Rafael from the beginning that I wouldn't kill any kids. His family has nothing to do with this anyway. This is between me and Caleb."

"It's not all about you. He betrayed all of us, Vanessa. We have to send a message. To the police, to the news, to the other cartels, to the other rats. Everyone needs to know that they *can't* fuck with us."

"I can send that message without killing his family."

"You can't."

"I can."

Diego said, "Vanessa, *you can't*. Listen, most people in this business know they're either going to die young or end up in prison. Killing them, torturing them... you're just giving them what they always knew they'd get. The only way to really hurt these guys is by hurting the people they love. Look at what happened between the boss and Gustavo. They've been at war for *years* because of what they did to each other's families. That's why a lot of the guys don't even fuck around like that anymore. All that family shit... It wasn't meant for us. This is the way we do things. And this is what the boss wants."

"It doesn't have to be like this," Vanessa replied in a sad tone.

The disquieting silence returned. Although he didn't have a family of his own, Diego partially understood her reluctance. From his experience mothers were supposed to be nurturing, not torturing. At the same time, he saw something different in Vanessa. Her eyes told stories of unending grief, unadulterated rage, and extreme violence.

"An eye for an eye," he said. "You've heard it before, haven't you? This is like... like an angel for an angel. Don't forget about what Gustavo did to your family—*to your angels.*"

"I got Gustavo already."

"Gustavo was no angel. That wasn't a... a fair trade. Leah and Nathan, *they* are angels. Once they're out of the picture, you're free. You can rest."

I'll never be free, Vanessa thought. She took some tissue from the box on the neighboring nightstand and wiped her nose.

Diego continued, "Look, I'll give you a hand, all right? The boss wants you to take care of all of them, but... if you finish Caleb and Leah—and I mean you have to *really* finish 'em—I'll handle the boy for you. You don't even have to watch me do it. But if you can't do your part, I think you should just go back to Mexico. And you have to make a decision soon because we have to get to work. I don't want to argue about this again. I don't have time for that shit. So, tell me now: What do you want to do? You wanna finish what they started or do you wanna go back?"

Guilt and shame ignited a throbbing pain in Vanessa's chest, matching the rhythm of her heartbeat. She tried to assure herself that Caleb's family deserved to suffer like she did, but she couldn't think about Nathan without thinking about her children. She wondered if Lucía and Joaquín were watching her in disgust from heaven. She agreed with Diego, though. She couldn't even start to think about resting until she saw Caleb die with her own eyes.

She said, "I'll... I'll do it. I'll kill Caleb and... and his wife."

Diego pressed the POWER button on his phone. He walked over to the window to his left and looked out at the street below their second-floor room. There were more vehicles parked on the street than pedestrians on the sidewalk.

He said, "I've got a place in Koreatown. It used to be some sort of clinic, but it's abandoned now. My guys are going to kick out the homeless that stay there and make sure they stay out all night. That's where we're going to do it. When we're done with them, we're going to put their bodies in the car and drive up to Griffith Park. Shouldn't take longer than thirty minutes to get there. We'll dump them there so the hikers can find them. Griffith Park is, uh... iconic, y'know? Everyone knows it, so everyone will get the message."

Vanessa asked, "How are we going to get them? We can't just take them out of their house, right?"

Diego said, "We've been watching them for a while, so we know how they move. We're going to get them while they're separated. I'll take care of the woman. You... All you have to do is pick the boy up from school." Noticing the alarm in her growing eyes, Diego raised a hand at her and said, "I'm not saying you have to hurt him or anything. You don't even have to touch him. Just tell him that his mom sent you to grab him."

"He won't believe it."

"I'll take care of that part. When we have them, I'll call Caleb and tell him to meet us at the clinic."

"And what if he doesn't come? What if he brings the police? Or other people? People like you?"

"You mean people like us?"

The response silenced her. Despite formally joining Rafael's cartel and receiving aid from the gang, she continued to see herself as an outsider—*a lone wolf*. She felt like she was bringing shame to her children's names by working as a *sicario*.

Diego moved away from the window. He stood between the coffee table in front of the sofa and a desk hugging the wall next to the bathroom door.

He said, "If he does anything other than what I tell him to do, we'll kill his family. We have a couple of escape plans. You just follow my lead and I'll get us out of there. But Caleb's going to follow my instructions like the good bitch he is. I know that for a fact because... he's like you. I saw the same thing in his eyes that I see in yours: Love. That man loves his wife and boy. And you wanna know something else?" He walked around the coffee table and returned to his seat next to Vanessa. He said, "He told them about us—*about you*—because Gustavo was going to kill his family if he didn't give him something. I know you would have done the same thing if you were in his shoes. And if you *were* in his shoes today, if your kids were still here and I was holding 'em hostage, you would have followed my instructions, right?"

'*Yes.*' The answer was stuck in Vanessa's throat. Diego was correct in his assessment. She would have betrayed anyone to protect her family. She was starting to understand Caleb's decision.

"*Permítame,*" she croaked out.

'Excuse me.'

She hurried into the bathroom and slammed the door behind her. She went to the sink and turned on the faucet, then she staggered over to the bathtub and turned on the shower. Hands over her face, she dropped to her knees in front of the toilet and wept. Mixed emotions left her head spinning. She hated Caleb as much as she pitied him. She felt bad for Leah and Nathan. The ice around her heart was melting and the black cloud in her head was dissipating.

She had felt nothing but anger and sadness for so long that she forgot what it was like to feel other emotions. She was still capable of feeling sympathy and seeing the good in people.

"*N–No s–soy como ellos,*" she said, barely able to hear her voice over the running water.

'I–I'm n–not like them.'

Diego stood on the other side of the door listening to her sobbing. Her unstable emotions concerned him. He saw her empathy as a weakness. He took note of it and returned to the sofa, drawing up alternate plans in his head in case she decided to betray him again.

Vanessa grabbed the edge of the bathtub in one hand and the toilet seat with the other, then she pushed herself up. She frowned at her reflection in the mirror. Blood was smeared on her face and palms. She washed it off with the hot water, then she turned the faucet off. The shower kept running.

She planted her palms on the countertop and leaned over the sink. She gazed into her own eyes as if she were looking into a stranger's.

"*Se lo merece porque yo me lo merecía,*" she whispered. It translated to: 'He deserves it because I deserved it.' She licked the water off her lips, then, switching back to English, she said, "Not Leah. Not Nathan. Not... Not Lucía. Not Joaquín. They're innocent. Me and Caleb... we deserve this."

A half-hearted smile came to her tired face as she tamed her emotions. She had convinced herself that every cartel member, including herself, deserved to die. In fact, she believed they all died the moment they joined the criminal underworld. They sold their souls to the devil, and Mexico was their hell on earth.

She splashed more water on her face, then dried herself off with a towel. She turned off the shower, then opened the bathroom door. She found Diego sitting on the sofa, toying with his phone.

"You good?" he asked.

"Yes," Vanessa said.

"Any, um... problems?"

"No. I know what I have to do."

"Yeah, okay," Diego said, voice laced with doubt. "Then let's get to work. We've got some planning to do."

25

CATCHING BAIT

THE CARTERS' AVERAGE WEEKDAY BEGAN AT SIX O'CLOCK in the morning. Parked across the street a few houses down, Diego could see activity in the house through the windows. Leah made breakfast and helped Nathan get ready for his day at school. Meanwhile, Caleb prepared for work in his office upstairs, answering emails and making phone calls. Caleb was out of the house by seven. He left in a black luxury sedan. Leah and Nathan followed thirty minutes later in the white SUV.

Rafael's men had been surveilling the home for weeks, so Diego was confident in their intel. He waited in his car, sipping on his coffee and playing with his phone.

As expected, after dropping Nathan off at school, Leah returned home a quarter after eight and continued her morning routine. She cleaned up the first floor of the house, starting with the mess in the kitchen, then worked her way up to the bedrooms on the second floor. Then she read a book in the living room while waiting for the laundry. She finished the housework shortly before noon. Right on schedule, she left her home again to meet a friend for lunch as she normally did on Mondays.

Although he wasn't planning on abducting her from the home, Diego stayed in his car all morning and kept his eyes on the house. He ate potato chips and snack cakes and drank room-temperature water and Coke. And when he ran out of drinks, he refilled the bottles with his urine. Everything had gone as planned. He followed Leah out of the gated community. They ended up at a diner in a small, quiet neighborhood with no buildings over two stories tall in sight. The restaurant was located between a chiropractic clinic and a café.

Diego parked in the alley across the street next to a vacant building. The women spent an hour and a half at the diner. They were parked next to each other in front of the restaurant. After saying their goodbyes, Leah's friend departed first. Leah sat in her SUV and made a phone call. Diego saw an opportunity to confront her, but he refused to take the risk. If she was talking to Caleb, he couldn't interrupt the call without foiling their plot. He decided to let her slide and wait for a more appropriate opening.

After the phone call he trailed her to a supermarket. Instead of waiting in the parking lot, he followed her into the store. He observed her from afar while pretending to read the nutritional labels on any product within arm's reach. Leah filled her shopping cart with fish, chicken, and fresh vegetables and fruit—mostly organic. She had a tendency to pick a product up, study it, put it back, then return and pick it up again after browsing for a little while.

At the register, she donated money to feed the hungry and packed her groceries in three reusable shopping bags. While putting her bags in the back of the SUV, she saw an elderly woman across the aisle in the parking lot struggling to put her groceries away. She went over to help her. She spent a few minutes chatting with her, then she went back to her car and watched the little old lady drive off, ensuring she was safe.

Outgoing and caring, Leah didn't have a bad bone in her body. Diego approached the SUV as she put her last bag in the cargo space.

"Leah Carter?" he said with a smile.

"Yes?" she responded. She gave him a quick look-see, then stepped back and narrowed an eye. She closed the trunk and said, "I'm sorry, do I know you?"

"No, ma'am, you don't. All you have to know is: I know your husband, Caleb."

"Caleb? What is this a–"

"And I have a gun."

Leah was left with her mouth ajar. She shook her

head and blinked rapidly, then she smiled and laughed in disbelief. *It has to be a joke,* she told herself. But she saw the seriousness on Diego's steady face. She took another step back and peeked over his shoulder. She saw a couple of customers walking through the parking lot and a supermarket employee collecting shopping carts.

"Don't scream," Diego said. "I'm going to reach into my pocket, take my phone out, and show you something. You're going to stay quiet, right?"

Leah didn't say anything. She was too busy arguing with herself in her head. She told herself to run. Then she thought she would probably fare better if she threw her purse at him before running. Then she considered throwing her purse at him, pushing the cart his way, *then* running around him and screaming for help.

Before she could make a decision, Diego held his phone out in front of him and showed her the screen. She gasped and slapped her hands over her mouth. Tears stood out in her wide, bulging eyes. There was a picture on Diego's phone. Shot from across the street a week earlier, the image depicted Nathan standing by himself in front of his elementary school.

"Don't. Scream," Diego said sternly. "Take your hands off your mouth and smile. Act like we're friends and I'll be friendly. Treat me like a stranger with a gun... and I'll act like one."

The picture left Leah lightheaded. She leaned

against the SUV's trunk door to stop herself from collapsing.

Words shooting out of her mouth, she said, "I'll do whatever you say. I–I'll do anything you want. Wha–What is this about?"

"Start by lowering your voice."

"Please don't hurt my family. Oh God, *please*. I'll do–"

"Shut your fucking mouth," Diego said with a smile. "Nothing's going to happen to you or your son as long as you don't cause a scene. You have my word. But if you make any noise, if you do anything I don't want you to do, he'll die. Even if a cop arrested me right here, your boy would die. Don't make us hurt him."

Leah didn't trust him, but she certainly feared him. '*Us.*' That simple two-letter word made her shiver. *Who is 'us?'* she thought. *Do they have my little Natty? Did they take him after I dropped him off at school?* The sound of a shopping cart's rattling interrupted her thoughts. She leaned away from her SUV and forced a smile as a man pushed a cart towards them.

"Okay, okay," she said. "I hear you."

"Happy to hear that," Diego said, matching her friendly tone. "So, how's your husband's business going?"

"It's... fine. He's doing, um... It's going well. He doesn't tell me everything, but..."

She stopped speaking as the man pushed his shopping cart past them. Earbuds plugged deep in his ears, he paid them no mind.

She stuttered, "Wha–What is this? What do you want from me?"

"I only want to speak to your husband."

"My–My husband? Caleb? Okay, um… Okay, I–I can give you his phone number."

"No. We need to speak in person."

"Then go speak to *him* and leave *my* child alone. His office is–"

"I know where his office is," Diego interrupted. "I found you here in this random parking lot. Shit, lady, I have a picture of your kid at his school. Don't you think I know where your husband works? I need you to get his attention. That's all there is to it. I can think of other ways to do it if you want, though. I could cut your son's ear off and mail it to Caleb."

"Oh my God, no," Leah gasped.

"Or you can come with me and we can do this the easy way. What's it going to be?"

Leah only thought about her son. Diego didn't show her his gun, but she knew he wasn't bluffing.

She said, "I'll do whatever you say. Just don't hurt Nathan. *Please*."

"He'll be fine. C'mon, follow me to my car."

"What about mine?"

"Leave it. C'mon, let's go. Your boy's waiting for you."

Arms crossed and shoulders raised, she followed

him to a silver sedan parked at the other end of the parking lot. Diego opened the passenger door for her. Standing behind the car, she looked back at her SUV, then at the supermarket's entrance. Customers walked in and out of the store, blind to the kidnapping occurring next to them.

"I can send him the boy's heart if you want to try anything stupid," Diego said.

Leah whimpered and shambled towards him. She sat in the passenger's seat. The cartel member went to the other side of the sedan and sat in the driver's seat.

He said, "Put your seat belt on and hand me your cell phone." Head down, Leah followed his instructions. With her phone in hand, Diego asked, "What's the pin?"

"Zero, eight..."

Halfway through the pin, a lump crawled up Leah's throat and the tears finally descended from her eyes. Her pin was her son's birth month and day.

Diego said, "The rest of it. Spit it out."

"Zero, eight, two, three," Leah responded.

The phone unlocked. Diego went through her contact list. His thumb stopped over a name: *Natty*. He didn't find a Nathan in her contacts, so he assumed Natty was the boy's nickname. He started the car and reversed out of the parking space.

Facing a large tree, Nathan sat by himself on a blue metal bench in front of his school's cafeteria. He played Minecraft on his cell phone. More kids—as young as five and as old as eleven—sat on the other benches surrounding the tree. Some children played on the grass behind the seats as they waited for their guardians. A tall chain-link fence enclosed the property. The gates were open, allowing students and parents to waltz in and out of the campus.

The PE teacher, a man named Gary Feathers, stood in front of the school. He was supposed to be keeping guard, but he was a chatterbox. He enjoyed speaking to the kids' guardians—especially the young single mothers. A crossing guard, a young lady named Erica Pulido, stood at an uncontrolled crosswalk in front of the school, helping everyone cross the narrow street every few minutes. She was more vigilant than Gary, but she could barely see the waiting area around the tree through the chain-link fence.

Vanessa strolled onto the campus. She stopped behind the bench and stared at Nathan. She wasn't surprised to find him there. *He'll be next to the tree,* Diego had told her. *He's always there when his mom's late.* She was, however, surprised by her bad case of nerves. She didn't plan on hurting the kid, but she knew she was putting him in harm's way just by being there. Her doubts were aggravated by the fact that every child on the campus reminded her of Lucía and Joaquín.

She saw Gary chatting and laughing with a woman. Fearing she was sticking out like a child predator in a kindergarten classroom, she sat on the bench with Nathan. She kept her distance. He sat on one end of the bench, and she sat on the other. The tree shielded her from the faculty. Nathan didn't notice her. He continued playing his video game, building a castle on top of a mountain.

Vanessa smiled and said, "Hello."

Nathan's eyes darted to her, then back to his cell phone. He scooted closer to the edge of the bench, as if preparing to run.

"You're Nathan, right? Nathan Carter?" Vanessa asked.

The boy looked at her, puzzled. He had never seen her before in his life. His parents were proactive. They taught him to ignore *and* report strangers. But Vanessa knew his name. And she smiled a mother's smile at him. He glanced at the PE teacher, then down at his phone, trying to remember everything his parents told him. He exited the video game and went to his contact list.

As the child called his mother's number, Vanessa said, "My name is Vanessa. You can call me Vani if you want." She waited for him to introduce himself, but she only heard the ringing tone over the phone's speaker. Vanessa said, "I'm your mom's friend. I've known Leah for a very long time now. I knew... I *know* your dad, too. I know him very well, actually. I met Caleb in Mexico."

The call didn't connect. Nathan looked at her again with his head tilted to the side. He was starting to believe her. She knew too much to be a total stranger.

In a meek voice, he stuttered, "Ha–Hi…"

Vanessa couldn't help but grin upon hearing that one word. She felt like she was meeting her shy son, Joaquín, for the first time. A swarm of butterflies filled her stomach and a pleasant warmth spread across her chest. She looked away from the boy as tears came to her eyes. She wiped them off with the back of her hand. She was amazed to see the tears didn't leave any bloodstains.

Am I better now? she wondered.

"It's nice to meet you, Nathan," she said as she turned to face him.

"It's nice to meet you, too, Va… Vani?"

"Yes, Vani. You can call me Vani."

"Do you live close to us?"

"I don't live in your neighborhood, no. But I live here in, um… in Rancho Cucamonga."

"Oh," Nathan said.

He ran his eyes over his classmates. The crowd in front of the school was thinning as parents and guardians picked up their kids.

He asked, "Am I friends with your son?"

Vanessa's teeth went to her bottom lip. His question stung a little, but she knew it came from an innocent place. She believed Nathan would have been great friends with Lucía and Joaquín if they were still alive.

"I don't have children, Nathan," she said.

"Oh."

"Listen, your mom wanted me to come pick you up. She's stuck at home waiting for a repairman. Looks like your dirty socks broke the laundry machine. Too stinky, I think."

She giggled while waving her hand in front of her nose, as if to say: *P-U!* She was trying to lighten the mood, but Nathan didn't laugh. Instead, he looked at Gary. He was talking to a pair of kids now, asking them about their guardians. Instead of reaching out to the PE teacher for guidance, Nathan sent a text message to his mother since he didn't feel like he was in danger.

It read: *Do I go with Vany* (He misspelled her nickname and forgot to use a question mark.)

"Just let me know whenever you're ready to go," Vanessa said.

She could see he was anxious—foot tapping, lips twitching—so she didn't want to pressure him. Nathan's cell phone buzzed as he received a text message. It came from his mother's phone, but it was written by Diego.

It read: *Good, she's there already. Go with mommy's friend. I'll see you in a minute.* Seconds later, another message arrived: *Love you.* It was followed by a heart emoji.

Nathan replied: *Ok.*

"I can go," he said as he stood from the bench. He put his backpack on and asked, "Do you have money?"

"Money?" Vanessa repeated. "What do you need money for, sweetheart?"

"Ice cream. It's hot."

"Yeah, it is. We can stop at a convenience store on our way to your house, okay?"

"Cool, thanks."

Vanessa put her hand on his back and asked, "What's your favorite kind of ice cream?"

Nathan said, "Hmm... I like Strawberry Shortcake."

"Really? I like that one, too."

They chatted as she led him away from the school. As if she were a ghost, the PE teacher and the crossing guard never saw her. She escorted Nathan to a blue sedan parked at the end of the block.

26

AN INVITATION TO VENGEANCE

Stifled cries echoed through the abandoned clinic's dark corridors. The windows were weather-stripped and boarded up. The makeshift sound-proofing couldn't stop all of the noise from reaching the surrounding streets, but it was enough to weaken it. The weeping was lost in Los Angeles' natural night-time ruckus—roaring car engines, emergency sirens, screaming from the homeless, mewling from the stray animals.

The clinic's entrance—now blocked by planks of plywood and two metal trash cans overflowing with garbage—opened to a lobby with a check-in counter and a waiting area. The counter was still there but all of the furniture had been removed. To the right a door led to the clinic's exam rooms. The exam rooms were furnished with torn sleeping bags; dirty tarps; and homes made of soggy, flimsy cardboard boxes.

On the left side of the lobby there was a dispensary.
The pass-through window at the counter was replaced
by a thick sheet of wood. Like the other intact walls in
the clinic, it was decorated with graffiti and bodily
fluids. Bright shafts of white light escaped the dispensary and entered the lobby through fist-sized holes on
the wooden barrier. It was the only light in the abandoned building.

Diego and his men had converted the dispensary's
back room into a stage. Work lights stood in the
corners of the room, illuminating every inch of the
place. Duffel bags and suitcases were stacked up near
the walls. Cords snaked out of the room, leading to a
portable generator in an office down the hall. Hooked
up to a tripod an action camera was pointed at the
center of the back room where Leah and Nathan were
bound and gagged on the floor.

Earlier in the evening Diego had contacted Caleb
through three cell phones. With his burner phone, he
sent a text message that read: *Meet tonight. Let's talk
business. No police. No friends. Only family. From your old
business partners*. He followed it up with the address to
the clinic. With Leah's phone he sent Caleb a picture of
his captive wife. And with Nathan's phone he sent a
picture of the boy's screaming face.

Discomposed, Vanessa watched the captives in the
back room from the doorway. Although she couldn't
hold him in her arms with her hands zip-tied behind
her back, Leah stayed close to Nathan. The boy rocked

every which way, his pink face coated in sweat. The duct tape over their mouths smothered their cries.

Diego walked around the room and rummaged through the supplies in the duffel bags. The suitcases were empty. The plan was to use them to transport the human remains to Griffith Park. The thug was unfazed by the crying.

Vanessa scanned the rest of the room. Wires stuck out of holes on the dusty, grimy walls and ceiling in frizzled loops. At the back of the room, a dilapidated sheet of plywood covered a huge opening on the floor like a manhole cover. The room was cleaned prior to their arrival, but some trash lingered—torn plastic bags, food wrappers, threadbare clothing. A big dead rat lay on its back under one of the work lights.

Gustavo and his men were executed in a hotel room, a restaurant, and a garage without any of their loved ones around. Meanwhile, Caleb and his family were scheduled to be tortured in an abandoned building. It didn't seem fair to Vanessa. She sought vengeance against the people who wronged her, but she didn't want another senseless tragedy on her conscience.

She said, "Diego, can I talk to you?"

Diego was crouched in front of a duffel bag at the other side of the room, inspecting the chainsaw inside. He zipped up the bag, then walked over to the doorway.

On his way to Vanessa, he pointed at Leah and said,

"You try anything stupid and I'll take that little fucker's head."

Despite the tape over her mouth, Leah's horrified response was clear: "Oh my God!" Nathan didn't understand the threat, he didn't even hear most of Diego's words over his crying, but he was still terrified.

Diego joined Vanessa in the hallway. They left the old, decrepit door open to keep an eye on their hostages.

"What's up?" Diego asked.

Vanessa said, "They don't deserve this."

"They don't... *What?* Are you serious? We've been through this crap already. Angels for angels, remember?"

"*My* angels wouldn't want this. I can't trade one life for another. I know that now. No, I've always known that. Killing them changes nothing."

"But killing Gustavo did? Or Ricardo? Or any of those other motherfuckers?"

The past murders made Vanessa feel better, but she was too ashamed to admit it. She told herself she was doing the right thing by killing bad people. The killings were acts of vigilante justice after all. But by murdering innocent people, she felt like she would have been no better than a serial killer—no better than her fellow cartel members.

She pointed at the lobby door and said, "They deserved it. That's the difference, Diego. This... This isn't right. They shouldn't be here."

"Deserve, deserve, deserve. You keep saying that word. Let me teach you something, Vani. No one in this fucked-up life deserves anything. We *earn* it. Some people have it all given to them. Luck, y'know? And some people never get a thing from anyone. Born poor and alone. Unlucky, right? We get dealt good hands and bad hands in this game. But it's all about how you play your cards. Think about it. Did your kids 'deserve' to be drowned? You think that was their fate or some shit?"

Vanessa said, "You... You're saying they..." Her voice cracked as she choked up. She coughed, then said, "You're saying my *kids* 'earned' their... their deaths? They did something to–to get killed like *that?!*"

"No. *You did*. You played your cards and you put them in that position. They were unlucky. And just like you, Caleb earned his family's deaths and his own. And you wanna know something else? None of this even matters. Remember who's boss, girl. Rafael wants them dead, so that's all there is to it. Now, toughen up and get your head straight. He'll be here soon. Don't let that punk see your weakness. He played you before and he'll try to do it again. He might even try to sell out his own wife and kid."

Diego returned to the back room and continued checking the bags. His rant left Vanessa speechless and heartbroken. She agreed with him, though. From the beginning, she blamed herself for her children's deaths. *I earned it,* she thought. She returned to the

JON ATHAN

doorway and checked on the Carters. Nathan was now leaning against his mother, his face buried in her chest as he bellowed. Leah nuzzled the back of his head. Her tears soaked the duct tape over her mouth and his hair.

"*Lo siento,*" she whispered.

'I'm sorry.'

———

Caleb parked his sedan on the street in front of the clinic. In the two-story building across the street, there was a travel agency, a barbershop, a massage parlor, and a cell phone repair shop. All of the signs were in English and Korean. Even at the dead of night, there was still some light traffic in the area.

From the driver's seat the clinic looked dark and desolate—not a soul or light bulb in sight. It was quiet now, too.

Hands trembling, Caleb opened the backpack on the passenger seat. It was filled with bundles of cash amounting to a little over one hundred thousand dollars. It was money from the emergency stash he hid in his cellar. He laundered most of his illicit funds through discreet investments in real estate and cryptocurrency.

There were no demands for money, but he was hoping he could buy his way out of trouble. He was of the opinion that money could fix anything.

He zipped up the bag, then opened the glove

compartment and took a small black pistol out. His hand was shaking so badly that he couldn't flick the safety lever. He looked like he was having a thumb war with the gun. Once he turned the safety off, he racked the slide, sending a cartridge into the chamber.

He leaned forward and put the pistol in the back of his waistband while inspecting the surrounding buildings. He only saw two tall office buildings beyond the intersection down the street—one was about fifteen floors tall, the other over thirty. Chest against the steering wheel, he looked up at their roofs.

He wondered if someone was watching him through a sniper rifle's scope. He expected a gang of cartel members to riddle his car with bullets from every angle. The normality of the night unnerved him. *The calm before the storm,* he thought.

Caleb got out of the car with the backpack slung over his shoulder. As he walked over to the rusty gate leading to the clinic's parking lot, he checked the other vehicles parked on the street. They were all empty. He stopped next to a blue sedan and looked through its windshield. There were two strawberry shortcake ice cream bar wrappers crumpled up on the dashboard.

"Nathan?" he said, stunned.

It could have been a coincidence, but he was convinced his son had been in that car—and he was right. He peered into the back seat, then he placed his ear against the trunk. He didn't hear a peep in the car. He rushed to the gate. It made a screeching sound as he pushed it. He glanced around, fearing he was drawing too much attention to himself with the noise.

The gas station next door was also abandoned. Some light shone through the windows on the three-story apartment building behind the clinic. He crouched as a car cruised down the street. The driver didn't notice him.

Caleb rammed the gate with his shoulder until there was enough space for him to squeeze through. The screeching and clattering echoed through the streets. Treated like a local landfill, the parking lot was flooded with trash. He walked between mounds of garbage with shards of glass crackling, plastic crinkling, and liquids splashing under his dress shoes.

He saw weathered mattresses, broken-down tents, old sofas and chairs with missing legs, and even a broken toilet. A lot of the trash looked like it had been thrown over the fence by the neighbors.

At the clinic, Caleb tackled the plywood blocking the entrance. More screeching and banging noises came from the trash cans behind the barrier. He gazed into the lobby as the gap between the plywood and the doorframe widened. The moonlight could hardly pierce the darkness, though. He took off his backpack and sidestepped through the gap.

As he slung the backpack over his shoulder again, he shouted, "Rafael! I'm here!"

He dug his hand into his pocket to grab his cell phone. Before he could pull it out, he heard whimpering to his left. He pulled his hand out of his pocket and reached for the pistol in the back of his waistband. He saw the rays of light beaming out through the holes on the plywood at the dispensary.

"Rafael," he said, lowering his voice but not quite whispering.

He drew his pistol and crept over to the dispensary. He kept the handgun down to his side, pointed at the floor. Shooting was a last resort for him. He walked faster as the crying grew louder. He peeked through one of the holes on the plywood. He saw Leah and Nathan sitting on the floor in the middle of the room. They looked like they were roughed up, faces red and hair messy.

"No!" he yelled.

He tackled the barrier twice before noticing the neighboring door. He opened it and found himself in a hallway. He didn't think about why the door was unlocked or why his family was in the back room unsupervised. Hurtling into danger, he only thought about saving Leah and Nathan. The first door to his left, wide open as if in invitation, led to the back room.

"Leah, baby," he said.

He tucked the pistol in the back of his waistband, dropped the backpack, and ran into the room. He fell to his knees in front of them and hugged them. They kept sobbing, feeling no relief from his presence.

He leaned away from them, looked Leah in the eye, and said, "I'm going to get you out of here. Everything's going to be okay." He looked at Nathan and said, "You hear me, buddy? Everything's–"

"Put your hands up, Caleb. I have a gun pointed at your back. You move, I shoot."

The male voice came from the doorway. Caleb could tell the man wasn't lying by the fear in his wife's eyes. She was shaking her head frantically. Nathan shut his eyes and pressed his face against her chest again, trying to hide from the world.

Caleb said, "There's money in the–"

"Just do what I say," the man interrupted. "I can see the gun in your waistband. We're not talking until we take care of that."

Caleb knew how to handle a gun, but he was well aware of his limitations. He couldn't draw his pistol, spin around, and shoot his attacker in one move. On his knees with his back to the door, he was already at a massive disadvantage. Unwilling to take any risks, he raised his hands slowly. He heard footsteps behind him.

He said, "Don't worry, I'm going to get you out of this. I won't let them hurt you."

The pistol was taken out of his waistband. His arms were pulled behind his back and he was handcuffed. His ankles were bound with zip ties, too. Then he was spun around and pushed down between his wife and son. Leah yelped as Caleb's hard shoulder hit her chin. They all fell back. Caleb's stomach turned over as he looked up.

Diego stood over the Carters, pointing a handgun down at them. Caleb had been part of his cartel, so he knew the hierarchy. Diego wasn't an average hitman or smuggler. He was one of Rafael's lieutenants. Many in the organization—and within government agencies—saw him as the drug lord's right-hand man, helping design the cartel's international business strategy.

Diego's presence in the abandoned clinic told Caleb that they meant serious business—and serious business translated to serious trouble. He could manipulate a random *sicario* or pay off a local American gangbanger, but guys like Diego were a different story. Like a cult member, Diego was too loyal to his boss to be deprogrammed.

"There's money in the bag," Caleb said.

"Get in here!" Diego hollered, keeping his eyes and the gun on the hostages.

"A hundred grand in *cash*. A–And I can get you more. A *lot* more. I can get you... gold... diamonds... fucking Bitcoin, man. I–I can give you more than Rafael's ever given you."

Walking backwards, Diego looked at the door and murmured, "Where the hell is she?"

Caleb didn't catch his words over the sniveling from his family. He sat up and scooted forward a little.

"Watch yourself, *güey*," Diego said as he wagged the pistol at him.

"Are you listening to me? Fuck, man, think about it. Think for yourself for once, Diego. Rafael doesn't give a fuck about you. He paid me more to move his product than he ever paid you. And you... you worked for him longer than I did! And you're Mexican, man! I'm a–a... a '*pinche gringo*' but I got paid more than you. That sits right with you, brother? You're okay with that?"

Smiling smugly, Diego said, "We're not 'brothers.' A man like *me* can't be a brother to a rat like *you*." He crouched and poked Caleb's forehead with the muzzle of the pistol, causing him to draw back. He said, "And that's the problem with people like you. You think you know everything, but you don't know shit. You don't know how much I got paid. You think we'd tell you that? Rafael put some bullshit in your head, man. He wanted to... make you feel special. You get me? It's not like you were gonna go around Mexico asking other cartels to pay you more anyway."

Leah heard every word over Nathan's harsh cries. She could see her husband had gotten involved with some very bad people during his business trips south of the border. She learned all of her knowledge about cartels from television shows on Netflix and sensation-alized news. But reality was worse than anything on TV. She was certain of only one thing: They were going to die. She wasn't expecting any torture, though. She slithered her way to Nathan and leaned over him, hoping to shield him with her body.

Caleb said, "I fucked up. I know that. Take me to Mexico. Let me speak to Rafael. I can make this right.

I'm worth more to him alive than I am dead. And if he doesn't believe it... I'll take it like a man."

"Get in here or I start shooting!" Diego shouted.

Ignoring him, Caleb said, "But leave my family out of this. Take everything else from me. Take my life, man, but don't take them. Please, Diego. For old times' sake, let's just..."

He stopped mid-sentence as he spotted movement in the corner of his eye. He was about to continue his plea, but shock stole his voice as he looked over at the doorway. Tears fogged his vision. His blinking sped up to two times a second. Forgetting about his handcuffs, he tried to raise his hands to rub his eyes. He wanted to clear his vision to make sure he wasn't hallucinating. He was seeing a revenant.

He was seeing *Vanessa*.

Hanging her head she stepped into the back room and said, "I'm ready."

27

YOU WATCH MY BACK, I WATCH YOURS

SNIFFLING.

The sound of pain and sadness.

It was the only noise in the dispensary. Vanessa locked eyes with Caleb. Despite the thicker beard, he looked exactly how she remembered him—tall, fit, handsome. His confidence was gone, though. Caleb was still having a hard time believing his eyes. He felt like he was staring at an old lover and a menacing stranger at the same time.

"What took you so long?" Diego muttered. "Watch them. We don't have time to waste."

He tucked his pistol in his waistband and approached a duffel bag to his left. Leah and Nathan continued to snivel. Nathan quietened a little after seeing Vanessa. She deceived and betrayed him, but he felt safer with her around. He could tell she didn't want to harm him. There was a good person under her battle-hardened exterior.

"Vanessa," Caleb said, breaking the tense silence between them.

Rifling through the supplies in a bag, Diego said, "Ignore him."

"Vanessa," Caleb repeated, as if saying her name would remind her of her old self. "I... I know you don't want to do this. This isn't like you. This *isn't* you. I know I messed up, but they didn't give me a choice. They were going to... to hurt them. And you know what they're capable of. You've seen it with your own eyes."

"I have," Vanessa said. "And do you know what they did to me? What they *showed* me?"

"They said they were only going to ask you a couple of questions. I told them you didn't know much more than me."

Vanessa crouched in front of him and said, "They killed my kids. He drowned them and made me watch. *Mis lindos hijos, Caleb.*"

The Spanish translated to: 'My beautiful kids, Caleb.'

"N–No," he stuttered, face contorted in bewilderment. "No! I never told them about your kids, Vanessa! I–I barely even mentioned your name! I would never—*never*, Vani—do that to you or your kids. If I knew... Oh God, if I knew he was going to do that, I would have told him something else. I was just trying to protect my family. You have to believe me."

"You told me you didn't have a family."

"Because I didn't want them to know! I didn't want it to end like this!"

"You said you were going to protect me."

"I tried. I really did."

"Don't listen to this rat," Diego said as he returned to the hostages. "He'll tell you whatever you want to hear. Anything to stay alive, even if it means trading someone else's kids for his."

Caleb said, "I didn't know he was going to touch your kids. Vanessa, listen to me. I didn't…"

His eyes grew and bulged from his face as he spotted the syringe in Diego's hand. He knew the deal. Cartel hitmen often injected their victims with a mix of drugs to keep them conscious during acts of torture.

Caleb flopped back and shouted, "No! Vanessa, please! Don't let him do this! Don't do this!"

Diego dug his knee into Caleb's lower abdomen to stop him from wiggling away, then he stabbed the captive's outer thigh through his slacks with the syringe. Pushing down on the plunger, he injected the clear liquid into his limb. Fear was contagious. Caleb's panic spread into Leah and Nathan. They screamed together like a family on a roller coaster. Their muffled cries reached the street outside, but no one was around to hear them.

"No! Stop! Let us go! Stop!" Caleb bawled.

Diego threw the syringe aside, then beckoned to Vanessa and said, "Get the boy ready."

He mounted Leah's legs and took a metal case out of his pocket. He popped it open and retrieved another syringe. He injected her arm, right under the short sleeve of her shirt. She tried to slide out from under him, but he was too heavy for her. As he prepared the next syringe, she started to feel a hot tingly sensation in her injected arm. She felt like an army of fire ants was marching up to her shoulder and down to her elbow, stinging her with every step.

Diego glared at Vanessa and asked, "What the hell's wrong with you, girl? I told you to grab this little shit."

He took hold of Nathan's neck and forced the boy onto his side. The kid screamed and swung his legs wildly. Although the duct tape distorted his voice, his words were clear enough: "Mom! Dad!"

As he stabbed the boy's thigh through his jeans with the needle, Diego said, "Stop standing there like a stupid bitch, Vani. Give me a hand or start recording."

Vanessa dragged her feet to the action camera on the tripod. Just as Diego pushed on the syringe's plunger, shooting some of the liquid into Nathan's leg, Leah leapt towards him and headbutted his back. He elbowed her face to push her away, then injected the rest of the liquid into the boy. Leah headbutted him again. Meanwhile, with limited options, Caleb chomped at Diego's leg. His teeth sank into his boot, like a dog playing with his owner's shoes.

Diego shook him off, then stomped on his face. Stunned, Caleb rolled onto his back. Blood leaked out of his busted nose, streaming through his beard and into his mouth. Diego turned around and slapped Leah, stopping her mid-headbutt and sending her down to the floor. Fueled by her protective instincts and the adrenaline flowing through her, she sat up right away. Diego slapped her again. This time he kept his hand on her face and thrust her head down at the floor.

The *thud* of her head hitting the floor echoed through the clinic. She blacked out for three seconds, but it felt like three minutes. She awoke on her back, staring up at the dusty ceiling while rolling from side to side like an overturned turtle. She could hear her husband's groans to her right, but her son's whimpers were drowned out by the ceaseless, painful ringing in her left ear. Blood dribbled out of a small cut on her left temple, leaving a red streak in her blonde hair.

Diego was up on his feet already with a roll of duct tape in his hand. He ripped a strip off, then slapped it over Caleb's mouth.

"Enough talking," he said.

He sounded tired and annoyed from the wrestling. He took a machete out of a duffel bag, then he returned to the center of the room with the Carters behind him.

He asked, "Is it recording?"

Vanessa nodded. Diego adjusted his clothing, ran

his fingers through his slick hair, and cleared his throat. He looked back at the incapacitated family, then he took two steps to his right.

Eyes on the camera's lens, he pointed his machete at Caleb and said, "*Óyeme bien. Este mensaje va para todos los chismosos que van contra Rafael 'El Decapitador' Vàsquez. Por última vez, ratas, perras, federales—mexicanos o gringos—déjense de mamadas y no se metan en nuestros asuntos. Si nos jodes, van a ir terminando asi como esta bola de imbéciles.*"

'Listen carefully. This message goes out to all the snitches who go against Rafael 'El Decapitador' Vàsquez. For the last time, rats, bitches, feds—Mexicans or foreign—stop your bullshit and stay out of our business. If you fuck with us, you're going to end up just like this bunch of assholes.'

Vanessa stood in awe behind the camera, like a director watching a star in the making. Diego's speech, delivered calmly but firmly, disturbed her. She could tell it wasn't his first time in front of the camera. With his status as *El Decapitador*'s right-hand man and his reputation as a performer in many snuff films, some of his peers took to calling him 'Leonardo DiCAPITATOR.'

Diego gestured at her and said, "Get your knife. We start with him."

Laying on his back, Caleb screamed at the top of his lungs. Diego stood over him with his foot on his chest. Leah and Nathan were huddled together nearby. The ringing continued in Leah's ear. Dizzy and weak, she had trouble sitting up. Her son unwittingly kept her from falling, propping her up with his body. Vanessa was standing near Caleb's feet. She held a hunting knife with a five-inch surgical steel blade in her right hand. The blade had a serrated edge along its spine.

Diego said, "We have to get them outta here before sunrise. Get to work." Deep in thought, Vanessa didn't move. Diego asked, "What are you waiting for? This is what you've been fighting for, no? Just think about your kids, Vani. This guy right here, he got your little Lucía and Joaquín killed. It's like that saying, y'know? 'Throw someone under the bus.' He threw *them* in that *water*. He knew what he was doing when he said your name. You know it, too."

Vanessa saw eye to eye with Diego, but it wasn't the idea of hurting Caleb that bothered her. She was worried about Caleb's family. As soon as they were finished with the traitor, she knew Diego was going to move on to Leah and Nathan. She wasn't sure she could stop him from torturing them.

"*Muévete,*" Diego hissed.

'Move it.'

Vanessa straddled Caleb's thighs. With the knife she ripped his shirt open down the middle from the bottom hem to the collar. Diego lifted his foot an inch for a second so Vanessa could pull the shirt away, then he stomped on his chest again. The captive's torso was rugged with muscles. A vertical strip of hair ran from his belly button to his pubic region.

"You killed my babies," Vanessa said. "You're no good. You're like the rest of them. You're like... me."

Caleb raised his head from the floor and looked up at her, goggle-eyed. He screamed and screamed and screamed some more. In his mind he was making a valid case for mercy. Everyone else heard a garble of noise.

Vanessa stabbed him under the right side of his rib cage. She watched the tip of the blade sink into his external oblique—the outermost abdominal muscle—but she stopped before it could skewer it and enter his abdominal cavity. She dragged the blade down two inches, then took it out. She stabbed him near the initial incision, cut him horizontally to the right, dragged the blade down an inch, then brought it back and connected it to the original gash. It looked like a capital 'P.' With another quick diagonal slash, she turned it into a bloody capital 'R.'

Next to it, she carved a lowercase 'a.' Then she sliced a lowercase 't' followed by another lowercase 'a' into his upper abs.

'*Rata.*'

In English, it meant 'rat.'

"Why did you tell him *anything* about me?" Vanessa asked agitatedly. "You *knew* I didn't know anything. You *knew* I was only working for my babies. You *knew* I trusted you!"

As Caleb moaned Vanessa cut him again. She started at his upper abs on the other side of his torso and stopped at the external oblique. She slashed him ten times to write a six-letter word: '*Cabron.*' She was trying to write '*cabrón,*' which translated to 'bastard,' but she forgot the acute accent mark above the 'o.' It wasn't because she wanted to spare him of additional pain. She was just too furious to notice.

As soon as she finished the second word, she moved on to his lower abdomen. Over her noisy breathing and his groans, she could hear the skin and muscle fibers tearing with each slice. Across his lower abs, in all capital letters, she carved: '*NARCO.*' It was short for '*narcotraficante,*' which translated to 'drug traf-ficker.' Blood filled the ridges between his abdominal muscles. It made it look like his muscles were airbrushed.

"Move," Vanessa said as she slapped Diego's leg.

The hitman took his foot off him. Caleb had an opportunity to fight, but he didn't take it. He stopped floundering due to the hot, aching pain in his abdomen. Every movement—*every breath*—amplified it. Diego was happy to make things worse for him, though. He stepped on Caleb's abdomen. The gashes stretched and widened. Caleb lifted his head from the floor and gasped, snorting blood through his busted nose.

Vanessa sat on his face and said, "Remember when you paid me to do this for you? Remember when you went to Mexico to fuck hookers like me?!" She glared at Leah and shouted, "Did you know?! Did he tell you what he did?! Did you... Did..."

She stopped as she noticed Leah's inattentive condition. Leah was conscious but distant. She was scared but she didn't seem to know why. The blow to the head left her in a befuddled state. Nathan kept crying as he fought to support her.

Holding the knife in the icepick grip, Vanessa screamed as she thrust the blade at Caleb's chest. It cut through his firm pectoral muscle. With a little more force, she could have snapped his rib. She felt his head shaking under her ass as he struggled to breathe. One on top of the other, she cut two words onto the right side of his chest: '*Drug Dealer.*' On the other side, she carved: '*Child Killer.*' The blade scraped his ribs with each slice.

Although the messages were upside down, she wrote them in English because she wanted to expose his true identity to the world.

Vanessa dismounted his face. She stood next to him and examined the damage. Multiple streams of blood flowed across his torso in every direction. His eyes appeared to be swiveling under his sealed eyelids. His shoulders moved like a seesaw, taking turns rising and descending. He couldn't lay still due to the blistering pain, and he couldn't fall unconscious due to the drugs flowing through him.

"He can't breathe," she said.

Keeping his foot on his stomach, Diego bent over and pried Caleb's eye open with his fingers. His pupil was dilated and his eye was moving. He was awake and alert. He rolled Caleb onto his stomach. The captive screamed as his gashes touched the floor. Dirt, dust, and animal droppings entered the wounds. Diego cut into the back of his shirt with the machete. He even nicked his lower back while tearing his shirt off.

"He's good," Diego said as he tossed the torn garment aside. "Keep going. I'll deal with the little fucker's crying."

"Hey," Vanessa said. Diego ignored her and walked to a duffel bag behind the other hostages. Switching to Spanish and raising her voice, she said, "*¡Oye!*"

"What?"

"Don't hurt the kid. I'll take care of them when I'm done with him."

"I'm just going to stop him from crying. But if you don't want me to waste him, you better stop wasting my time. Keep going."

Vanessa took a knee on the small of Caleb's back, causing the cuts on his stomach to grind up against the floor. He shuddered and whined. She pressed the blade against his upper back horizontally, then she tilted the blade and started sawing into him. Shudders turned into convulsions as pain rocketed through his body. She clutched the back of his neck with her free hand to control him.

Breaking a sweat, she had trouble cutting through his thick back muscles. Every few seconds, the blade got stuck in his mutilated flesh. As she made her way down, she heard a loud *buzz* to her right. She glanced over at the other hostages. Diego had strapped a shock collar to Nathan's neck. The boy yelped again, but it came to a quick end as the collar electrified him. He toppled over and his dazed mother followed him to the floor.

He's going to kill him, Vanessa thought.

Realizing he had stopped fighting, she released Caleb's neck. She sawed faster while digging her free hand *into* the wound to help loosen the muscle. She heard the muscle crinkling as it rose from his body. At the center of his back, she turned the blade and started cutting towards his spine. The supraspinous ligament —which connected the trapezius muscle to the spine —was too durable for the blade's straight edge.

So, she spun the blade around and used the serrated edge to cut through the ligament, making her way back up to the original incision. She severed his trapezius muscle as well as chunks from others.

There was another buzz from the shock collar. Despite the pain the boy kept crying out to his parents. The electrocution jumbled his thoughts. He couldn't link the pain to the collar, so he started screaming as soon as he recovered from each shock.

Trying to ignore the boy's suffering, Vanessa leaned close to Caleb's ear and asked, "Do you remember what you said to me? 'I'll watch your back as long as you watch mine.' I trusted you. I thought you were going to protect us." She cringed as the collar buzzed again. Bloody tears warmed her eyes. She said, "But you only watched your own back. Now I'll help you see it without a mirror."

Eyes half-lidded, Caleb could only respond with a weak moan. Vanessa threw the severed flesh at the floor next to the captive's head. The muscles hit the floor with a *splat*. She grabbed a fistful of Caleb's hair and lifted his head so he could see his own back. He heard Vanessa's speech, but he couldn't comprehend the situation or recognize his skin. In the clinic he only understood—*only felt*—one thing: *Agony*. Again, all he could do was moan.

With traces of blood on her cheeks, she cut into the other side of his back. She sniffled and shuddered while listening to Caleb's muscles tear and Nathan's collar buzz. The man and his son got weaker and weaker with each slice and each shock. Laying on her side next to him, Leah sounded like she was trying to say something to her son to help him. Diego stomped on the side of her breast, crushing them both under his boot.

Leah's sudden shriek made her son scream. The collar shocked him again. Unable to tolerate it, he fell unconscious and pissed himself. His legs shook while the muscles on his neck spasmed. Leah couldn't slip out from under Diego's foot. He was stepping hard on her breasts. The hot pain was endless. She felt like magma was flowing through her chest, blood about to erupt from her nipples like lava.

Vanessa was physically and mentally exhausted. So, she stopped halfway through Caleb's other trapezius muscle. Once again, she sawed through the supraspinous ligament with the blade's serrated edge. After removing the chunk of muscle, she picked his head up, slid the piece of flesh under him, then pushed his face back down. He nuzzled his back skin, as if it were the softest pillow he had ever rested his head on.

"I watch your back... you watch your back," Vanessa said as she struggled to her feet.

She stumbled over to a bag to her left. She took a bottle of rubbing alcohol out, then returned to Caleb's side. She unscrewed the cap as she stared down at the bloody, pulpy, massive craters on his back.

Voice heavy with hesitance, she said, "Let me... clean that for you."

She poured the rubbing alcohol onto his back. Caleb bounced and threw his head up as soon as the first drop touched his mutilated muscle, screaming with thick veins jutting out from his face and neck. Vanessa wagged the bottle while moving it over Caleb's body, making sure she wet every inch of his open wounds. The burning pain was unbearable. The drugs couldn't keep Caleb awake. His head fell forward, face hitting his detached back.

Vanessa looked at Leah. She was the last conscious hostage. She understood Leah's pain. She had been in a similar position before. She saw herself back in the deserted airfield, pinned down under David's boot.

"Help me," Vanessa said as she threw the bottle of rubbing alcohol aside and beckoned to Diego.

"You finished already?"

"Not yet. One more thing. Flip him over and take the tape off his mouth."

"*Sí, seguro.*"

'Sure.'

Leah felt some relief as Diego took his boot off her crushed breasts. The hot, aching pain lingered, though. Crying, she inched closer to her unconscious son. Diego rolled Caleb onto his back and ripped the tape off his mouth. Caleb drew shallow, raspy breaths while his head moved in circles on the pillow of muscle.

Vanessa went to the corner of the room and picked up the dead rat from under the work light. She cut its body open down the middle with her knife, as if she were dissecting it for a biology class.

As she returned to the center of the room, Diego said, "What are you–"

Mid-sentence she shoved the rat into Caleb's mouth headfirst. Caleb gagged as the rat's nose hit his uvula. Vanessa slapped the rat's bottom, trying to mash its entire body into his mouth. Caleb kept hacking it out, though. The rat's hind legs stuck out of his mouth; its scaly, crusty tail dangling over his chin. Caleb's cheeks expanded as the rat's innards spilled out. He swallowed some of it.

Vanessa grabbed a roll of duct tape and ripped another strip off. She secured it over Caleb's mouth, stopping him from spitting the rat out. He swallowed another mouthful of guts while the rat's whiskers tickled the back of his throat. Floating between consciousness and unconsciousness, he had no idea there was a rat in his mouth.

"I'm finished," Vanessa said. "You can, um... You can cut his hands and feet off with the chainsaw. That's what he deserves. Then... Then leave him."

"Huh?" Diego responded.

"Leave him and his family. If he lives... he'll have to live with everyone knowing what he did. He'll live... *discapacitado y asustado*. It's enough. And if he dies... he dies."

The Spanish translated to: 'Disabled and afraid.'

"*¡Chale!*" Diego exclaimed. The term was used to express disagreement or disapproval. He said, "We're not here to fuckin' scare them, Vani. We're here to kill."

"I don't want them to die. If he dies now, he's not even going to feel it. Just look at him. I want them to feel my pain for the rest of their lives. I should have done the same to Gustavo and the rest of them. They knew they were going to die violently. All of you know you're going to die like that, no? The bosses—*los patrones*—they never tell you, but you know it. I hurt Gustavo and his people for a few minutes, then I gave them the easy way out. This... *This* is the way we should have been doing it. Mark their bodies so the world knows who they are, take their hands and feet so they never work again, and let them live with their sins for the rest of their pathetic lives."

"You know what? You're right. No, for real, I like the way you think. Pain for life? I can fuck with that, Vanessa. *But...* it doesn't matter. The boss wants them dead, remember? You didn't forget who's boss, did you?"

"Let me handle it," Vanessa said as Diego approached a duffel bag behind him. The hitman took the chainsaw out of it. The engine was already primed. Vanessa said, "I'll tell him that it was *my* decision and, if he doesn't like it, *I* will deal with the punishment. I am here because Rafael wanted me to get justice for my babies and his sister. I already took care of Gustavo for him just like he asked, and now I've got my revenge on Caleb. Cut off his feet and hands if you want, but that's it. We're not touching his family again. It's over."

"Goddammit," Diego muttered. "He's not going to like this."

"We'll see."

Diego shrugged, then he pulled on the starter cord. The chainsaw came to life, roaring and rattling. The racket reached the street. Some neighbors heard it from their homes. They just slammed their windows and ignored it. Tired of the violence, Vanessa turned to leave. But from the periphery of her vision, she saw Diego thrust the chainsaw at Caleb's neck.

"No!" she shouted.

The blade ate through Caleb's throat with the utmost ease. As soon as it entered his neck, he instinctively clenched his jaw, crushing the rat in his mouth. In the blink of an eye, a puddle of blood surrounded his head. The blood covered his face and chest in an instant, too. It blew out of his neck in a crimson haze, splattering on Diego's legs and raining down on the other hostages.

Leah cried hysterically. She crawled over Nathan's unconscious body to shield him from the bloodshed.

Twelve seconds.

It only took Diego *twelve measly seconds* to behead Caleb. During those twelve seconds, a terrible realization came to Vanessa: Diego was going to behead them all. Words couldn't stop violence just like laws couldn't stop criminals.

As the chainsaw cut into the floor and Caleb's severed head rolled away from his body, Vanessa ran forward with her arms outstretched in front of her—both hands on the handle of her hunting knife. She felt like she was moving in slow motion, floating through a quiet room. Diego didn't see her coming.

As the chainsaw came to a grinding stop, the five-inch blade entered the side of his neck horizontally. It cut through his jugulars, sliced his trachea open, and split his esophagus in two. The entire blade disappeared in his neck. The tip was close to his cervical vertebrae.

Vanessa released the knife and time resumed at its regular pace. She felt the floor under her feet and she could hear Leah's crying again. She watched as Diego staggered away. A look of shock and rage spread across his face. He slid on Caleb's blood, feet zigging and zagging, then he fell to the floor.

He squirmed back until his head rested on a backpack. He reached for the knife in his throat, hand shaking slightly. With the gentlest touch of the knife's handle, a blaze of pain exploded in his neck. He opened his mouth as if he were screaming, but he could only retch. A gooey thread of blood ran out from each corner of his mouth.

He looked up as Vanessa closed in on him. From below, in his fading vision, she looked like a tall, menacing silhouette—a ghostly figure.

Estás muerta, he mouthed.

'You're dead.'

Even as his other hand wandered towards the gun in his waistband, Vanessa wasn't concerned by the threat. She just stood there and observed his suffering for about thirty seconds. When his hand finally reached his waistband, she crouched and took his pistol before he could touch it. She stood and pointed the gun at him while making eye contact.

I was right, she thought, failing to find any fear in his eyes.

After another thirty seconds she squeezed the trigger four times, shooting him twice in the chest and twice in the head. One bullet entered his skull between his eyes and stopped in his brain. The other entered his forehead and exited through the back of his skull. Bits of brain leaked out of the exit wound, piling up on the bag under his head.

———

Vanessa put the pistol down slowly, then turned her attention to the hostages. She had mixed feelings about Caleb's death, simultaneously relieved and saddened. She had avenged her children while making a widow out of Leah and turning Nathan into a fatherless boy. She was reminded of the ripple effect of violence. She was right about that, too.

After hearing the gunfire, Leah's panic increased tenfold. She was now laying on top of her son, using herself as a human shield. Nathan was barely conscious but unaware of his surroundings. His father's severed head was close to his feet, but he was oblivious of his gruesome death. He couldn't even remember how he ended up unconscious in the first place.

Vanessa slunk to the center of the room. She gazed at Caleb's severed head and shed a tear for him.

To her surprise it wasn't a bloody one. She took his head to the other side of the room and set it down next to an extra-large suitcase. Then she hooked her arms under Caleb's armpits and heaved his body from the floor. She could smell the blood and rubbing alcohol.

She spent ten minutes trying to put his body in the suitcase. Only his torso and arms—still cuffed behind his back—fit inside. She tried to fold his legs, but they straightened out and fell out each time. She eyed the chainsaw and thought about cutting him into smaller pieces. She didn't want to traumatize Leah and Nathan further, though.

She pulled the backpack out from under Diego, put Caleb's head inside the bag, then threw the backpack on. With his legs hanging out, she put the suitcase's hard shell down to cover his body. Then she dragged the suitcase out of the room. She left it near the door leading to the lobby.

As she returned to the family, she said, "Don't fight me. I'm going to help you. Get off him." Leah screamed and swung her head madly. Speaking over her sobbing, Vanessa said, "It will shock him again if he starts screaming. It could kill him. Let me help him."

Despite witnessing Diego's murder, Leah didn't trust her. Caleb's blood was on Vanessa's hands—literally and figuratively. But she didn't have to trust her to share the same opinion as her. She was concerned Nathan would cry again as soon as he regained his strength. She wasn't sure his heart could handle another shock. She rolled off of him.

Vanessa unlatched the shock collar and threw it aside, then she took the tape off his mouth. She was relieved to hear his whiny breathing. She scrambled to a duffel bag nearby. After rifling through the supplies for a moment, she took a pocketknife out of one of the bag's side pockets.

"No," Leah cried through the crinkled tape over her mouth.

She lunged at Vanessa. Vanessa pushed her back, so Leah jumped at her again. She was begging her to spare Nathan.

Vanessa pushed her back once more and said, "Shh. It's okay. I'm not going to hurt him. Please calm down."

Leah sat next to her son, eyes fixed on the knife. Vanessa cut the zip ties around Nathan's ankles first, then she rolled him onto his side and cut the zip ties around his wrists. She laid him down on his back carefully and pulled his arms to his sides. He was going to survive.

Vanessa caressed his forehead and whispered, "*Perdóname, por favor.*" It translated to: 'Please forgive me.' She looked at Leah and said, "I'll take the tape off your mouth. Please don't scream. I don't want to hurt you. Okay?"

With puffy, protruding eyes, Leah nodded. Vanessa peeled the tape off her mouth.

"Na–Na–Nathan," Leah stammered in a weak, grating voice. "Hon–Honey, can you hear me?"

Vanessa said, "I'll call–"

"Please don't hurt him. He–He's just a boy. A–A good boy. I'll do anything you say, I swear. I'm not screaming, you s–s–see?"

Vanessa could see Leah was on the verge of a panic attack. She was overwhelmed by her emotions. Her heart wanted to grieve for Caleb while her motherly instincts told her to focus on protecting Nathan.

"I'll call an ambulance after I leave," Vanessa said. She put the knife down next to Nathan, then said, "If you can, you can cut yourself loose when I'm gone. If you can't, tell your son to do it for you. You'll both be fine. I'll move Caleb's body, so your son doesn't have to see him like that. Please don't try to follow me."

Leah had millions of questions—*Who are you? Why are you letting us live? What's going to happen to us?*—but she only had time for one.

She asked, "Did... Did he really do what you said he did?"

Vanessa looked at Nathan, then back at Leah. She gave a single nod. Leah's world came crashing down around her. There were times where she suspected Caleb of cheating during his lengthy business trips, but she never imagined he was down in Mexico mingling with cartel members. At a loss for words, she bent over and kissed her son's forehead.

Vanessa took the microSD card out of the action

camera. As she headed to the door, she saw Caleb's backpack next to the doorway. She opened it and found his cash inside. She strapped the backpack across her chest and walked out, leaving the survivors to wallow in their grief. In order to get her 'luggage' off the property, she had to clear the obstacles in every doorway.

She pushed the garbage, trash cans, abandoned furniture, and sheets of plywood out of the way. It was still dark outside, but she noticed more vehicles in the area. She even spotted a small group of pedestrians taking a stroll on the sidewalk across the street. She waited until the pedestrians were out of sight, then she dragged the suitcase to the blue sedan.

Behind the car she sat the suitcase up and squatted in front of it, using her body to stop it from flying open and revealing the corpse inside. She leaned forward, squeezing the suitcase between her body and the sedan's rear bumper. Then she slowly lifted it up, legs shaking uncontrollably. She had to lean back against the truck parked behind her to stop herself from collapsing.

She took a short break after a van cruised past her. Once she caught her breath, she continued lifting the luggage. It took her nearly five minutes to get it done. She felt like her legs were made of paper afterward, about to fold and crumple with the next step. She slammed the trunk shut, then hobbled over to the driver's side of the car.

She put the backpacks in the back seat before settling into the driver's seat. She froze with her hands on the steering wheel and the key in the ignition. The ice cream wrappers on the dashboard caught her eye. The trash sparked a sense of guilt within her. She tricked Nathan and murdered his father. She spared Leah and Nathan, but she didn't think it made her much better than Gustavo.

After all, Gustavo had spared the Carters as well.

She threw the trash out the window, then continued with Diego's plan. She followed his map to a designated area in Griffith Park. Thanks to the cartel's prior arrangements, the area was clear for her. She didn't see any park rangers or homeless campers. She drove up a dirt hiking trail for about two minutes. Then she dumped the suitcase and the backpack with Caleb's head on top of a set of bushes.

The morning hikers were in for a grotesque surprise.

Driving in reverse she made her way back to the road. Then she headed back to her hotel. The front desk clerk—a young, chubby guy covered in tattoos with gauged earlobes—welcomed her with a smile. He didn't seem concerned about Diego's absence. She went up to her room, secured every lock on the door, then called Yolanda with the emergency burner phone that Diego had stashed in one of the nightstands.

"Talk," Yolanda answered bluntly after two rings.

Vanessa hadn't thought about what she was going

to say. The truth was out of the question. She wasn't ready to die or live a life on the run. She had unfinished business in Mexico.

Yolanda said, "I'm hanging–"

"It's done," Vanessa interrupted.

"Then why are you calling me?"

"Diego... They got him."

The line fell silent. The silence went on for so long that Vanessa checked the phone to see if the call had ended. It was still going.

"How?" Yolanda asked, breaking the silence after thirty seconds.

"Someone followed us," Vanessa said with confidence. "It was one of Caleb's people. We were almost done with the job, but I didn't want to 'finish' him in front of his family. Diego said he would take care of it. So, I left the room for a little while, then I heard gunshots over the chainsaw. When I came back, Diego and Caleb were already dead."

"And what about the other one? The one who killed Diego?"

"I got him. Two in the head. Two in the chest."

The silence returned, but it was shorter this time.

Yolanda said, "Come back. Let's talk in person. We'll pick you up at the same place."

"When?"

"We'll be there whenever you get there."

Vanessa said, "I have Caleb's money. I can't bring it with me. What should I do?"

"Leave it. Only take your shit. Your clothes, your papers, whatever you need to get across. And don't worry about checking out of the hotel. We'll take care of everything."

"*Te oigo. Hasta luego.*"

'I hear you. See you later.'

The call ended.

Vanessa tossed the phone aside and sat in silence for a while, contemplating her next move. She took the microSD card out of her pocket. She used her knife to crack the plastic and scrape the chip, then she burned it with a lighter for a few minutes, and then she flushed it down the toilet. She gathered her belongings, then headed out.

In the car she set a route on her phone's map app to El Paso, Texas. After taking a break there, she planned on traveling to Progreso, Texas, then crossing into Mexico via the Progreso International Bridge. It was the same route she took with Diego. A cloud of uncertainty followed her during her trip. She wondered what was waiting for her on the other side of the border.

Friends or foes.

Applause or gunfire.

Life or death.

Either way, she was ready to face the consequences of her actions.

28

WHEN SHE WEEPS

La Bomba by Azul Azul played in the dingy bar. Patrons packed every table and sat shoulder to shoulder at the crowded counter. Some women—prostitutes trying to turn a trick—sat *on* the tables with groups of drunk, horny men. The chatter and laughter were almost as loud as the music. There were some arguments; alcohol tended to open the door to aggression, but the overall mood was cheerful.

"*Muévanse. muévanse,*" David Carrillo said as he elbowed his way to the counter.

'Move it, move it.'

He stood out in the room thanks to his red polo shirt and his wide roly-poly figure. He had a pleasant buzz going, all smiles and snickers. The other patrons made room for him. Despite laying low after the massacre at the airfield, he was well known in the area. He experienced a period of peace after Gustavo's death, so he assumed he wasn't being targeted like the rest of his associates. While waiting to be assigned to a new hit squad, he spent his nights frequenting bars, nightclubs, and brothels.

He complained to the bartender about the poor service at his table. His big grin made it look like he was joking. His eyes, on the other hand, appeared feral. He knocked on the table and ordered another round of drinks. As he turned to leave, the young woman next to him fondled his arm. She was wearing tight short shorts, a tighter crop top, and high heels. He was instantly attracted to her curvy figure. She was his type.

He leaned back against the counter and asked, "*¿Cómo vas?*"

'How are you?'

"*Bien,*" the woman responded. "*¿Y tú, guapo?*"

'Fine. And you, handsome?'

David said, "*Pues ahora mismo estoy muy bien contigo, linda. ¿Cómo te llamas?*"

'Well, right now I'm very fine with you, sweetie. What's your name?'

"*Me llamo Isabel,*" the woman said. It translated to: 'My name is Isabel.' She took a sip of her piña colada, then said, "*Oye. ¿Quieres conocer a mi amiga?*"

'Hey. Do you want to meet my friend?'

Isabel pointed at the other end of the bar. David leaned farther back over the counter to follow her finger, hitting a couple of glasses with his elbows.

Vanessa sat there, dressed in all black—a jacket, a tank top, a small skirt, and knee-high boots. There was a martini on the counter in front of her. She winked and waved at him.

"*Tenemos un cuarto arriba,*" Isabel said.

'We have a room upstairs.'

David kept staring at Vanessa. He couldn't put a name to her face, but he was sure he had seen her before.

"*¿Es una actriz del porno?*" he asked.

'Is she a pornstar?'

"*Claro que no,*" Isabel said, giggling. She stroked his arm again and said, "*Nosotros lo hacemos mejor.*"

'Of course not. We do it better.'

David rubbed the back of his neck. The offer was tempting, he was attracted to both women, but his gut told him something was off.

"*Déjame pensarlo,*" he said.

'Let me think about it.'

As he walked away, Isabel ran her hand across his crotch and said, "*No nos hagas esperar.*"

'Don't keep us waiting.'

David smiled nervously. He returned to his table in the middle of the bar. His friends—low-level cartel members—poked fun at him, believing he was rejected by the woman. He tried to explain to them that *he* rejected *her*, but they were too drunk to listen. A waitress brought them another round of beer. They finished it quickly, as if racing against each other, then ordered another round.

While drinking, David took occasional glances at Vanessa. The more he saw her, the more he wanted her. And the more he drank, the more he imagined himself ripping her clothes off.

Isabel approached the table with a blue margarita. She placed it in front of David and said, "*De mi amiga.*"

'From my friend.'

Some of the other men joked about the drink. They saw it as feminine. They also believed men were supposed to buy women drinks, not the other way around. David stopped paying attention to them, though. He took a swig of the margarita and waved at Vanessa. She waved back at him.

Isabel asked, "*¿Ya has terminado de pensar? Nos vamos a ir pronto si no quieres jugar.*"

'Are you finished thinking? We're leaving soon if you don't want to play.'

While his friends goaded him on, David glanced at Vanessa. She got up from her seat and spoke to a bartender. He realized he was running out of time.

"*A la chingada,*" he said before chugging the rest of the margarita. "*Hagámoslo.*"

'Fuck it. Let's do it.'

While the other men cheered for him, Isabel smiled and said, "*Dame un minuto.*"

'Give me a minute.'

Ignoring his friends David watched her strut back

to the bar. Her hips moved like a pendulum, hypnotizing him. She spoke to Vanessa and the bartender. David wasn't stupid. He knew Isabel was a prostitute. He wasn't expecting a woman like her to fall in love with him at first sight in a bar known for its prostitution. Their conversation went on for about ten minutes. He believed they were talking business.

Once they were finished, the women beckoned to him. He received another half-joking, half-serious round of applause from his friends as he departed from the table. He followed the prostitutes up a flight of stairs next to the bar. While heading up he leered at Isabel's ass and peeked up Vanessa's skirt. Unable to resist them, he grasped at their legs and asses. They just slapped his hands away while giggling.

On his way up to the third floor, David began to feel drowsy. His legs started to wobble with each step, too. He grabbed onto the handrails.

"*¿Estás bien?*" Isabel asked.

'Are you okay?'

"*Sí... Sí,*" David responded.

'Yeah... yeah.'

They ended up in a hallway at the top of the stairs. Arm in arm, Vanessa and Isabel walked to the first door to their right. Isabel dug through her purse while complaining about the room key. David leaned against the wall at the top of the stairs and breathed heavily. Sweat darkened the armpits of his shirt. He squinted and shook his head. The walls appeared to be tilting, then the hallway looked like it was twisting into a spiral.

"*¿Qué pasa?*" Vanessa asked as she walked over to him.

'What's wrong?'

One arm over his stomach, David stuttered, "*A–A–Al... go es–es...*"

He was trying to say '*algo está mal*' which translated to 'something's wrong.' Mid-sentence, his eyes rolled up and he fell forward. His body hit the floor with a thunderous *bang*. The prostitutes and Johns in the other rooms heard it, but they didn't care about the noise outside. No one in the bar noticed it.

Staring down at him, Vanessa said, "*Eso fue más fácil de lo que pensé.*"

'That was easier than I thought.'

David raised his limp head. His eyes struggled open to a canvas of orange and black. He squeezed his eyes shut and groaned. He had a pounding headache and a sour stomach. He felt like there was a rock in his abdomen. He could taste vomit in his mouth, but he couldn't remember anything from the previous night. He lifted his head and forced his eyes open again. He saw shadows moving and heard hushed voices. The light exacerbated his headache, forcing his eyelids to slam shut once more.

He heard a *creaking* sound above him and a *plopping* noise below him. He could tell he was nude thanks to the breeze hitting his warm skin.

He tried to reach for his face to rub his temples, hoping it would relieve the pain, but his arms were handcuffed behind his back. And when he attempted to move his arms, he felt his entire body swing. Cuffed at the ankles he couldn't move his legs either. Then he noticed the rope scratching his chest, waist, and shins. He screamed, but it was stifled by the tape over his mouth.

"*Ya está despierto,*" a man said.

'He's awake already.'

David swung his head in a frenzy, causing his body to glide in every direction. He saw the sun rising beyond some hills on the horizon. He noticed the ruins of two razed buildings to his left. As his vision cleared, he saw a pond of filthy water under him and the tree to his right. His heart raced, outpacing the throbbing in his temples.

He finally realized he was suspended in midair, hanging from a tree branch above him. He recognized the area, too—the deserted airfield.

"*¡Cálmate, panzón!*" a woman hollered. "*¡Vas a destruir el árbol!*"

'Calm down, fatso! You're going to break the tree!'

David homed in on the voice. He saw four shadowy humanoid figures standing near the pond with a technical parked behind them. Two of the people were wearing military uniforms and ski masks, armed with assault rifles. He immediately recognized one of the women in the group—*Yolanda 'La Muñeca de la Muerte' Torres*. Vanessa was there, too, but he still couldn't put a name to her face. He squirmed in the air and mumbled unintelligibly.

It had been three months since Caleb's execution. Rafael was suspicious of her version of the events, but most of her story checked out. The whole world had heard about the headless body found in Griffith Park. He was satisfied with her work, and he was proud of her for returning to Mexico to face him. He knew it wasn't easy for her to trust him or anyone else in the business. He returned the favor, hiring her as one of his assassins and letting her keep Caleb's money.

Like Rafael, Yolanda was skeptical. Diego wasn't known to make mistakes. He was cunning and methodical. But she agreed to follow her boss' orders and help Vanessa eradicate the rest of their enemies. She was loyal to Rafael, so she was willing to do anything for him. And Vanessa was growing on her.

After being invited to join Rafael's cartel, Vanessa spent some time at her children's graves. She told them stories of her trips to the United States—excluding all of the violent parts. She brought them toys and flowers as well. She was convinced she wasn't going to join them in heaven. She believed she was better off alive. She wanted to kill as many assassins and smugglers as possible. But she promised Lucía and Joaquín she would never hurt another child.

In a booming, fearless voice, Vanessa said, "*¡David Carrillo! ¡La perra de Gustavo! ¿Sabes por qué estás aquí, marrano?*"

'David Carrillo! Gustavo's bitch! Do you know why you're here, you pig?'

David responded with nonsense. He swung around like a chandelier during an earthquake. The tree was groaning with him.

Vanessa pointed at the mud under her feet and said, "*Aquí... Aquí es donde ustedes mataron a Alicia.*" It translated to: 'Here... This is where you people killed Alicia.' She pointed at the pond and said, "*Y ahí...Ahí es donde Gustavo mató... a Lucía y Joaquín. Y tú, David, lo ayudaste. Me pegaste. Me paraste. Me hiciste ver morir a... a mis hijos.*"

'And there... That's where Gustavo killed... Lucía and Joaquín. And you, David, helped him. You beat me. You held me down. You made me watch... my kids die.'

She saw flashes from her past and heard voices from the dead. She lowered her arm and shifted her gaze to David's eyes.

"*¿Me recuerdas?*" she asked.

'Do you remember me?'

David's eyes were filled with fear—childlike but *real* fear. The color faded from his face. If it weren't for the tape, his mouth would have fallen agape. It was his first time seeing a ghost.

"*¿Me recuerdas?*" Vanessa repeated. David nodded rapidly. Vanessa said, "*Bueno. Ahora, voy a mandarte a tus amigos. En pedazos, cabrón. Y seguiré mandando a más de ustedes al infierno mientras viva. Se va a llenar de narcos allá abajo.*"

'Good. Now, I'm going to send you to your friends. In pieces, bastard. And I'll keep sending more of you down to hell as long as I'm alive. It's going to get crowded with narcos down there.'

While David screamed, Yolanda said, "*Te gusta comer, ¿eh? Bueno, te dimos algo de comer mientras dormías. Tu última comida.*"

'You like to eat, huh? Well, we gave you something to eat while you were sleeping. Your last meal.'

She raised her right hand and showed him a wireless detonator. He could connect the pieces. The pain in his stomach made sense all of a sudden. He kicked his legs, sending him swinging through the air. Yolanda tossed the detonator at Vanessa. Vanessa caught it, then waggled it at David, as if showing it off and waving goodbye at the same time.

While torturing Caleb, she had concluded that it was better to leave her victims permanently disabled, disfigured, and disturbed than to give them the easy way out by killing them. She couldn't disobey Rafael's orders, though, especially in his own territory with several of his most trusted killers around her. She had to settle for murder.

As they walked to the technical, Vanessa yelled, "*¡Ponle música! ¡Que muera con comodidad!*"

'Play him some music! Let him die with some comfort!'

David kept screaming and swinging helplessly. One of the armed men sat in the technical's driver seat. Yolanda sat in the front passenger seat and Vanessa took the seat behind her. The other man stood in the back, his hands on the mounted .50 caliber machine gun. As the truck rolled away, *Wake Me Up Before You Go-Go* by Wham! played through its speakers.

Without looking back Vanessa flipped the detonator's toggle switch. A piece of C-4 in David's stomach exploded. The blast sent a wave of water and blood into the air. His torso was blown open from his lower rib cage to his waist. Mutilated organs fell out of the massive wound like pieces of candy from a broken piñata, splashing in the pond. His spinal cord snapped in multiple locations. His upper body was only just attached to his lower half.

His body descended little by little as the tree branch sagged, weakened by the explosion. The rope around his waist slid into his abdomen, causing him to spin and tilt aimlessly through the air like a helicopter struggling to land. Despite all of the pain, loss of blood, and missing organs, he lived for an impressive fifteen seconds after the blast.

The technical continued cruising away. Vanessa wiped the bloody tears off her face with a handkerchief.

Watching her from the rearview mirror, Yolanda asked, "*¿Estás bien?*"

'You good?'

Vanessa poked her head out the window and looked back at the pond. David's death didn't bother her. She just thought about her children and their place of death. She leaned back into the truck, rolled the window up, then blew her nose.

She sniffled, then said, "*Estoy bien. Vámonos de aquí. Tenemos narcos que matar.*"

'I'm fine. Let's get out of here. We have more narcos to kill.'

JOIN THE MAILING LIST

'When She Weeps' is a standalone novel, although you could say I've left the door open for a sequel. I already have a plan for my next twisted romance novel, though. I can't guarantee that I'll go through with it, but if you've enjoyed these stories and if you have an interest in Japanese culture, I highly recommend signing up for my mailing list. (Just to temper expectations, I'm not teasing a sequel to 'Am I Beautiful?' I'm talking about another Japanese urban legend.) I continue to tackle new characters, themes, settings, and subgenres every year.

So, want to learn more about my books and stay up to date with my latest releases? Please consider signing up for my mailing list. By signing up, you won't miss any of my huge book sales or my new books. I usually send one email a month, but you may receive two or three during busier months—or none at all during uneventful months. And this isn't a personal blog. I won't be spamming you with world news, personal opinions, or life updates (unless I'm on my deathbed). This newsletter is strictly about my books. And it's completely free. Visit this link to sign up: http://eepurl.com/bNl1CP.

DEAR READER

The legend of *La Llorona*—also known as 'The Weeping Woman' in English—is probably the first horror story I was ever told. I remember sitting on a white plastic chair in the backyard of my grandmother's house at night, surrounded by my siblings and cousins. I believe one of my uncles swung by and started telling scary stories. I don't remember any of the other tales I heard that night, but the legend of *La Llorona* stuck with me. I didn't want to go out at night by myself out of fear that *La Llorona* would catch me.

That childlike fear sparked my lifelong infatuation with horror.

In previous letters, I've mentioned an unreleased collection called 'Legends of the Extreme.' If this is your first time hearing about it, it was supposed to be a collection of classic urban legends reimagined as extreme horror stories. When I wrote the outline, I stuck close to the source material. So, my outlines for the *Kuchisake-onna*, *La Llorona*, and *Teke Teke* stories had supernatural elements to them—and I think we all know I'm not really skilled at writing supernatural horror stories. So, I scrapped the whole book.

But my mind kept wandering back to those ideas. And when the pandemic started back in 2020, I found the piece I had been looking for: *Reality*. I started to reimagine the supernatural as natural—ghosts as people, hauntings as violence. That was how I finished writing my *Kuchisake-onna* reimagining, *Am I Beautiful?*, which I had been stuck on since 2018. And that's how I finished this book.

For the next book in this series of standalone twisted romance stories, I plan on returning to Japan. Again, the story is planned to have a very real human horror element. I'd like to mix in some more psychological terror as well. I don't want to get too deep into it because it's so early in development, but I wanted to mention this for two reasons: To let you know what I'm working on, and to segue into a related topic.

After I published '*Am I Beautiful?*' I received some flak. Now, I don't mind criticism. I wouldn't be writing today if I ignored the negative reviews I received at the beginning of my career. But I'm talking about something a little bit different here. In several discussions, I saw people saying—and I am paraphrasing here—that I couldn't write a good *Kuchisake-onna* story because I'm just a guy from California while also assuming I was Caucasian. I even received some messages saying I wasn't 'allowed' to write that story.

Most of these comments came from people who did *not* read the book, so at the end of the day, I didn't let them bother me too much. But I just want to make something clear. *Am I Beautiful?* and *When She Weeps* were written with respect for culture and a passion for storytelling. And, in my defense, I am from California, but I've lived in Japan for years. (I also pay taxes here, and somehow, I still owed a dollar to California last year. What's up with that, huh?)

And, just in case anyone is wondering about my 'credentials' for writing *When She Weeps,* here's some news for you: I am Mexican American.

[*Gasp!*]

Enough ranting about that, though. This was one of the hardest books I ever had to write. It gave me flashbacks to my experience writing *The Groomer*. You might be thinking 'there's no way anyone could survive that' or maybe something like 'no way someone could do that to a person.' Well, a lot of the death scenes in this book were inspired by real cartel snuff videos. Yes, I watched some very, *very* dark stuff in hopes of creating a grim, unforgettable experience for you.

I won't mention any video titles for the same reason I didn't mention any actual cartels or real people in this book: Cartels scare the *crap* out of me. You may think I'm exaggerating, but for my own safety, I don't want to push things too far. I wrote this book because it scared *me*. And when an idea scares me, it reinvigorates my love for writing and horror. It makes me feel like I'm breaking new ground.

On my decision to use Spanish dialogue, I hope you understand it was meant to add a layer of authenticity to the story. I tried writing it with all English dialogue at first, but it just didn't bode well with me. I know I probably shouldn't, but I picture my books like movies when I'm writing them. I just can't imagine a movie set in Mexico with all of the characters speaking English all of the time.

I sincerely hope you enjoyed this book. If you did, please—don't make me beg because I will! —take a moment to leave an honest review on Amazon. As usual, reviews on Goodreads, Bookbub, Facebook, Twitter, TikTok, and your blogs and vlogs are also appreciated. Aside from my translated books, I am still independent. I don't have a publisher to support me or market my books. So, word-of-mouth is very important.

Need some help writing your review? Try answering questions like these: *Did you enjoy the story? Were the characters interesting or memorable? Were you satisfied with the ending? Would you like to see more nonsupernatural reimaginings of classic urban legends from Jon Athan?* You can also try to guess which urban legend I might tackle next. Good or bad, your reviews help other readers find my books and help me improve.

I'm writing this letter on February 26th, 2022. If you follow me on social media, you probably noticed I haven't been very active recently. For the last month, I have been focused only on this book, writing from eight in the morning to nine at night. Of course, there were a couple of breaks spread throughout the day, but I spent most of my time writing. It was simultaneously rewarding and punishing. Usually, after I finish writing a book, I jump right into the outlining process for the next story. And if I already have an outline prepared, I start typing up the next book. I have quite a few outlines ready right now, but I'm out of energy, so I might take a few days off after the revising process for this book.

Up next, I'll be focusing on finishing *The President's Son*. It's an ambitious extreme horror epic I've been working on for years. I've never written anything like it before. I'll save the 'making-of' details for that book's letter, though. I was originally planning on releasing an Author's Enhanced Edition of *The Harbinger of Vengeance*—my first long piece of fiction—this summer. Due to some issues with the distribution of my most recent enhanced book, those plans may change. But, like I mentioned earlier, I already have a stack of outlines waiting for me anyway. I'll always have something to write. I should be announcing the next batch of books shortly before the release of *The President's Son*.

Thank you for reading my 53rd novel. If you'd like

to read more of my books, please check out my Amazon's author page. I write extreme horror novels. If you have a morbid interest in the dark side of humanity, I think you'll enjoy my work. The next book on my schedule is *The President's Son*. You can pre-order it today. If you like slashers and killer clowns, I just released *Do Not Disturb 2: The Platinum Palace* in January. It's a sequel, but it can also be enjoyed as a standalone slasher. I might even be planning a third book in that series. Thanks again!

Until our next venture into the dark and disturbing,
   Jon Athan

P.S. If you have any questions or comments, feel free to contact me directly using my business email: info@jon-athan.com. You can also contact me via Twitter @Jonny_Athan, my Facebook page, or Instagram @AuthorJonnyAthan. I can't promise that I'll reply right away, but I always try to respond. Thank you for your patience!

Printed in Great Britain
by Amazon

81637623R00236